My name is Terasa Dower. I have been writing since I was 16. I have always dreamed of having writing as a career. When I started the *Look for the Dragon* series, I promised my father I would get them published. And when my father fell ill, I promised that I would complete *Look for the Dragon* and get it published. This is what I'm doing now.

Everyone has some bad things happen to them in their lives, I am no exception, but I think it's better to think of the positives and none of the negatives. I enjoy writing fantasy fiction; it gives me time to dream about a world that is blessed.

To Dad, a promise made is a promise kept.

For my family whose love and support have meant the world to me. Even through the darkest times in my life, you were always there—thank you. Tammy, without whom this book would never have been finished, and to Leeroy—the man with all the heart and patience in the world; I will forever thank and love you.

Terasa Dower

LOOK FOR THE DRAGON

AUSTIN MACAULEY PUBLISHERS™

LONDON * CAMBRIDGE * NEW YORK * SHARJAH

A CIP catalogue record for this title is available from the British Library.

ISBN 9781398427266 (Paperback)
ISBN 9781398427273 (Hardback)
ISBN 9781398427280 (ePub e-book)

First Published 2023
Austin Macauley Publishers Ltd®
1 Canada Square
Canary Wharf
London
E14 5AA

Chapter 1

The Accident

It was late, Sarah was supposed to be home hours ago, but she was having too good a time with her friends. Looking at the watch on her wrist she noticed that it was gone at midnight, the harp had closed its doors hours ago, but the party remained strong. Finally, she decided that it was time she made her way home, knowing that her father would be awake waiting for her. She knew she was in so much trouble, but she didn't often stay out late plus she was eighteen, even so, she called her friends letting them know she was leaving. Andy walked over smiling sweetly his bright white teeth shining under the strobe light, "OK, my sweety, just make sure to let us know your home safe, OK?" he said with a wink but also serious.

"I will once I get in, I'll send you a text to show I'm home." With a kiss on the cheek, she was off.

Walking outside she looked at the car park, should she risk driving she had only had a couple of drinks, while she stood there pondering on the question. She heard her name being called from behind turning around, "Mike, hi." It was her father's co-worker Mike, bending her head slightly so he couldn't see her eyes, but Mike had already seen her leave the pub. "Well, well, well what do we have here don't tell me sergeant Dailies daughter is thinking of driving after having a drink." He had seen her she knew she was caught looking at him he caught under her arm, "come on young lady I'm taking you home, the serge would have my head if he found out I'd let you go off on your own." Sarah tried to pull away "Oh mike I've only had a couple and how's Dad supposed to find out anyway."

"Because I'd tell him that's how now move or do I have to call him and let him know his daughter was going to drive home after drinking."

Looking at him she knew he was dead serious he would tell him in a heartbeat, letting her arms fall she followed him to where his car was parked.

Like the gentleman he always was he opened her door first letting her slide into the passenger's seat then closed it, walking around he climbed behind the wheel looking at her he smiled. Reaching over he touched her leg, "don't worry I won't say a word OK." He patted her knee and then started the car up, as he pulled out, he didn't notice the car tailing them Sarah reached over grabbing his arm, "Mike I think we're being followed that black sedan has been with us since we left the harp." Mike looked in his rear-view mirror then took the Abercynon turning it seemed she was right the Sedan took the turn with them.

Mike sped up and the Sedan did the same looking around he could have kicked himself why did he have to have his car, if he had his police-issued one, then he would have a radio. His first thought was to get Sarah home safe "Sarah do you have your phone at hand?" she looked at him and nodded fear had constricted her vocal cords, "OK, here's what I want you to do, get it out don't dial nine instead I want you to dial the station OK." Tell them that you're with me and we are being followed, can you see what model it is." shaking her head she fumbled for her phone, dialling the station she got through to the captain. "Captain Davies" his voice was deep, with just the slightest Irish twang in it, Sarah looked at Mike who once again patted her knee, "We're going to be fine, just tell whoever is on the phone my name and badge number and let them know what's going on OK."

He sounded completely normal as if this was an everyday occurrence, what she didn't realise was he in fact was terrified, but his training had taught him how to stay calm under pressure, they had already made one lap and he had passed Lamben and had gone up towards the heads of the valleys. "Hi Captain, this is Sarah Daily, sir."

"Oh Sarah, your father's not here, sweetie, are you OK?"

"No sir I'm not, I'm with Mike Driscoll and we are being chased by a black Sedan, he told me to phone you," she heard the phone drop on the desk next thing she heard was him shouting orders to the men that were there, finally he came back to the phone. "Right Sarah, Hun I want you to hang up from me and dial through to the emergency line they are waiting to pick the call up, OK." "OK, Captain, thank you."

After putting the phone down, she dialled the emergency services, upon getting through she told them who she was and was immediately patched through to one of the operators. Who told her to put it on loudspeaker so she could speak to Mike; Sarah did as she was told? Then spent the next twenty minutes listening to Mike explain to the operator where exactly they were, but without realising it he had taken the turning that led them to the beacons. The car that had been just tailing them now started to shunt the back of the car, Sarah screamed Mike sped up, but the Sedan easily kept pace with him ramming them over and over.

"Mike why are they after us!" Mike looked at her; he had been put on this case. He always disagreed with the way this was being handled they knew that someone was after Sarah that was why she was under surveillance, however they were under strict orders that Conner was not to be told. They were unsure whether the threat was real or not, but they had to know, it was no Meer coincidence that he had been there tonight he was making sure that she was OK. Looking in his rear-view again he tried to make out faces but it was too dark, there was no way to tell who was driving, as he came around dead man's curve almost losing control, just managing to get the grip under the tires and pulling the car as hard to the right as he could the back wheel skimmed the edge of the ninety-foot cliff, Sarah by this point had crawled down under the dash huddled there. Praying it would be over soon.

The last thing she remembered was a loud noise then feeling weightless, then nothing. The operator was calling Mikes name, over and over but there was no answer the trace they had put on Sarah's phone told them exactly where they were. The Sedan drove off leaving them Sarah was sure she heard them say they were dead, but she wasn't she was alive. She tried to groan but her breathing was laboured she could feel something pressing against her chest her breathing getting heavier, she could see a light but turned away from it she wasn't ready yet. She heard the voice of her mother telling her to hold on. But her body felt heavy.

It had taken the police just over fifteen minutes to get to where they were, Officer Llewellyn looked inside he could see Mike and Sarah, reaching in he pressed his hand to Mike's neck there was a slight pulse, looking at the others, "We need fire and rescue, but I'm telling you I don't think she will make it. Look at her she is caught under twisted metal," the ambulance was first on the scene getting down they went to Mike his pulse was still there but weakened. Walking around Dean managed to feel Sarah's neck he was shocked to discover her pulse was surprisingly strong, climbing back up he looked at the fire chief who had just arrived "we need to get them out now, his pulse is thready he won't last much longer I have already called for the air ambulance. The girl on the other hand someone must be watching over her, her pulse is strong for now…we'll keep monitoring it" the fire chief nodded his head then ordered his men to work.

It took them fifteen minutes to get Mike out looking over to where she was, they didn't know where to start; she seemed to be enveloped by the metal. Tye stepped forwards, "if we start from this side, we should be able to cut around her," Ivor, standing next to Tye, looked into the car, "no if we start there, we have more chance of hurting her more." While the men stood there discussing the strategy on how best to get to her dean put his hand in once more and felt for a pulse, it was weaker than before. "Guys enough talking, we have to get her out now, her pulse is dropping," Chief Edwards walked down the embankment to where his men were standing. "OK, guys, what's the plan." Tye stepped forward and explained what he had suggested but it had been dismissed, looking he noted that Tye's suggestion was the best alternative, "OK," he slapped cracker on the back, "cracks if you climb in through the gap there Tye, you're the smallest if you climb to the back seat just behind, we will go with your suggestion."

The other men did as they were told, slowly they started cutting, and it turned out Tye was right. it was easier and quicker, even with them cutting slowly it took half the time it would have if they had gone with Ivor's suggestion, but like a team they worked efficiently and quickly, half hour after they had started they could see the twisted metal coming away, Dean leaned in her pulse was even weaker, "Guys we're losing her, she needs to get out now." finally after forty five minutes she was freed, slowly and gingerly they lifted her onto the back board rushing her to the waiting helicopter.

Captain Davies was on scene and looking to Simon and his partner, "OK, we have to get ahead of this. You two are going to head to Conner's home let him know that Sarah has been in an accident. Don't tell him anything other than that, understand as far as he will be concerned it was an RTA nothing more." Simon and James looked at him then nodded getting in the car they made their way to Conner's, dreading it the entire drive was silent, only the noise of their radios bursting into life intermittently, finally they made it to Lamben driving to the top of the site up past the many houses, they came to Conner's it was the large white house.

Simon and James climbed out of the cruiser, looking at each other they could see the light was still on. Conner was awake slowly they walked to the door; Simon took a deep breath reaching out he pressed the button. The outside light came on as the door opened; Conner went white "what is it…what's happened."

10

Simon looked at him, "Umm serge, your daughter has been in an RTA…" he didn't have chance to say anything else Conner was out the door shaking him. "What do you mean an RTA…Where…When" Simon's head lolloped back and forth as Conner kept thrusting to and fro, finally James stepped in, "Serge. She has been taken to queen's memorial hospital, in Lindes" with that Conner dropped Simon who fell to the floor. James helped him up "Should we go with him?" Simon grabbed him and walked out of ear shot, "are you crazy, the captain said he's only to be told about the RTA, what do you think will happen when he gets there if we accompany him?" "He'll want to know what happened" "Correct so we will leave him go and report back to Captain Davies OK."

It didn't take Conner long before he was out the door and, in the car, he didn't even look in Simon and James's direction, he rushed to the hospital, he took the A470 it was the quickest route to the hospital, as he pulled into the parking lot, he looked up praying that she was going to be OK.

Rushing through the doors he ran to the reception desk, Jackie who was the nurse on that night saw him thundering through the door he made his way to her slamming his hands down on the desk he took a long deep breath, "my daughter was brought here this evening, please can you tell me where she is?" Jackie looked at him for a moment then to the monitor in front of her.

"Name?" was all she said polite but formally Conner looked at her, "Sarah…Sarah Dailey" she punched the name into the system, then looking at Conner "She's in the I.C.U" Conner looked at her and rushed from the desk only to stop a few paces ahead turning he walked back. "Ummm, could you tell me how to get there please." smiling sweetly and pointed to the wall behind him if you follow the green line to the elevators then go up to the second floor. Take the second corridor and that will lead you to the intensive care unit."

Conner looked at her and smiled then resumed his course he followed the line that led to the elevators finally he got to the second floor, he took the second corridor and came to a pair of doors pushing the button he waited for an answer after what seemed like an hour when in reality was actually about five minutes he said who he was and why he was there, it wasn't long before the door opened walking through he followed the corridor turning the corner he saw the nurses' station he walked with determination to where he saw two nurses and what looked like a young man in a doctors coat, he remembered thinking that they sure start young these days. As he got to them the man turned, "I'm Conner Daily my daughter was brought in here earlier this evening she was in a car accident." The doctor looked at him he knew exactly what he was talking about for he had already had a discussion with the police who had accompanied the girl, and was given strict instructions that if asked anything then he was to say that she was the only one in the car for some reason they did not want it known that Mike had been with her, the doctor looked at him and smiled "Mr Daily if you would just follow me, there is something that You need to know before you see your daughter." Conner stiffened and a million thoughts raced through his head he had no idea what this man was about to tell him. He followed without a word the Doctor led him into a quiet room, looking around the floors were a lime green and the wall they seemed cold for some reason there was a desk and two chairs one in front and the other behind. The Doctor walked over to the chair and pointed "if you'll just take a seat this won't take too much longer," Conner walked over and sat on the chair the Doctor took up the other seat Conner looked about him the walls had certificates on them he wondered if they were the Doctors or if they were someone else's finally the Doctor broke through his thoughts.

"My name is Ryonoskie Itchia, I am the one who is taking care of your daughter." without thinking Conner jumped to his feet cutting the doctor off, "please is she OK? What's wrong with her?" Ryonoskie raised his hand stemming Conner's barrage of questions, "Mr Daily please, you don't seem to understand the gravity of the situation. Your daughter has sustained many injuries the fact that she is still alive is a miracle... I just wanted to speak to you before you see her, I need you to understand that when you go in there you probably won't recognise the girl that you know... she has sustained fractures and breaks to her entire body her face is swollen and bruised..." he stopped speaking when he saw the colour drain from Conner's face. Conner looked at him his eyes were awash with unshod tears, finally Ryonoskie stood up and started pacing back and forth he wasn't sure if he should tell Conner everything he knew.

He knew that for some reason they wanted him kept in the dark they didn't want him to know everything but since he was her father, didn't he have the right to know? The thought made him think of home he remembered a similar situation happening and it turned out they were using the person as bate, it didn't end well, the person they used ended up getting killed. What was he going to do he couldn't just stand there and let another innocent person die he looked at Conner but by the looks of him there was no way that he could tell him know he was going to have to wait at least let him see his child let him get over the shock of it first?

As they walked, they walked in silence Ryonoskie didn't even look at Conner he wanted to get this over with as soon as possible they weren't even sure if she was going to survive. Her body was broken plus there was swelling in her brain and on top of that she was in a coma. He had finally explained all of this to Conner before taking him to see her. As they came to the room where Sarah was Ryonoskie turned and placed a hand on Conner's shoulder, "You have to understand that she may not even know you are there." Conner just nodded there was no way that he would not recognise his own daughter.

As he walked through the door the sight stopped him cold it was more than he could take there in front of him was his little girl hooked up to all different types of machines how was he going to do this, his knees buckled under him the strain was too much he couldn't do it, raising his fists he pounded the tiled floor letting out a blood-curdling cry, "No this is not my daughter this is not my child. No!" He could not go on; tears fell in torrents down his face Ryonoskie came to his side kneeling he put a hand on his shoulder. "Mr Daily, this is not what she needs right now, she does not need your self-pity she needs your strength." Conner stretched out his hand and grabbed the bottom of the bed, slowly he pulled himself to his feet with the help of Ryonoskie. Standing there at the bottom looking up at her he could not believe that this was his daughter her face looked so bad he wasn't sure, walking up the bed he placed his hand on her cheek. Then moving her hair there, it was just above her eyebrow the scar she had gotten when she fell off the swing. There was no denying it this was his beloved daughter, tears once again rolled down his cheeks Ryonoskie walked over and bowed his head, "I am so sorry," was all he said then left the room.

As he walked down the corridor, he thought about the time his sister was used as bait by the police to lure and catch a serial killer that was stalking young women. His sister had managed to get away and made it into the street where she was struck by a slow-moving car, she had been taken to the hospital his father was a police captain over there then and had given the go-ahead to use her, but no one had known the serial killer was actually a police officer, the men guarding her had been called away, giving him the opportunity, he needed to get to her. She could identify him, so he had no choice but to try and finish her off.

What he hadn't been counting on was for her snot nose brother to be there when he had come in, as he walked over to the bed knife raised above his head ready to end her life, Ryonoskie had seen him. Wanting nothing more than to protect his sister he had gotten between them; he felt the knife plunged into his chest just missing his heart. He managed to cry out alerting the staff that something was wrong but by the time help had come she was dead, and he was close to death. They had worked hard and, in the end, managed to save him raising his hand he placed it where the scar he would carry for the rest of his life was. It was thanks to him that the man had been caught in the end but missed his trial deciding to end his own life in his cell the night before it was due to take place, Ryonoskie had always wondered if his father had anything to do with it.

One of the nurses broke him out of his thoughts it seemed that the boy in room six had woken up finally, he had been in a coma for over a month, walking past her he went to the boy's room he was actually sat up and looking around, his mother who had never left his side was crying, Ryonoskie smiled it was the end of his shift and he was happy that it was ended on such a joyous note.

Chapter 2

The Recovery

Conner looked at Sarah he wondered if she was in any pain, grasping a chair he moved it to the side of the bed sitting down he took hold of her hand bending his head down he kissed it, with tears in his eyes he looked up at her finally he was able to speak.

"They say you can't hear me, but I don't believe it I have heard of people in coma's waking up and telling of what they remembered, so I think you can hear me. Now you listen to me you will not die; do you hear me you will not die."

A tear rolled down his cheek, but he continued. "Do you remember when we lost your mother, I was inconsolable, you walked into the room, you were still so young, but it didn't stop you from coming over and jumping onto my lap, do you remember what you said? You said Dad don't worry mam will always be with us and I will always be with you I promise, then at her funeral, you stood there holding a white rose in one hand and the other firmly in mine as we walked over to her, you placed the flower on her coffin you said don't worry mam I will take care of Daddy…well I'm holding you to that promise I can't lose you…p…please wake up, please my darling wake up." he had no choice at this point the raw emotion took over and he just sat there holding her hand and cried.

Julie had been outside and had heard everything Conner had said there was no way she could go in now she put her hand over her mouth as she walked away so that he did not hear the sob that broke from her. She could not let anyone see her like this walking past the nurses' station she went into the lounge by this time the tears were rolling down her face she could not believe anyone could feel so much hurt in their life.

As she looked up Jess was standing by the window looking at her. "What's going on?" Julie looked at her and took a seat near her, "the girl that was in room five her father is with her oh Jess if only you could have heard what he said," with that, the head nurse walked into the room looking at both girls.

Julie wished that the floor would open up and swallow her whole, this was the worst thing that could have happened everyone referred to her as the ice queen, she was always sweet and helpful when it comes to patients, but you would swear she was a nurse from the fifties, she didn't believe that personal lives should interfere with work-life something Julie agreed with but she always seemed cold when it came to her co-workers.

Looking at Julie, she fixed her with a steely gaze, "What's wrong with you?" She asked in a very cold manner Julie looked at her and then away what was she going to say, was she going to tell her the truth well she always seemed to see through people when they were lying so the truth seemed to be the best option, sitting up she explained everything once she had finished Miranda just stood there for a moment, she seemed to be thinking about something but neither Julie nor Jess could read her expression she seemed completely guarded.

Finally, after a moment she looked up at them both, "people go through a lot of things in their lives, you will learn as you get older there are no straight lines in life," walking over she took the seat next to Julie patting her hand. "Listen to me yes there are times in one's life where you will face adversity, but it is up to you how you will deal with it... when something bad happens you can take one of two paths one is to allow it to destroy you. The other is to allow it to shape you... I have gone through a lot in my life that left me feeling sometimes I couldn't go on. I have a reason too, and that reason is my children... I know that I may seem hard sometimes. But you must understand the only reason I am is so that I can help you; now dry your eyes the patients are sick enough as it is and the last thing, they need is a puffy eyed nurse," with that she stood smiled and walked away leaving the girls looking after her.

Conner was stood looking out of the window as Jack entered the room his shoulders sagged slightly, Jack recalled the first time they met when he walked into the captain's office; there he was he looked like a mountain, Jack thought he must be over seven feet tall while he was just standing there no real expression on his face it looked hard, his shoulders were broad. He wore a well fitted suit that hugged his masculine frame. Jack remembered thinking that he would probably be able to crush a man's head with his bare hands if he wanted to, there were few times in one's life where you were actually thankful that someone was on your side, and this was one of them.

The captain introduced them and Jack who was a big man himself saw his hand get dwarfed by Conner's, when he found out that he was his new partner you could have blown him over with a feather. Conner had just transferred there from America it was him and his daughter there was no wife and Conner never elaborated on what had happened, all anyone knew for sure was that he had custody of their only daughter it did cause a rise of speculation on what had happened and why he had transferred over here but none of them could be verified so they were just rumours.

He remembered the first time that he had met Sarah he had gone to pick Conner up as he pulled into the drive way and there she was sat on the step in front of the house, he remembered thinking how beautiful she was, her hair had been down just the front pinned back so that you could see her face, she had the bluest of eyes they were as clear as the ocean her hair fell down past her breast it was the colour of corn syrup, he always wondered how someone with olive skin could have her colouring. When he had pulled up, she got up walking down the drive to where he was. She held out her hand, "You must be Jack" it was more of a statement than a question he had smiled and took it. She was nine years younger than him she had only been fourteen when they had moved here that was four years ago, he walked behind her as she led the way up to the house thinking the whole way could she really be his daughter, she was nothing like him.

He was jolted out of the memory by Conner speaking, he hadn't realised that he had moved from the door and was now standing at the foot of her bed, he looked at Conner for a moment then back to Sarah, "How's she doing today?" he asked thankful that his voice was normal.

"There has been no change" Conner said as he took his spot back by the window Jack was wondering what he was looking at as he drew nearer he could see nothing except the remnants of the east wing that had burned down over twenty years ago killing ten patients and three staff members, he was only a child then but he still remembered the news coverage of it, one of the heating exchanges had blown, the fire had spread quickly before anyone had noticed, it completely consumed the first floor the evacuation had taken hours. There had been three fire trucks he remembered his father coming home telling his mother something he didn't quite hear what it was, but she started to cry, he found out later that her uncle had been one of the patients that perished in the fire. Finally, after all these years they had decided to knock down and completely refurbish it.

"That building and I are the same" Conner said bringing Jack back to the present Jack thought for a moment but didn't quite understand what he was talking about however, before he had the chance to say anything Conner started to speak again. "Yes, we are the same, there is nothing we would like more than to crumble down, and just lie there but we can't all we have is people leaning on us... Expecting us to stay strong for them, not once realising that we have weathered too many storms; we have gone through too much we want nothing more than to just fall..."

He stopped, with tears in his eyes Jack stepped forward shaking his head. "No Conner you're not, you're like the grand old oak tree, with roots long and deep with branches that stretch for miles you are the beacon of hope for all those who have none left, they lean on you because you give them strength. So, no you are not like that building out there, you are the beacon. The one everyone knows will still be standing tall and strong in years to come."

Conner looked at him then to Sarah then back shaking his head, "No I'm not a grand old oak don't you understand that I have been through too much, I can't take it anymore I have already lost her mother if I lose her too then that will be it. I don't think that I could ever recover from that," he could no longer speak the tears that had threatened to fall were trailing their way down his cheek he fell back against the wall his body wracked with grief, his head hurting he put his hands up to his face as a sob broke from him slowly he slid down the wall until he was sitting on the floor his knees bent he was there for the longest of time, Jack didn't know what to do walking over to Sarah he grasped hold of her hand. Turned back to Conner closing his eyes he said a silent prayer that he would be able to find the right words that would help Conner at this time, finally he opened them and looked at him. Letting go of Sarah's hand he walked in front of Conner he had never seen him look so dejected.

He had to find a way of getting him out of this depressive mood, but how after all she was his daughter the one thing that always kept him grounded and now there was a very real chance that he may lose her, at that thought Jack stopped, *she might die,* he thought it over and over and the gravity hit him like someone had just dropped a house on him. Stopping he could not believe it but somewhere along the line, he had fallen in love with his partners daughter. Looking at Conner he had no idea what he was going to say, with that thought he made an excuse and left.

Over the next three weeks Jack would go over to the hospital and check on Sarah's progress to the doctor's surprise she was starting to mend but she still hadn't opened her eyes yet and Conner was always there, what was he going to do he was in love with her, but she didn't know it. He hadn't told her or her father he was the one that made him even more nervous than anything, looking at the clock it was just gone six visiting ended at eight and he hadn't been over yet, he usually went over in the afternoon but he had been so busy today he hadn't got the chance, if he left now at least he would be able to see her even if it was for a short time, making his way through the rush hour traffic was a nightmare. He kept looking at the clock on the dash finally he got there it was ten to seven good there was still an hour left. Getting out of the car he headed into the main entrance, then taking the elevator to the second floor he was finally there. As he walked through the door of her room, he noticed that Conner was nowhere in sight, slowly he walked over to the bed bending he kissed her forehead.

"Hi there my sweet girl," he said gently caressing her cheek the breathing tube had been removed she just had the strip going across her nose, the bruises were almost gone her beauty shone through once more, tears stung his eyes at the thought of not having her in his life, she was his the one woman he truly wanted, the doctors had said that even though her body was healing there was no way to know if she would ever wake up again, she may just stay like that forever never moving never talking just in a timeless sleep.

Finally, his legs gave way under him and he sank to his knees, "Sarah I love you, please wake up don't leave me" the words rang from him but after saying them he was awash with a whole new type of feeling, one of anger at the thought she will never hear him say those words to her, standing he looked at her no. This wasn't going to happen she was going to wake bending low he kissed her lips, lifting his head he looked at her "Sarah do you remember the first day we met? You were sat on the step outside your house and when I pulled in, I truly thought that there was an angel in front of me. I could not conceive the idea that you were Conner's daughter, how was it possible that the daughter of a black man could have golden hair, and eyes the colour of the ocean on a sunny day, I loved you the moment I saw you sat there" gently he laughed, "I remember that stupid Christmas party, where you fell onto my lap if it hadn't been for your father I don't think I would have let you go, I just wanted to keep you there" once again he let out a laugh sitting down in the chair by the bed, "The one thing I always remember even when I don't want to is that red and black dress the one you

19

bought for Halloween, you came down the stairs like a vision your father took one look and hit the roof, that was the day you clung to my arm insisting to your father, that I was going with you, I on the other had had no idea what you were talking about. Until you dragged me out the door, I have to say that was one of the best accidental dates that I have been on. I had so much fun your father grilled me about it the following day wanting to know exactly where we had been and why you were so late getting home. That was the night you kissed me," A noise from behind him stopped his speaking slowly he rose turning around he was face to face with Conner.

Oh man please ground just open and swallow me whole, he thought but Conner just stood there silent, like a centurion on the front lines holding his cutlass standing tall and proud ready to pounce when the word was given. "Should I leave? How much did he hear? Oh god what am I going to do?" These thoughts just kept going round and round for the longest time, finally Conner stepped forward as he raised his arm Jack thought "this is it he's going to give me one hell of a right." But he was wrong Conner just let the hand fall hard onto his shoulder squeezing it slightly he smiled, "So you finally said it did you?" was all Conner said Jack just stood there looking at him he couldn't believe his ears, "You knew?" Conner dropped his arm down to his side laughing "Of course I knew. you look at her the way I used to look at her mother, I'd know it anywhere" Jack stepped back even he had to look up when looking at Conner Jack was six foot five and Conner towered him, looking at the bed to where Sarah was, he couldn't take it her father knew but there was a chance that Sarah would never find out it wasn't right it wasn't fair.

Another week had past and still Sarah had not woken up, the doctors kept saying the same thing it takes time; but even if she was to awaken there were no guarantees that she would remember anything from the accident. They didn't know if there was going to be any long-term brain damage all they could do was wait.

Every week Conner would ask if there was any news, and every week the captain would say that nothing significant had happened, he was still being kept in the dark. He still didn't know that Sarah hadn't been alone in the car, he was still under the assumption that it was nothing more than an accident, and that was the way they wanted to keep it, they knew that if he found out the truth then all hell would break loose and that was the last thing they needed.

Jack woke up and looked at the clock, on the table at the side of his bed six oh he didn't have to be in work for another two hours. He and Conner were on the early shift, they were both going to see Sarah after their shift ended. Conner had already taken a lot of time off; he could not afford to take anymore. The captain for some reason always seemed to send them on the long journeys lately like yesterday, for example, there were documents that needed picking up and instead of sending one of the uniforms, the captain had asked if he and Conner would go.

Climbing out of the bed he stretched, he knew that he would not be able to sleep any longer no matter how much he tried, walking to the bathroom he climbed into the shower, the water felt good as it rolled down his masculine body, he stood there for a moment and just let it cascade down him the heat permeated him, washing away the dream he had, his shoulders were starting to relax he was feeling so much better. The sound of his phone ringing brought him out of the daze he was in, climbing out he grabbed the towel from the rail and hung it around his waist. Walking back into the bedroom he lifted the receiver, it was Williams on the other end reminding him that he and Conner were to be at the crown courts, in Lindes by ten Jack looked at the clock it wasn't even seven o'clock and he was phoning.

"Williams are you out of your mind, its only seven I'm not in work for another hour." he complained down the phone Williams laughed, "I know that it's just the captain asked me to phone you to tell you instead of coming straight to the office that you should go straight to the courts, the judge wants a word before he hears the case." Jack looked at the phone for a moment, "ai OK," he put the phone down getting back in the shower he scrubbed himself. Finishing he got out opening his cupboard he grabbed the grey suit, he couldn't help but laugh for a moment, he knew that if this was Sarah she would have been up hours ago and would probably still be trying to figure out what to wear, there had been many a row in the house because of that Conner would be shouting for her to move, and she would be shouting that she was almost done and it would still take an hour before they would be leaving. Whereas he just grabs his suit.

Finally, he was ready running down the stairs he grabbed the keys out of the bowl he always kept them in, it was the one that Sarah had picked out, she was fed up with him always complaining that he lost his keys. So, she had gone out and bought that bowl, she had given it to him with a word of warning; that if he complained one more time about losing his keys, she was going to hit him with it, and the way that she had said it made him believe that it was true.

As he pulled into the driveway Conner was waiting on the door for him, walking over he got into the car, and they set off there was a lot they had to do today they had to go to the courts; then they had to talk to one of the confidential informants they had. Even though the captain had told them they were not to go near the case, they could not help themselves they had to try and find out exactly what went on.

After everything they had heard so far, made them start thinking there was more than they had been told. The last person they had spoken to had said something about a chase, but every time they tried to get any information out of anyone assigned the case, they could not get any answer from them they just said it was being treated as an R.T.A, but every one of the informants had all said the same thing about a chase, they just didn't understand it. Finally, the day was over they had done everything they needed to do; the last thing on their list was to talk to Ray the informant that said he had information for them, they were going to meet at the old mill. As they turned into the mill, they didn't notice anyone there, they waited for some time and still nothing. After an hour they decided to leave it was almost visiting time at the hospital.

It didn't take them long to get there the old mill was only a mile or so away from the hospital, finally they pulled into the parking lot; finding a space they parked, as they were heading for the ward doctor Ryonoskie stopped them. "Mr Daily may I have a word with you?" Conner looked at him and nodded Jack went to Sarah's room while Conner followed behind the doctor. As he entered the room there was a nurse taking her stats, by the time she had finished Conner was walking into the room, Jack waited until the nurse had left, "What did the doctor say? Is there any change? Do they know if she is going to wake up?" Conner raised his hand to stem Jacks torrent of questions, "Just calm down, it was just to say that they had done another M.R.I and x-rays; her arm and legs seems to have healed and the swelling has subsided all that's left know is for her to wake up, they said that she is out of danger." Jack sighed heavily that was the first bit of good news they'd had.

They were still talking when they noticed that Sarah was starting to moan, her head was turning as though she was having a nightmare. Then she suddenly stopped she was just lying there Conner and Jack resumed talking.

Without a moment's notice Sarah let out a loud shriek jumping up in the bed causing both men to jump and ran to her Conner grasped hold of her calling her name, but all Sarah could shout was "Mike, where's Mike?" Conner looked at Jack then back to Sarah she managed to push him away, climbing out of the bed she found that her legs couldn't hold her weight the pain was too much and she fell with a thud into Jacks arms. He had raced to her side, there they were both on the floor he was holding her tightly Conner had run to get the doctor, she wasn't making any sense, she was babbling about mike and the cliff. Something about men chasing them, the doctor ran into the room with Conner finally they managed to subdue her long enough for the doctor to give her an injection to calm her down.

After they got her onto the bed, she was just lying there they were not sure at all what was going on, they knew that Mike had been off just as long as Sarah had been in the coma, but they were told that he was on an undercover investigation. Neither man moved from the room slowly after three hours she started to wake up she was groggy, Conner and Jack both went to her; Conner grabbed her hand. "Sweetie, its dad you're OK. You're in the hospital, you were in an accident."

Sarah looked at her father this time instead of jumping or doing anything frantic she spoke quietly. "Dad is Mike, OK?" Once again, she had mentioned to mike; "Sarah what are you on about love? You were alone in the car" this time Sarah jumped up shaking her head, "No! Mike was with me there were men chasing us that was how we ended up in the accident." Conner and Jack both looked at each other in shocked disbelief, they could not understand what was going on, until this point, they believed that Sarah had just been in an accident.

Conner and Jack had left the room, they thought that maybe it was just the coma, for some reason thought that there was someone with her. When in fact she had been alone, but why Mike, out of all the people why would it be him she believed was with her.

Conner walked down the Corridor towards the vending machine, for the first time he looked about him, it was then he noticed something; a room further down, standing outside the door was Mike's wife, but why would she be here he hadn't heard of any of their children being in hospital, walking down to where she stood. "Maria" she turned and looked at him giving him a weak smile; as with everyone involved, she had also been asked not to speak to Conner, but what was she supposed to do she was happy that Mike was finally awake.

"Hi" was all she said then looked down, Conner looked past her through the gap in the door, he could see that there was someone laying in the bed but couldn't make out who it was, turning back to Maria, "who is that?" he knew the answer but he had to hear it from her she looked at him then away, "Mike" once again it was a one word answer, just his name no explanation, just his name he could also tell for some reason she was avoiding looking at him, they had been friends for years. If they were in the same hospital, why had she not gone to see him, why had nobody told him that Mike had been with Sarah. What was going on?

After some time, he realised that he was not going to get anything out of her and he didn't want to push her at this point, so he just smiled and walked away, he was going to have to get to the bottom of this himself, if it was the last thing, he did he was going to find out what happened that night.

It had been three days since Sarah had told them everything, she could remember about what had happened on that fateful night, but the boys at the station were screening his calls every time he tried to get even the slightest bit of information from any of them, he had not been able to get hold of captain Davies at all. It always seemed that he was out every time he called or went in, he was getting tired of this he had already had a run in with James and Jensen they were the ones heading up the investigation, as he had said to them he had not known any investigation to take this long, usually it was handled with in a matter of weeks not months, but they were still making on-going inquiries, what was up with that they just looked at him and told him to stay out of it they wouldn't even give him the file on the case. What was going on why was everyone trying to keep him out of this.

As he walked onto the hospital floor he noticed Captain Davies leaving Mike's room, this was it Conner was fed up of hearing everything from other people, he had managed to work most of it out with what Sarah had remembered, but he was not allowed to speak to mike and every time he tried he was kicked out, this time he was not going to be dissuaded he was going to find out the truth, even if he had to wring it out of him, with determination in his stride he walked to where Davies was grabbing him he slammed the Captain against the wall. "Right," he spat out "Now I think it's time that you and I had a discussion don't you…? What the hell is going on? You all said that it was a simple accident, yet the guys are still working on it, then you put Sarah into the equation she has told me everything that she remembers from that night. I know that Mike was with

24

her I know that there was some kind of chase and I know you know more than you are telling me. Now out with it or I swear to God I am going to beat it out of you!"

Captain Davies knew from the way Conner was acting that he would do as he had threatened; he knew that he was going to have to be told eventually, although he had hoped that they would have been able to give him at least an answer when they did finally find out. He raised his arms and pulled at Conner's arms "OK, OK, but you're not going to like it," Conner released him and as he found his footing, he looked at Conner he knew that he was going to have to tell him everything they knew starting from the beginning, raising a hand he placed it on Conner's arm. "Go and see your daughter, I will have all the information you want by the time you come back to the office OK." Conner would have preferred he tell him everything now, but he just nodded in agreeance, he knew that Jack would want to be there for this.

Walking down the corridor he walked to Sarah's room Jack was stood by the window, Conner could not help wondering if he had told Sarah that he was in love with her, Conner had accidentally heard his confession and he knew that there was an age gap between them, but there had been one between him and Sarah's mother as well. He didn't know if it would work but he knew he had no right to interfere, yes, he was her father, but he knew that if he told her that she was to stay away from him or asked for another partner then things would probably go downhill. He had decided that he was going to take a step back and allow nature to take her course, looking at Sarah she was just lying there. He could not believe she would still be laying there if he had told her,

Walking through the door he smiled, knowing there was no way that he had told her, walking over he kissed her on the forehead, "how are you doing my sweet?" He asked with a smile, but before he had the chance to say anymore or she answered the doctor walked in, walking over to where Sarah was, he smiled. "OK then little lady, how are you doing today?" He picked up her chart and looked at it seeming to know what Conner was about to say he turned to Conner. "Well, I have to say that your daughter must have someone looking out for her, I just don't understand it but by the looks of it she might actually be able to leave here tomorrow," Sarah sat up this time she had a large smile on her face. Ryonoskie looked at her and put his serious doctors face on, "Yes, but you have to follow the rules or you're going to end up back in here understood." Sarah nodded and clapped her hands, "Yes I understand, and the rules are?" Looking at her doctor Ryonoskie smiled, "OK, you have to rest no overexerting yourself; you don't have to stay in bed, but you are to stay on the sofa, only get up to use the bathroom then back on the sofa you go." Sarah pouted for a moment then thought "yes but at least I get to go home tomorrow."

As they left the room, Conner told Jack that they were going to see the captain that they were finally going to be let in on what had happened that night, even though so much time had passed for Conner and Jack they had been living with this now for months they had been doing their own investigation without telling anyone. Finally, they pulled into the police car lot parking the car they got out, as they walked through the door Jane who was on the desk just smiled and greeted them her usual way. They walked past her onto the main floor, the captain and the other two were waiting for them as they entered the room they noticed the board behind them, it had names and faces on it, Conner did not waist anytime.

"OK, what the hell is going on?" The Captain looked at them "you are going to have to sit down for this," Conner looked at him but could tell by the tension in his shoulders that this was going to be one of those conversations that would take a lot out of them, walking over he grabbed the chair making sure to take the one furthest away from them, he didn't know what they were about to say but he wanted to be further away for their safety not his, Jack took the seat next to him for exactly the same reason, finally with everyone seated it was time to start, James stood up walking over to the board he pointed to the name that was at the top of the pyramid this is Usagi Matsimoto, he goes by the name Kaijinbo," just as he finished speaking a man entered the room, all heads turned to him the captain stood, "Your late!" he spoke sternly the man bowed slightly "My apologies sir" He said walking over he stopped next to Conner and Jack, the captain turned to them pointing to the man that had entered, "This is Tommy Takahashia he is on loan to us from the Japanese police, he has been on this case for many years and it's not until now that Kaijinbo has resurfaced."

Conner and Jack still didn't understand what this had to do with the accident. They shook his hand and Tommy sat next to them, and they continued by about half way through Conner could feel his blood boiling they had been talking for over an hour about this bloody Kaijinbo but nothing about Sarah's accident, he had finally had enough standing he slammed his hands onto the table causing it to shake under his strength, "I don't give a damn about this bloody Kaijinbo, how about we get to the reason that I'm actually here, what happened the night of my daughters accident!?" All attention turned to him it was at this point Tommy stood and walked to where the captain was, turning he looked directly at Conner there was a slight strain on his face.

"Your daughter was the target that night, they believed that she was killed in the accident, and we have done everything in our power to let them keep believing that. However, the Captain informed me that she is being released from the hospital tomorrow. That does not bode well for her; if they were to find out that she has survived they are sure to try again." Conner was on his feet and had caught hold of Tommy without thinking.

The Captain and James both grabbed hold of him however Conner had questions that needed answering, and there was no way he was letting go until he had them. Conner lifted Tommy slowly off his feet, so they were eye to eye, "Why is this maniac after my daughter?" Tommy in a slightly shaky voice nervously replies "Conner we don't know why he is doing this" it was not the answer that he wanted slowly he set Tommy down "OK, tell me what you do know" he spat out, Tommy took a deep breath then with shaking legs he sat down, he had never been manhandled like that before and he didn't want to be again. But he knew that Conner had the right to know what had happened.

He sat there for a moment just looking at them; so, had the captain and James and Jensen who he had already met. Looking from Conner to Jack he could understand Conner being there however was still wondering why his partner had accompanied him, however thinking on it had it been his partners child he would also want to be there to support his friend at this difficult time.

Finally, he brought himself back to reality when he noticed all eyes were on him, standing he looked at the men. He had been wondering why, himself he didn't understand exactly what was going on, but he had to figure it out. He hadn't even met the girl this was all about yet. Things were surely getting more complicated; he had initially come over here for his brothers.

They had managed to get themselves involved with Kaijinbo while they were in Japan, upon him leaving to come to this country they had followed. At first everything had been fine but lately they had found themselves getting in too deep and wanted out, but Kaijinbo was a ruthless man, he never just let anyone walk away so they were trying to find a way out. It was during this time they had found out about the plan to kill this one girl; they didn't know why he was so determined but he had made it clear that she was not to live.

After they found this out, they phoned their father he was some big shot in the government in Japan, he had put the phone down after he had heard what they had to say, not even giving them an answer. He had given his children everything that they had wanted, he could not believe that they would do something like this, after hanging up the phone he had been the one to contact Tommy and tell him Well order him to sort it out and due to his connections, he had no problem swaying it with the police commissioner over there to put him on this case.

Tommy was already on the trail of Kaijinbo without his father ever knowing it and he didn't like the fact that his father was butting into his job. He'd had enough of that while he was growing up, he was the oldest son the one his father decided was going to take over the family business. He knew that there were only a few years between him and his brothers, but they could not be more different, from a young age Tommy had always known he wanted to help people; and the best way he thought he could do this was by joining the police academy. His father believing that it was just a faze, held no objections to it he would become a police officer, then after a short time realize that it wasn't his true calling then he would choose to leave and take his place at his father's side.

He had been groomed to take over the company when his father finally retired, all his schooling and college life was to make him ready. His mother was always too soft on him, his father used to say but all she had wanted was for her children to be happy, in whatever they chose to do when he had graduated from the police academy, his mother had been overjoyed and told him that she was proud of him, his father hadn't even gone to the falling out parade.

Once again, he turned his attention back to the men that were in the room Conner was still standing, he was waiting for him to start talking, *OK, here goes*, he thought, finally he decided that being totally up front with everyone would be the best choice right now. Even though he knew that they would want to take his brothers into custody, it didn't matter, at least they would be safe, then looking at Conner he thought maybe not.

He however did not have the luxury of leaving anything out; he was going to have to tell them everything, no matter where it would lead. He started explaining everything to them he knew about Kaijinbo and all that his brothers had said, but it still left one important question why? it was one that nobody had the answer to. But one that no one other than Kaijinbo himself could answer, could it be something that Conner had done had he angered him somehow? But going through everything there was no way that their paths had crossed.

Finally, he had finished, but even after being told everything they were all still none the wiser, on what was going on, Sarah was attending Linde's university so is there some way that they had crossed paths that way? But Conner was sure that if anything had happened, she would have told him, Tommy interrupted his thoughts. "Umm Sargent, would I possibly be able to meet your daughter. After all she if she is the one that they are after she is going to need protection." Conner thought on it for a moment, he was right he would have to meet her at some point but not yet. He wanted her to be fully recovered before that happened. "Yes, you are right but let us get her back fighting fit before that OK," they agreed that they would sort the meeting out after she was back on her feet.

As they left the office curiosity got the better of him Conner had to know turning to Jack, "have you told her yet?" Jack looked at him slightly puzzled, "told her what?" Conner could not believe his ears "have you told my daughter that you are in love with her yet?" Jack went red then looked away; Conner knew from that reaction that the answer to the question was no, laughing he got into the car, Jack climbed in, "Umm…I want her to make sure that umm… She is back on her feet before we have that type of discussion" Conner was thankful although he wasn't sure why.

Finally, the day had arrived for Sarah to come home, Conner and Jack were wheeling her out of the hospital, but it didn't stop Conner from fussing, as they got to the car Conner opened the door while Jack lifted her out of the wheelchair, "I can walk you know?" she said with slight annoyance in her voice. Jack didn't have to say anything, Conner was doing a good job of telling her off, sitting in the car she folded her arms and pouted, and she couldn't believe that they were treating her like a porcelain doll, she was eighteen not eight. The ride home was slightly sombre as she complained because her father said that she was not walking from the car to the house, reminding her what the doctor had said about not overexerting herself, finally they were crossing the bridge into Uialben as they passed the old cemetery they noticed once again she closed her eyes, they had always wondered why she did that. Conner turning to her asked "Why do you do that?" Sarah looked at him "do what Dad?" "Well, every time we pass a cemetery you always do the same thing you close your eyes" Sarah looked at him and smiled, "Just saying a prayer for the souls of the dead." Conner looked at her then back to Jack who just shrugged.

As they went up Lamben Sarah noticed that the bouncy castle was up again, the family always inflated it on sunny days and allowed all the children of the site to play on it, Sarah had always liked the family that lived there. They were kind to everyone even though they had gone through a tragedy, it had only been a few months since they had lost their father but being the family that they were they held their head high and carried on they were amazing.

Finally, they were pulling into the drive Conner put the car into park then got out opening the back door he looked at Sarah, "OK, you have a choice is Jack going to carry you and I open the door, or do you want Daddy to carry you and Jack open the door?" Sarah looked at him his expression held no argument she was going to have to choose, heaving she looked at her father, "You can open the door" she said pouting Conner laughed and walked away jack bent down and picked her up with ease, as he made his way up the path Conner was once again fussing "Don't drop her," he said as he walked through the door Jack just looked at him. "Are you trying to say that your daughter is too heavy for me to carry?" he winked; Sarah just burst out laughing, "Gee thanks you know how to make a girl feel special don't you." Jack looked at her "hey don't blame me; your father is the one who said it not me." Conner looked at them both, "OK, that's enough you two," as they entered the living room Sarah noticed that the sofa was already made up waiting for her. She looked at both Jack and her father she could not believe that they were seriously going to make her stay on the sofa.

Jack put her gently down, looking up at him she smiled she was happy that he had been the one that carried her, she would never tell him, but she had fallen in love with him months ago. It was that stupid Halloween party the one where her father had gone nuts over the dress she had chosen, without thinking she had grabbed Jack by the arm, and convinced her father that he was the one who was accompanying her. It was only after they got outside that she realised that he was going to have to go with her.

She had dragged him along to the party, and when anyone asked, she would introduce him as her friend, wanting nothing more than to say boyfriend. The longer he was with her that night the more she realised that she liked him, then when he had taken her home, he had walked her to the door she leaned in and kissed him. She wasn't sure but it felt as though for a moment that he had kissed her back, that was before he had abruptly pulled away and left, she remembered feeling so rejected at that moment in time, the more that she tried to push her feelings away the more she wanted him.

Chapter 3
The Truth

It had been almost three weeks since she had come home, she couldn't understand why there seemed to be so many men at the house all day and even at night; they always left when her father got home but they were always there, she was starting to get concerned.

Conner walked through the door and Jax the officer who had been there all day said his goodbyes and left, she noticed that there was someone that she had never met before with her father she could not see him clearly, what she could see of him made her think of her friend back in America. He had been a Japanese transfer student, she noticed that he seemed out of place not comfortable at all, she decided that during recess she was going to talk to him, that day was one of the best days she had, as they left school that day she had asked if he wanted to walk home with her, but as they got outside there had been a black limousine outside waiting for him, they had remained friends until her father had transferred over to Wales but they still kept in regular contact.

Tommy and Conner walked into the living room where she was sitting on the sofa still on rest mode, she was getting sick of it, looking up she smiled at them her father walked over bringing tommy with him, she could see him clearly now. He was very handsome about six-foot one quite slim, but she imagined that under that nicely made suit was a toned body. He had high cheek bones and grey eyes, his hair was black not short but not too long either, her father interrupted her thoughts, "Sarah this Is Tommy Takahashia," Tommy held out his hand and Sarah took it, tommy looked at Sarah then at Conner he wondered if she was adopted, she seemed nothing like her father well maybe around the eyes but her skin was dark yes but more tanned than anything, as though she had been out in the sun all day and gone that nice golden brown. "Hi how are you feeling?" he asked. *Man, she was gorgeous an absolute beauty,* he thought to himself.

She smiled, "Hello, there it's nice to meet you," she said her voice was like hearing a chorus of angels singing.

He had been there for about an hour but not once had the subject of the accident come up, Jack opened the door as he walked in, Conner shouted, "We're in here" Tommy stood looking at the door waiting for whom ever it was to come in; as Jack entered the room Tommy tensed slightly but it was enough for Sarah to notice, as Jack walked in, she'd had enough of this. "I may be on this sofa but I'm not stupid you know," she said in rather a brisk tone that made all the men turn to look at her, "What are you talking about?" Conner asked innocently, "Don't give me the innocent act... you know very well what I'm talking about! Men here every day while you're out only leaving when you come home. And if your working nights there are men outside all night long until you come home. What... you thought that I wouldn't notice! Now instead of treating me like a child, how about you tell me what the hell is going on." Conner was actually shocked at her outburst she was usually so mild mannered when she spoke even when she was complaining but this was different she had actually raised her voice at him, he didn't like it walking over he sat on the edge of the sofa, "OK, what's gotten into you?" looking at him she lowered her head she couldn't actually believe that she had shouted like that it was so unlike her, well it was their fault they were the ones who were treating her like a child, and she'd had enough of it, looking her father square in the face so he would know that she was serious about what she was saying. "Listen you guys have been acting strange since I came home, you are always whispering about something, there are men in and out of the house at all hours please just tell me what's going on," As she said that she stretched out her hand touching her father's face.

Tommy looked at her he noticed a mark on her arm, at first, he thought it might be a scar from the accident but as he focused on it, he noticed it looked more like a fish. He couldn't believe it. He had heard about this mark from grandmaster Yamatoya. "Tommy is everything OK?" Jack asked bringing him out of his thoughts, "Umm yes I'm fine thank you" Jack looked at him he was sure that there was something wrong but if he didn't want to discuss it then he thought he had no right to push the subject. He will leave it for now, but he just didn't know how he looked at Sarah.

Conner looked at her smiling he grasped hold of her hand, "I know you're not a child... but you have to understand that there are some things that I cannot talk to you about and this is one of those times, you will just have to take my word for it." Sarah looked at him there was something he was not telling her, something that they were all keeping from her, like this new man who was he, why was he here? she knew all her father's friends and all those he worked with. This was the first time that she had seen him, walking over Jack sat down on the chair opposite Sarah; her father had moved to his chair and Tommy was sat in between them both. Sarah couldn't help but think of piggy in the middle, when she looked at them.

"How are you feeling now?" Tommy asked breaking the uncomfortable silence, Sarah looked at him and smiled, "I'm fine still not happy that I'm being kept in the dark about what's going on though," Conner sighed he knew that she would eventually have to be told but he wanted her to stay innocent for just a little longer before he totally shattered her world, "there are times for talking, and times for remaining silent. But knowing which time the best is not easy to understand," they all looked at Tommy "Did you understand a word of that?" Conner asked Jack who was just sat there still trying to work out what he meant; he just looked at Conner and shrugged.

"Sarah. May I ask you about that mark on your arm?" Tommy asked looking at her, "mark on my arm?" she asked quizzically "yes, the one on the inside of your left arm, Sarah looked at him then raised her arm looking at her birth mark she pointed "Oh this thing you mean... I was born with it" Tommy's eyes widened now he could see it clearly, there was no mistaking it standing he made his excuses then left, as he got into his car, he looked in the mirror. It wasn't possible there was no way that it was possible, reaching into his jacket he pulled out his phone punching Yamatoya's number into the phone it rang for a moment, then came the dorsal tones of Master Yamatoya Tommy explained that he needed to see him but was unsure on how to get to where he was, Yamatoya told him to go to Lindes and once he was near the castle to let him know and he would have one of the young monks pick him up.

Tommy drove for about an hour finally he got the castle, letting Yamatoya know he was there he waited, finally a man approached him, "are you Tommy?" Tommy looked at him "It's the rainy days that are the worst" Tommy said, "Yes, but when the snow falls it's so beautiful" the man replied, Tommy smiled and followed him they made their way to where the cars were, Tommy followed him back upon to the A470, as they travelled Tommy noticed the man driving put his indicator on, tommy followed they turned off the road onto what looked like an old horse trail. They had followed the path for over an hour when they finally stopped, climbing out Jack went to where the man was standing. He didn't understand why they were stopping, the man walked over to the hedge moving some moss on a tree he pushed what looked like a button slowly the hedge started to open, it was then Tommy noticed that there was a monastery, through the opening it was then he realised how it was that no one knew it was there it was built in the trees, not one had been cut down instead they built the monastery so the trees would mask it from view, so even if you flew over it you would not know it was there, all you would see would be trees.

As he entered Tommy noted that the court yard was spacious but the answer was simple to see, the trees that would have been in the court yard were still there but somehow they had managed to move them, and arrange them in such a way that they would have more than enough room for training, Plus they didn't have to worry about rainy days due to the dense coverage the rain never really got through so they remained dry most of the time, he followed behind the man who led him to two large doors, upon entering he noticed it was a large room, how the hell did they manage to get all these statues up here without anyone noticing, there were men knelt in prayer on either side, not one of them looked up when they entered, they walked through the hall into one of the smaller rooms and there he noticed Yamatoya, who was standing talking to the junior monks that were there. Once he noticed Tommy, he sent them away and walked over to where they were standing.

"Renji, you may leave us now" he said looking to the man who had accompanied him, Renji bowed then left, Yamatoya smiled raising his hand he placed it on Tommy's shoulder, "Tommy it's been too long, how is Tetsu doing these days?" Tetsu was Tommy's uncle, it was through him that he knew Master Yamatoya, as he grew into a young man, he was often told the stories of him by his uncle Tetsu who had been young when he met Master Yamatoya, their meeting was quite by chance. Tetsu was going through a hard time always getting into trouble, one of the times he had run away and was hiding in the mountains, that was where he met Master Yamatoya who saw promise in the young boy.

Tommy remembered the story of that first encounter, Tetsu had been in another fight again and gotten into a big argument with his father, after that he had stormed out making his way up the mountain; he was full of anger and resentment he didn't know why he was feeling like this but the anger was the worst, while he had been up there Yamatoya had happened to come across him he was hitting a tree with a stick, "May I ask what that tree has done to you?"

Yamatoya asked, Tetsu just spun around "Get out of here old man, before I hit you with it, Yamatoya laughed that made Tetsu even angrier. "If you think you can hit me, why don't you try" Tetsu had heard enough spinning around he swung the stick, but Yamatoya wasn't there it was then he felt someone take his legs out from under him, as he landed on his back an looked up Yamatoya was standing over him laughing.

Even angrier Tetsu jumped up and tried to hit him again but once again ended up on his back with the man laughing at him, he couldn't believe it how was this guy able to do this he didn't look anything special, Tetsu decided that he would try one more time; but once again he was the one that ended up on the floor, this time instead of laughing Yamatoya sat on a log, "do you know why you fell?" he asked, Tetsu just sat up and looked at him. He waited a moment then up with his cane and hit Tetsu on the head, "Do you know why you fell?" he repeated Tetsu looked at him then down at the floor, "No I don't" the man laughed "you fell because your too clumsy," Tetsu jumped to his feet "No I fell because you hit me!" he shouted, Yamatoya laughed "why were you hitting that tree?" he asked, Tetsu looked at him "I don't know I just get angry and I need to hit something.

"What is your name?" Tetsu looked at him thought about it for a moment "My name is Tetsu Takahshia," the man smiled "OK, lad off you go," Yamatoya said as he walked off Tetsu remembered leaving feeling a little down that he had not gotten the man's name, the next time they met the man was talking to Tetsu's father they seemed to be having a lengthy conversation, once they had finished his father had called him to them. It was then he found out that he was to be leaving with the man, he had tried to argue but his father would not hear of it, finally it was time for them to go. As they left his mother was crying Tetsu had stayed and trained with the man for sixteen years when suddenly the old man announced that he would be leaving, it wasn't long after that he totally disappeared, the only news they had was a letter every month. That was the only way they knew that he was in Wales because of those letters Tetsu had wanted to leave and join him but his father would not allow it instead he was given a job in his father's company.

Yamatoya broke him out of his thoughts, "Master why did you come to Wales?" the question just popped out, Yamatoya looked at him and smiled, "Well my boy it's a long story," "Well couldn't you shorten it? I know uncle Tetsu has always wondered why you left Japan the way you did, you were there one day and then you announced that you were leaving, you didn't even tell them when you were going. One day you were just gone" Yamatoya looked at him sighing he sat down. "Master Teruo asked me to leave and come here, you see this monastery has actually been here for thousands of years it was built by Master Takegami back in 1509, and it was decided that he would be the one to leave, his soul mission was to bring peace to their worlds but it seemed as though once he had found Wales, he decided that was where he wanted to be, back in those days there were no mobile phones or the internet so there was no way of letting the others know where he was so he started this monastery. It was him and two disciples they left and were never heard from again, it seemed as though he found this place so bewitching that he built what you now see before you. I left to come here after this place was found. One of the disciples from here made his way back over to Japan, he was put through many tests before they would accept him, but it seemed that he passed them all, leaving no doubt... the only way he could have learned the techniques was from someone that had already mastered them... it was then that I was ordered to come here and check things out... I must say I understand what he wanted... I have been here ever since." It didn't really answer his question, but Tommy knew that one thing Yamatoya was good at was turning everything one their head.

Tommy remembered why he had gone there in the first place; it was that damn mark on Sarah's arm, "Master do you remember about the nine protectors?" Yamatoya looked at him then nodded "Of course I do I learn about them while I was a young disciple back in Japan... It was something that we all learned it has been passed down through the centuries once every thousand years a person is born with the mark of the protector, they say that's where the astrological signs come from, each of the protectors are born with the mark of what they protect. Why do you ask?" "Umm what would the mark of the fish mean?" Yamatoya looked at him "That is the mark of nature, the one who bares this mark is the protector of earth...but once again I ask why you are asking me this?" Tommy looked at him, he was wondering what he should tell him after all it was folk law, it's not like these people truly existed there was no way magic didn't exist. If it did then it would be found out by now wouldn't it, Yamatoya popped him on the head bringing him out of his thoughts, "Tommy have you seen this mark?" he asked quizzically Tommy looked at him and just nodded, "Come with me," Yamatoya stood and led tommy down into the lowest part of the monastery, there were a lot of old scrolls and other manuals and such there, walking over he went through some scrolls then choosing the one he wanted, he walked over to the table in the centre of the room. "Come here," he commanded in a more authoritative tone. One that tommy had never heard him use before; but did as he was told, looking at the parchment he noticed the symbols that were on it and there on the right was the same sign that was on Sarah's arm.

"That's the mark I saw" Tommy said without thinking, Yamatoya looked at him grasping him by the shoulders "Where, where did you see this sign?" He asked with urgency, Tommy pulled away it was as though he had been sucked into a dream. This was not possible there was no way. Looking at Yamatoya he saw that he was deadly serious, "Umm there was a girl she was in an accident, and she had that mark on the inside of her left arm." Yamatoya looked at him "A girl...A girl had this mark?" Tommy looked at him and nodded, Yamatoya looked at him "are you sure that she had this mark on her?" "Yes, I am positive that was the mark on her arm" Yamatoya looked at him "You will take me to this woman" Tommy looked after him as he walked out of the room, Tommy didn't have a clue what he was thinking, how in the hell was he supposed to introduce him to Sarah. Conner would not hear of it he knew that. "Are you coming?" He heard Yamatoya shout, running out of the room he caught up with him, "Master how am I going to introduce you to her for one her father will insist on meeting you first...no one gets near her without his say so." Yamatoya looked at him and smiled, "OK, then I will meet him first...umm Tommy did you notice if there was a mark on her father at all?" Tommy was taken aback for a moment at the question, "no I didn't why?" Yamatoya looked at him he knew that if she was who he was thinking then there was no doubting it Conner would have to have the mark on him, maybe Tommy just hadn't noticed it.

As they left the monastery Yamatoya left instructions with the high priest, then they were on their way they took Tommy's car, the drive was made in silence as they made their way from Lindes to Uialben, Tommy was happy about it in a way he was still trying to think of a way to introduce Master Yamatoya to Conner, then they were going to have to find a way of getting Conner to agree. Finally, they were there they had made their way to Lamben as they headed up the site Tommy still had no idea how he was going to pull this off.

He was disappointed that when he had called the station, they told him that Conner was not in today, it seemed as though it was his day off; why did he have to be off today of all days. He would have preferred that he see Conner outside of the home instead of going there, but master Yamatoya would not be dissuaded he was intent on meeting this girl. Finally, he pulled into the driveway of the house, getting out of the car they made their way up the driveway to the front door. Tommy pressed the button, and they waited finally Conner answered the door Tommy and master Yamatoya stood there patiently, "Hi Tommy it's been a while what can I do for you?" He asked eyeing Yamatoya suspiciously, Yamatoya stepped forward and stretched out his hand Conner took it, the two men introduced each other tommy noticed that Master Yamatoya was looking at Conner's wrist.

Looking up he smiled at Conner "I am Master Yamatoya," Conner looked at him, "Master of what?" he asked casually Yamatoya just laughed, "Oh my I am getting old, I am the Grand master of the frost monastery, that is why they call me master Yamatoya" Conner looked at him and smiled "Oh so you're like a monk then?" Once again Yamatoya laughed, "Yes I am a monk," Conner stood to one side and welcomed them both in, Yamatoya followed him into the living room, Sarah was sat on the window seat looking up the mountain, he noticed a ghostly figure sitting next to her, one thing she loved doing was just sitting there looking up at the mountain. Conner interrupted her thoughts, "Sarah honey this is Master Yamatoya, and you have met Tommy before" she turned seeing the old man she smiled and stood up walking across she stretched out her hand to him, "Well hello there, would you like to sit down?" she said as she led him to the chair near to where she herself was sitting.

She didn't know why but she liked this old guy, Yamatoya smiled and sat down, "Would you like tea or coffee?" she asked looking at all who were there, Yamatoya thought for a moment "What type of tea do you have?" Sarah smiled "well we have normal or herbal" Yamatoya smiled once again, "Oh what type of herbal do you have?" Sarah rattled off a few, then she said the one he was waiting for Rosehip. "Oh may I have a rosehip please" Yamatoya asked "Honey or sugar?" she asked he smiled once again "honey please" Tommy sat down he said he would have a peppermint tea and her father wanted his usual coffee, and she would have a cup of coffee herself, as she made her way into the kitchen they noticed that she still had a slight limp, but other than that you would never have noticed that she had been in an accident, all her wounds were healed and she was almost back to her perky self, she had her days when she would be a bit down but she was looking forward to going back to university next month, it had taken a lot to get her father to agree; but what was she supposed to do just sit back and do nothing, there was no way she refused to do that.

As she put the kettle on, she heard the front door go walking into the living room there was Jack, she laughed "What smelled the kettle did you?" he looked at her and laughed he always had the habit of showing up when the kettle was just put on or just boiled, "Coffee please" he said Sarah laughed, "No you don't... get your butt in here and give me a hand would you?" Jack stood and walked into the kitchen with her.

Yamatoya decided that this would be the best opportunity he would have, pointing to Conner's wrist, "Could you tell me when you got that?" Conner looked at him then at his wrist "That has been there since I was a child I don't really know where it came from." Master Yamatoya smiled, "Do you know what that mark means?" Conner looked at him "No" he said shaking his head, Yamatoya sighed and reaching his hand up stroked his long beard, "Can we walk in the garden?" Conner looked at him smiled then led the way, walking through the kitchen Conner grabbed his Coffee, Yamatoya bowed slightly then leaving his tea on the counter followed Conner out to the back, the garden was massive Yamatoya smiled, Conner let the old man past him as he closed the door, as they walked up the garden a ways Yamatoya turned to Conner.

"You already know, don't you?" Conner looked at him, then away "You mean about my daughter, right?" Was all he said, Yamatoya knew at that moment that he was right the mark that was on Conner's arm was only given to those who possess protector abilities and the fact that the child that bore the mark was a female was something that only happened every ten thousand years, but it seemed that Conner was under the impression that she was just a normal protector, but he knew she wasn't.

He remembered from his years of training that once every ten thousand years a female was born with the mark of the protector, but she was unlike the other she would be endowed with the abilities of all protectors, she was the one that would keep the nine realms in order, looking at Conner he stood up straight, "Conner do you not realise, the significance of the fact that a female has been born with the mark,"

Conner looked at him for a moment then bent his head, "Yes I'm not stupid you know that I have gone through my training and part of that training was about a female being born with the mark and what that would signify, I never thought however that it would happen in my lifetime." He shook his head. The thought of when she had been born all the interest there was in her, he had been born with the mark of a protector and so had his wife they were told that a union between the two was prohibited but they fell in love, they didn't care about the rules they thought that it was a stupid rule, it wasn't like they were actual protectors not like the nine protectors, they were guardians ones who were born with the mark of protector guardians, they would raise protectors and train them once they received their abilities.

Never once did they think that their union would produce the Grand protector guardian, but they had not listened, they married against the wishes of everyone her family and his family had both been against the union. There had been a massive fight the night before the wedding, Conner and Miranda had feared that the families would try and step in and stop the wedding, so at the last minute they had eloped. They knew that once they had been married there was nothing the families could do, it was a legal union so even if they were unhappy they would be able to do nothing, they were right everything changed when she had fallen pregnant, they could not get rid of the family then all working out when the baby would be born and weather she would be male or female, Conner remembered the look on their faces when one of the others had brought up the fact that they might have a female child, The room had fallen silent.

Even if he and Miranda had known that there was a chance that she would be the great guardian protector it would not have changed who they were, once Sarah had been born and they had seen the mark on her there had been people in and out of her life for years, Sarah's mother asked him on her death bed to take her away some where they would never be able to find them. That way no one could take her away, we knew that her awakening would take place on her twenty first birthday and we decided that we would raise her as a normal girl only telling her when the time was right but when I almost lost her, I have been wondering what I should do…but how do you know about her?"

Yamatoya looked at him for a moment, "humph… Tommy told me that he had seen the mark on her arm, he had not realised what it was he was seeing at first that's why he sought me out… now tell me how could you have been so foolish raising her like this as though she was just a normal girl when you knew all along what she was destined for."

"I wasn't thinking about that, and neither was her mother we were just fed up with people coming back and forth looking at her, telling us how we were to raise our child, that she was to be shut away from the world not having contact with anyone, then going mad when we enrolled her into school saying that she would be jaded. She had to have complete isolation, I'm her father her mother

41

and I were going to take her away before she fell ill, and when she did, she made me promise that I would give our daughter a normal life, up until the point she had to be told." Master Yamatoya looked at him his face stern and foreboding, "How old is she?" Conner looked at him she will be nineteen in three weeks, "Nineteen in three weeks! Then she has to be told now, we have to start getting her prepared for what she is about to undertake…Conner you have to understand raising her the way you have has put her in more danger, than if she had been raised the way a protector is supposed to be raised, there is a reason behind everything…the reason behind them being raised in isolation is so that they will have no ties to this world so they will accept the awakening when it happened!" shaking his head he started to move towards the house, Conner caught up to him quickly.

"Wait! You don't have the right to come in here and demand anything! She is my child, and I will decide when it will be the most suitable time to tell her not you!" With that the door opened and standing there in front of them was Sarah looking at them puzzled "Tell me what?" Conner looked at her and then to Yamatoya then back to her, Yamatoya smiled and took her by the elbow leading her into the house, Conner coming up behind him trying to voice his objections, but he could tell that Yamatoya wasn't listening to him. Finally, he grabbed the old man by the arm, but in one swift motion, Yamatoya had moved twice, and Conner found himself looking up at the old guy, he didn't quite understand what or how that just happened, but Sarah was at his side. "Dad, are you OK?" Conner managed to get to his feet when he looked around, he noticed that Tommy and Jack were both standing there with shocked disbelief on their faces; they could not believe what they had just witnessed. Conner turned to Yamatoya, "how the hell, did you do that" "Quite simple you're to clumsy." This time Sarah and the others in the room laughed they couldn't believe that this unassuming man had put Conner on his back.

Yamatoya guided Sarah over to the window seat, she had been sitting on when they first arrived and took the seat next to her, looking to Conner, then to Sarah "Young lady there is something your father has to tell you." He turned and looked at Conner who was standing there wanting nothing more than to strangle the old codger, instead he walked across the room and sat on the seat next to Yamatoya, stretching out his hand he placed it on top of Sarah's. "Honey, do you remember the bedtime stories that we used to tell you when you were young about the nine protectors and that how that fish on your arm meant that you were one of them?" Sarah looked at him and laughed "Of course I do, I remember thinking that it would be great to protect everyone. Why?"

Yamatoya looked at him then realised that she had grown up with stories of the protectors even though she had no idea that she was one, she knew everything she needed to know. Because her mother and father had put it into story form for her, which meant that even though he wanted her to grow as a normal child she still learned of the path she was going to undertake.

Getting up she left the room, while they waited for her return, they filled Jack and Tommy in on what was going on, master Yamatoya had forbidden Jack to tell her how he felt, this was the worst thing that could happen right now, Jack didn't know how this could actually be true but he never thought that Conner would lie to him, so he agreed that until everything was decided he would say nothing. Though Conner could not understand why Jack had still not told her.

Finally, Sarah re-entered the room holding a choice of notebooks she handed them to her father, "Dad remember that box mam gave me the one that had a time lock on it," Conner looked at her then nodded "yes" "she said that it would open on my sixteenth birthday. Well, these are what was inside it," Conner opened the first book there was a letter from her mother it explained everything, also why her father was to take her away so that she would be able to grow up happy, Conner looked at her, "When did you read these?" Sarah smiled "I started reading them on my sixteenth birthday." "So, you know already?" "That I'm something that's called a grand guardian protector? Yes, the books explain everything... because you have gone through so much, I decided that I would not show you these until you were ready to tell me."

A tear fell from Conner's eye, to think that even now her mother was still protecting her, as he thumbed through the pages, he noticed that they were all written by her own hand, "so this is what she was working on," he said without thinking, "Dad?" Conner looked at her "I always wondered what it was she was working on, when she found out that she had cancer she started working on these books I always wondered what they were but she would never let me see them I assumed they were a journal or something...I would have never guessed that she was actually writing them to you explaining everything that I myself have been trying to work out what to say." Sarah just smiled I remember my sixteenth birthday like it was yesterday Watching the timer count down till I was able to open it." She reached into her pocket and pulled a disk out this was in there too, Conner looked at it, Sarah got up and walked over to the TV pushing the disk in they waited then her mother popped up on the screen, oh how he missed that smile.

"Sarah, my darling child I know that you must miss me as I will miss you. There is something that you need to know something that your father and I have been keeping from you. And if I know him, he is still trying to find a way of telling you everything that you need to know…well my darling I will explain everything to you now. But don't say anything to your father until he is ready to tell you, his self. Only on that day are you to show him this."

She went on to tell her all about the day her father and her met and the warning they had received but neither of them would listen, then the day that she had been born everyone being there, they had taken her away when they had noticed the mark and if it hadn't been for her father, they might not have seen her again. The disk finished with her mother speaking straight to Conner asking him to forgive her.

By the time that it ended her, and her father were in tears, watching her mother on the screen she looked so well the only realization that she was ill was the bandanna that she wore to cover her head.

Yamatoya smiled as it ended and turned to Conner and Sarah "OK, so you know. Now you must come with me we only have a short time to prepare you for what's to come." Sarah looked at him and laughed but I have already been preparing since my sixteenth birthday, when I found all this, the books told me everything that I needed to do, and I have been doing them." "May I have a look at those books?" he asked, Sarah nodded "Sure," she said handing them to him, he took up the seat he was originally sat in and started reading. The phone rang Conner answered not long after he and Jack left, leaving her there with Tommy and Yamatoya she just sat back on the window seat looking up at the mountain while Tommy watched over Yamatoya.

Dusk was beginning to fall and Master Yamatoya was still reading Sarah and Tommy were talking trying not to be too loud, so they didn't disturb him. They realised that they had a lot in common, so they passed the time talking about their favourite films and books they both liked Yestin Llandorags books they were full of action and suspense. They were looking forward to the next instalment of Loves lost it was a tragic love story the last one had ended with the hero and heroine being separated again, they were both hoping that the next instalment would have them reunite and finally tell each other that they loved them, but in all the books so far, each time it seemed to be heading in that direction he would put another plot twist in that would separate them.

Finally, Conner and Jack were back, master Yamatoya had fallen asleep on the chair, Sarah and tommy left him there he was an old man after all. It was getting late so Sarah brought a blanket down for master Yamatoya, she had told her father not to wake him up "just let him sleep," she whispered as she put the blanket over him, she turned to Tommy there is a guest bedroom upstairs you can sleep there, Tommy looked at her and smiled "It's OK, I think that it would be best if I wake him up and we go to my place." "Don't you dare" she said in an angry whisper "Let him be, now stop being so stubborn and sleep here." Tommy bowed his head and followed her up the stairs she led him into the guest room.

He settled himself down for the night the bed was so comfortable he fell asleep almost as soon as his head hit the pillows, he dreamed about the day he left to come here the argument that he had with his father. Then it went weird he started dreaming about Sarah about taking her in his arms just as he was about to kiss her the door to his room burst open. "Come on are you going to sleep all day," Tommy jumped up and came face to face with Sarah looking at the clock on the side table he was shocked to see that it was past ten. He pulled the covers closer to him the last thing he needed was for her to see what was happening beneath them, she put his clothes on the chair "I took these while you were sleeping, so hurry up and get dressed, we are heading to the monastery today."

Once she had left the room, he climbed out of the bed heading to the shower he climbed in what on earth was that dream about, he could hardly believe that he was dreaming about her. Could this mean that somewhere along the lines he found himself attracted to her, they do say that dreams are hidden desires. As the water washed over him, he found himself thinking about that dream and about Sarah it's impossible how could a woman he has only just met stir such emotions in him, shaking his head he tried pushing the image of her from his mind but the more he tried the stronger it got when he finally finished getting out, he dried putting his clothes on he joined the others downstairs.

Conner was working on a case as usual but luckily, he could work from home if he needed to or from the monastery, once they were all present and accounted for, they left Conner climbed into his car with Sarah and Jack while Tommy and master Yamatoya climbed into Tommy's car, as they headed out Sarah found herself looking for the castle, as they drove down there it was standing like a beacon drawing all the children to it, she loved watching their smiling faces.

They got to the monastery at just gone one Sarah looked about in wonder, it was amazing you could see how old it was by the design of it, she also loved the way that none of the trees had been cut down to place it there instead they had managed to build it around the trees so that the only ones who knew it was there those residing in it.

As she got out of the car all who were working on the grounds suddenly stopped, what they were doing and were looking in their direction, for some of them this was the first time they had seen a woman in the flesh. Sarah was starting to feel a little self-conscious, as they just stared at her master Yamatoya clapped his hands that seemed to work. It brought them all to their senses and they carried on with what they were doing when they first walked up, Tommy and Yamatoya led them into the grand hall where there were monks on either side sat in silent prayer, as with Tommy not one of them moved, when they came in they didn't even open their eyes to acknowledge that they were there, Master Yamatoya led them into a separate room, once they were in there he excused himself.

Yamatoya made his way to the prayer chamber where the internet was, he didn't waist anytime in contacting all the grand masters; letting them know that he was going to do a conference call with them at around seven that night, once that was done, he made his way back to where they were waiting. He didn't see the point in just beating about the bush she was going to have to start her training now, he knew that the books had taught her what to do but he was going to start from the beginning.

Walking over he tapped her on the shoulder "OK, now is a better time than ever, come with me." He said catching her by the arm he led her into the training grounds, looking around him he called one of the men that were training there over. "OK, I want you to show her to the obstacle course, the man looked at him then to Sarah, "Master Yamatoya, do you think that's a wise idea with the way she's dressed? Master Yamatoya looked at her it was only then he noticed that she was wearing a dress and heels. "Well, this will never do, why did you were a dress?" Sarah looked at him, "well I wasn't expecting you to start my training today, and I thought you would at least let me get used to the place first." "There's no time for that…do you have something else you can wear?" she looked at him and smiled walking over to the small travel case she had gotten out of the boot earlier, "Well I thought since I was going to be training here, I would also be staying here," Master Yamatoya went white he hadn't thought of that, a girl staying at the monastery. It was never heard of, but he had no choice because of who she was, she was going to have to stay there, but where the dorms were full of men, they didn't really have the facilities to accommodate a woman. Once again, the men that had been training had stopped at the Meer mention that she would be staying there, master Yamatoya clapped his hands, and they resumed training. "Follow me" Master Yamatoya said leading the way, walking behind him he walked her past the first set of dorms to the second, as they walked in she noticed beds lining the walls on either side he walked her past them into a smaller room, that was meant for visiting monks, there was no choice she was going to have to stay in the dorms; but at least this way she would be separated from the men the other added bonus was the room was built with a bathroom, leading her in "OK, this is where you will stay." She looked around the room a bed and a small table with a clock on it.

"Not used to catering for women, are you?" she said smiling at him, he looked at her "not usually we only have men at this temple, but this is one of the rooms set up for the visiting monks that is why it has a shower. So, you will stay here but I warn you that the room out there is full of men during the nights. So please be mindful of that," she looked at him a bit strange be mindful she didn't quite understand what he was talking about so she just smiled and nodded, "OK, get changed and meet us outside once you're ready, OK?" once again she nodded as he left getting her stuff together, she searched her bag for the clothes she always wore to the gym they should be fine for this, getting them out she changed, as she left the room, she grabbed her hair and put it into a tight ponytail. As she walked through the door to where everyone was, standing her father and Jack were used to her gym wear but when master Yamatoya looked at her he went white, what on earth was she thinking wearing something like that, with all these men around. Marching forward he stopped in front of her, "What on earth is this? Where are your clothes?" She looked at him in wonder "Umm these are my workout clothes nobody at the gym says anything about what I'm wearing," Master Yamatoya looked at her and shook his head there was no way he could leave her in the hands of one of the acolytes, he was going to have to take her and never once take his eyes off her, these men have had very little experience with women, and with her dressed this way he was going to have a stampede on his hands.

Finally, they were at the assault course, she looked for a moment she thought that her heart was going to stop. They call this an assault course Conner could not believe his eyes the police assault course was tough how the hell was he expecting her to get through this, with that he noticed some of the men were training they looked exhausted and by the looks of it they weren't even halfway through, "Umm Master Yamatoya, what the hell is this?" He looked at Conner and the others "Well you see this is what we call the assault course, you start there, and the course takes you in a complete circle, so you end at the same place." He called one of the men over.

"I want you to take her around the assault course," Conner stepped forward "Wait a minute you mean you want her to do this now?" Master Yamatoya looked at him "of course I do, this will let me judge her fitness level, I don't expect that she will finish it on her first try; but I want to see how far she will get before she has to give up," Sarah looked at him with annoyance "Oh is that so" she said briskly, causing him to look at her but she didn't even let him get a word out turning to the guy on her right, "Take me around this course" she said more of a command than a request. He stood there and just bowed his head slightly he could understand her frustration, at the thought that he didn't have faith that she would be able to finish it. They walked to the start as they got there, he handed her a watch. "Put this on, it will track your heart rate, you have to know that no one finishes it on their first go, we all fail in the beginning." Sarah looked at him and smiled.

As they took off, she went easily over the first two hurdles, then came the tree she stopped looking at it. *Just think of it like the climbing frame when you were a kid you go up one end and come down the other*, she thought looking at it she was a little daunted by it, for it was three times higher than any she had seen before. Slowly she started to climb she could feel the sweat running down her back, the further she climbed the more she could feel the perspiration finally, she was at the top now all she had to do was swing her leg over and climb down the other side, with quiet determination she lifted herself over and started her descent, as she reached the bottom, she could feel her legs trembling slightly, there was no way she was giving up yet. This was only her third obstacle no way; she carried on as she got to the swing bridge, she looked this was obviously to test your stability. She watched as Tim made his way across then stepping up he was on the other side, like with the others once he got to the other side he waited for her it was a bridge made up of one long pole attached to ropes that formed a

48

bridge, underneath was a slow moving stream grasping hold of the rope it swung slightly as she put her foot onto it, she could feel it sliding she gripped the ropes either side of her, she was not going to fall there is no way, she made her way across finally she was on the other side, thankful she had not fallen in, finally she was at the next obstacle as she made her way around the course her legs began to feel heavy. She was feeling as though she was going to throw up, she couldn't take anymore she was going to have to give up she was so angry at the fact, she found a new determination it was only then she noticed that her father and the others were looking at her, not only them but some of the monks that were training there as well.

Why had she done something wrong, Tim who had been with her the whole way was now at her side "Come on girl, you can do this…" Sarah looked at him slightly bemused; at what he had said only then did she realise that she was almost back at the start she was almost finished with that she stopped at the pit, she watched Tim expertly make his way across jumping from one pole to the next, "Come on! Really?" Tim looked at her "You can do this come on" there was no way she was going to be able to get this each pole was just wide enough for one foot. As Tim was about to make his way back master Yamatoya shouted at him, "Don't you dare she can work it out" they all waited finally she jumped on to the first pole her leg felt as though it was about to give under her, looking she noticed that some were shorter than the others, she had to concentrate slowly she made her way across, as she landed on the one pole it shook under her Tim run to the edge "quick jump to the other one, some of those are meant to make you lose your balance, if you fall you have to go back to the beginning," Sarah listened to him and swiftly made her way over the poles finally landing on the other side as she did she slipped slightly Tim reached out his hands and grasped hold of her, without thinking pulling her to him as he realised what he was doing he quickly released her, she stood there and looked there were two more obstacles and she would be back at the beginning, she was dreading what was to come each of the obstacles she had come across were more intense than the last, she still couldn't believe that all the men here had to go through this, she remembered that master Yamatoya and Tim had both said nobody makes it on their first try. Now she understood why, she got to the last but one obstacle this was for upper body strength it was a bit like the monkey bars but once again a lot higher and underneath was a pool of water it looked horrible and muddy the last thing she wanted was to fall into that, she climbed the ladder to get to the start position once again Tim went first, with ease he made his way across landing on the other side he looked at her, there had to be more than thirty bars here, there was no way she was going to be able to take them two at a time, with trepidation she caught hold of the first wrung her arms felt like lead she had to do this swinging she caught hold of the next one, then the next finally she had made it half way but her arms were feeling tired she could feel her muscles burning as she went as she caught hold of the next one she thought "I'm not going to make it," she could feel her hands slipping quickly she moved to the next one then the next she could see the end in sight, but this was hurting if she did manage to get to the end of this what was the last one going to be like, she found herself dreading it with that her arms seemed to stop working she was just hung there as she tried to release so she could grab the next it was as though her body was fighting against her. Oh no she was going to fall, and she only had a few wrung's left come on she willed her arms to move out of sheer determination she finally managed to get to the last wrung all that was left to do was swing onto the podium, and this would be over she swung and released her feet hit the hard surface it was only then did she realise how bad her legs actually felt the pain was bad the last time she felt pain like this was when she was healing from the accident, but she was determined to continue there was no way that she was going to give up now there was only one obstacle left. She remembered looking at it when she was standing next to it, master Yamatoya she was dreading this one even though it seemed simple, she knew that each of the others had gotten harder as she went along, the bars were the worst she had thought that with each new one she had gotten to, as she made her way to the next one she could feel her legs wobbling slightly; her shoulders were sagging she could feel her eyes getting heavier, was she going to pass out? No, come on there is one left you can do this she thought even though she knew that her body wanted to give in her spirit was unwilling. It pushed her harder than she would have ever thought it could, finally she was there it was then she realised the distance between the obstacles, she wondered if she could walk but she knew the answer there was no way, if she tried that Master Yamatoya would probably have her go back to the start she could feel how much she had slowed down looking at her watch she could hardly believe it, she had been at this for over three hours, the end was insight; come on just one more and it would be over, as they got to the last one she looked at it a log, all she had to do was walk across a log and she would be done, she watched as Tim approached it he expertly moved across it with ease, when she took up her position she realised the log looked like it was spinning, wait it was spinning, "Oh come on!" she shouted looking at where Master Yamatoya was, there wasn't just a few there this time it seemed that all of the men from the monastery were standing there, when she shouted they all seemed to form a line they looked at her all bowing slightly. OK, she could do this she had climbed a mountain run over three miles swung across a gorge the things she had done she knew she had the balance the poles had shown her that so had the stupid bridge thing just this time there was nothing for her to grab hold of, she was going to have to try and run across, no wait if she runs there was more chance of her falling, if only she had taken more notice of how Tim had done it. Then she would be able to do this with ease, but she was thinking about how much her body was hurting, right when he crossed he seemed to lean slightly to one side and his feet seemed to slide across rather than stepping, okay she could do this as she put her foot on she was glad that she hadn't put her full weight on it because it slipped there was no way this was impossible.

She was stood there trying to work it out when Master Yamatoya broke her thoughts, "If you don't move then you have to start over again!" "You have to be kidding me!" She shouted at him, he smiled and shook his head "you spent too much time on the other obstacles this course is meant to be finished in four hours of which you have just twenty minutes left." She looked at him he can't be serious "But this is my first time!" she complained, "Yes and you have done well, I would never have thought you would make it this far, that is why I never told you about the time limit, but since you are on the last obstacle, I think it only fair that you have the same amount of time the others have." "Oh, great gee thanks," now she was angry looking at her watch so there was a second purpose to this dammed thing it was only then she noticed that a timer seemed to be counting down, he was serious she wasn't sure if it was anger or pure frustration, the next thing she knew she was on the log her feet moving so she didn't fall. She could do this she would show him, finally, she got to the other side Tim tapped her on the arm quick we must get to the finish. She ran with him just as her hand landed on the log the watch started beeping, "Sorry you failed" she looked at Master Yamatoya. "But I made it to the finish." "Yes, but to complete the course you have to be on this side, not that side, but well done for your first attempt."

Sarah wanted nothing more than to fall into bed as she followed Master Yamatoya, she pouted she couldn't believe it she had finished yes; she was on the wrong side of the log, but he could have given in for her first time. This was so unfair, the men that had been there having all cheered for her when she had gotten to the end, they had all found her amazing, but she had been going to the gym every day, she ran five miles, but this was new to her this was the first time she had attempted anything like this before. She was a bit amazed that she had finished it. As the night drew in she found herself wandering around the temple it was magnificent, she loved the old carvings there were symbols on the walls they looked like some kind of writing as she ventured into one of the other rooms she noticed one of the other monks there, he turned and bowed slightly smiling she walked over to where he was standing, "Hi" he looked at her for a moment then "hello" came his response, "what is this place?" she asked looking around the room there was a large sculpture of Buddha on the back wall and many different wall hangings the monk smiled, "This is the room of reflection, we come here when there is something we need to meditate on," "oh you mean like a question you want the answer to but can't find one" "yes something like that" "but how do you meditate on something? where do you start?" the monk once again smiled, "well do you see that space over there" he pointed to what looked like a mat, "Yes," "we sit there and meditate it's through mediation we find enlightenment." "So you mean if there is something that I want to find the answer to then, I can just sit there and it will come to me," the monk laughed slightly "I'm sorry, I don't mean to laugh but you do ask the strangest of questions, when you meditate you put yourself into a trance like state, once you have completely relaxed only then can you start to meditate on the question that you want answered," "Can you show me how to meditate?" the monk looked at her then smiled, "Come with me" he led her out of the room into a weird looking chamber, "To be able to meditate you must be able to have complete focus, this is where you can train for that," "Umm what do you mean train to have focus, I already know how to focus myself," he walked into the room, she watched as he climbed up onto a the podium in the middle of the room she watched in awe as he raised his leg and just stood there he was only there for a few moments when the first of many items started falling, not once did he move even when the one came very close to hitting him. He just stood there after about ten minutes he climbed back down and walked over to where she was standing. "You see only when you can have complete focus can you start to truly meditate," she didn't quite understand what he meant, with that, he bowed and left leaving her in the room, she could do that she was sure she could. Walking over she climbed onto the podium standing there she looked about her, then just like the monk things started falling she stood there watching them, they looked like bean bags in different colours and shapes, but she was sure they were bean bags she stretched out her hand as one fell close to her, as it hit her hand it stung slightly she could imagine what it would be like if they hit over and over again. She would imagine that after a while they would hurt. Standing still she closed her eyes, not moving slowly she started drowning everything out the only thing she could hear was the slight whooshing noise the bags made as they fell, she could tell how close they were by the loudness of the whoosh.

She had been there for some time, when she heard someone calling her name opening her eyes there was Master Yamatoya and her father, then just like the monk when she climbed down the bags stopped there has to be something on the podium that told them when to fall, she thought, walking over to where Master Yamatoya was standing, she smiled at him, but he was looking at her quite unusually. "What's wrong?" She asked Master Yamatoya, who looked at her "Who told you to do that?" he asked, "Oh there was a monk in the other room I was in, when I asked him how to meditate, he brought me in here and showed me how to use that," she said pointing at the podium, "what did he look like?" Sarah looked at him "Well he was bald; he was wearing similar clothes to you, but he had a blue sash instead of the red one you are wearing." Master Yamatoya looked at her "are you sure he was wearing a blue sash?" "Yes, why?" He didn't answer her he just turned and walked out the door Sarah and Conner followed behind him, "Master Yamatoya what is it? Is there something wrong with him showing me that room?" Master Yamatoya was deep in thought so didn't answer her, he just kept walking.

He led them into the large dining hall it was time for them to eat, Sarah thought she would be sitting with the other men there but instead, she was led to the top end where the higher monks were seated, walking he pointed to an empty cushion, "you sit there" looking at him somewhat bemused "why do I have to sit here?" pointing to the picture above the cushion "is that the man who told you how to use the SheiKra?" looking up she smiled, "yes that is the man I met him in the meditation room, I asked him how he meditated on an answer that was when he took me to the SheiKra he stood on it and said that only when I could do that would I truly be able to meditate," master Yamatoya looked at her then back at the picture that was hanging there. "That is master Yakamoto he was one of the founding priests he has been dead for more than four hundred years, meaning you communed with the dead, he has been seen many times around the temple but only ever communicated with those who he deemed worthy. The last time he showed himself to someone, was over seventy years ago, to a young monk who had lost his way. You see back then this boy believed that being sent here was a punishment, it took for Yamatoya to show him how wrong he was, he left it at that not telling her anymore just telling her to sit. This was going to be a long night she thought why he was making her sit with them instead of with the others.

Finally, the night was over as she walked into her room she collapsed onto the bed it felt so good beneath her, she fell into a dreamless sleep, the sound of the clock on her bedside table woke her up, looking at it five o'clock no way hitting the buttoned to knock it off she turned over and went back to sleep, she hadn't been asleep long when she heard a knock on the door, "Umm yes who is it?" "It's time to get up miss," came the response looking at the clock six "OK, " she said weakly, slowly she sat up her arms and legs were aching, she groaned as she put her feet on the floor man she was dreading, what was she going to do the only thought she had was getting into the shower, slowly she made her way her legs felt so heavy, she hoped that Master Yamatoya didn't have a lot planned for her today. There was no way she could do too much her body hurt too badly, she turned the shower on the heat felt so good she washed once she had finished, she felt a lot better getting dressed she made her way down to the dining hall, it was mostly empty most of the men were already out training Master Yamatoya looked at her smiling. "How are you feeling this morning?" She looked at him, for some reason she was sure that he knew very well how she was feeling. She smiled sweetly "Fine thank you," she said "Good so are you up for another day on the obstacle course, maybe today you will finish it on time." Sarah stood there with shock on her face. *Please let that be a joke*, she thought but the look on his face said that it wasn't.

Walking over she grabbed her breakfast not speaking she was starving all that work yesterday had taken a lot out of her, she sat there eating she knew that they were looking at her. Even though they were in conversation there was no way she was going to look up, she was going to eat her breakfast then have another look around.

She was finally finished as she was about to excuse herself, Master Yamatoya stood and walked to where she was. "OK, now that you have finished it is time to start your training," she looked at him seeing that he was deadly serious she stood and followed him, she thought that he was taking her back to the obstacle course, but he didn't this time he took her into what looked like a pool, "OK, I think today we will start you off a bit slower. Get your muscles working properly again, do you have a bathing suit?" "Umm well I didn't think I would need it, so I never brought one," Master Yamatoya looked at her. Okay, there are bathing suits in there that you should be…" He stopped she was female all the bathing suits that were there were male. Shaking his head, he sent Tommy out to get one for her.

Tommy had been gone for about half an hour. She was grateful in a way because Master Yamatoya had not made her do anything for that half an hour, when he finally returned, he had a bathing suit with him one look she could see that he wasn't used to picking for women, it was more of a wetsuit than bathing suit. But at least it was functional. "Right now, go and get changed and we can get started," she listened and went to change by the time she got back she was horrified to find that there were all different things in the pool, Master Yamatoya walked over to her, "OK, all you have to do is get the flag," the flag? She looked around but she could see no flag Master Yamatoya pointed, she followed the path from his finger and there hanging from the ceiling was a flag, how the hell was she supposed to get that? "How?" He smiled at her "there are many different ways, but this is your trial you have to figure it out, oh and the only rule is you have to do it whilst you're in the confines of the pool," "you say what?" that's when she realised all those things must be there to help her get it, as she was about to get into the pool she stopped. "Wait a minute is there a time limit to this one too?" Master Yamatoya smiled "This one, not the time is up when you have retrieved the flag," he replied with a slight grin "OK," Sarah said with confidence walking over to the edge of the pool she dived in, swimming over she looked at the items that were there; okay maybe they fit together somehow and make a ladder or something, she tried many different ways but no matter what she tried they did not fit anyway. She climbed onto the larger of the object it was then she noticed that they were all shaped, you had a rectangle a circle all different shapes, okay what if she stacked them but how? diving off she swam over to the square taking it back she put it on top of the other one, okay now the circle slowly it started to fit together wait yes they were stacking but would she be able to climb it, there is only one way to find out, it was then she noticed there was no place to put her foot, she moved around she noticed there were notches at the top maybe if she used it like a climbing wall, grabbing hold she tried to pull herself up but it gave under her weight and she went tumbling into the water, she wasn't giving up there was no way climbing back up she tried again and for the second time ended back in the water. She was getting so frustrated now, maybe she could just pretend that she had done it, climb up and get the flag looking around she noticed that she was not as alone as she thought, maybe she could ask how it was done. Shaking her head there was no way that would mean she couldn't do it herself.

She had been there for over three hours her fingers were starting to look like old prunes, agghh what was she going to do, everything she tried didn't work. Was she going to give up tell them she couldn't do it, or maybe this was the test for her to give up; no that was stupid there is no way that Master Yamatoya would set her a task that she would not be able to complete. No there was a way to do this she just had to figure it out, before she knew it another two hours had passed, finally Master Yamatoya had come back smiling at her, "Umm I see the flag is still there?" She looked at him "This is impossible, there is no one who could possibly do this" "you are correct," What he didn't just say that did he? "What do you mean I'm correct I have been here all day and only now you tell me it can't be done!?" she was shouting, but Master Yamatoya just smiled that silly grin of his, "In life there are many obstacles that you have to overcome, not all of them are easy and even though it may seem impossible, there is always a path for you to take to make it work." "You are not making any sense." Master Yamatoya called one of the men to come to him, "Show her how to get the flag" was all he said, the guy jumped into the water grabbing the larger of the floats he made his way to the other end of the pool climbing upon to it he grabbed a hold of one of the ropes that were hanging down slowly he made his way across them once he grabbed the flag he let go landing in the water not far from where she was, coming up he handed her the flag then swam to the other side and got out bowing he left, she was standing there she hadn't noticed the ropes before.

"If one only sees straight ahead then the answer will surely avoid them," with that he left, no way was he just going to up and leave, what the hell was that supposed to mean. "Hey…wait, what do you mean only see in a straight line…Master Yamatoya!" With that he stopped turning to her he smiled, she was getting fed up with that stupid smile of his he never just gives her a straight answer, he always talked in riddles she was fed up with it. "Master Yamatoya please just tell me what I have to do give me a straight answer please?" Master Yamatoya could see her frustration, "Come with me." He said holding out his arm, she walked over to him and followed him into the meditation room he walked and stood in front of Buddha, turning he looked at her, "Sarah. If I were to give you all the answers, what would you learn? Buddha teaches us that wisdom comes from knowing oneself, and only by pushing ourselves can we truly know who we are?" Once again, he was talking in riddles, is it too much to ask for a straight answer? Bowing her head, she sighed what was the use. She thought.

Chapter 4

The Training

Sarah had been training at the monastery for over six months, now she could keep up with the others and found the training enjoyable. She also enjoyed the fact that they treated her the same as them, the fact that she was female had been a bump in the road at first, but now she got along with them all. It was like having brothers she loved the feeling she got when she was around them, they were even on the same training program when she had first arrived. She did everything on her own but slowly she was integrated into the group, she had even beaten the four-hour limit that was set on the assault course she had managed it in just under three hours, now all she had to do was beat Samuel's time of two hours twenty-five minutes, she was steadily getting better. She had noticed that there were men steadily appearing over time, soon there were more than twenty masters in the temple, she had not yet been introduced to any of them. Master Yamatoya who was always there when she was training always seemed to be preoccupied these days, she very rarely saw him anymore and when she did go looking for him, he was always with one of the newcomers who always gave her a cold look, she didn't know what she had done to them for them to be treating her this way, but she was getting tired of it.

"Sarah, earth to Sarah" it was Yestin calling her she looked at him "Umm, yes?" "What's wrong you seemed to space out for a moment there?" "Oh, it's nothing just thinking?" "What about?" "Oh, just about beating Samuel's time on the assault course" Yestin laughed. *We have all had those dreams, but until now his is one time that has never been beaten.* Sarah looked at him there must be a way she thought silently to herself. "Umm Yestin, do you know who all those men that came here are?" He looked at her "They are master's from other temples, there hasn't been a meeting like this since the temple was found," "What do you mean found?" "Well I don't know exactly what it means there is a legend that goes back over a thousand years, that this temple was actually created by a disgraced monk who had fled from his own temple, after coming to this country he found this place, and so no one would ever know of its existence he built it in the trees," Sarah looked at him she wondered if that was true but there again they say all legends start from a grain of truth.

After the days training was over, she was just sitting down to dinner with the others when Tommy came in, "Umm Sarah could you come with me please," Sarah stood and followed him he led her into a large room, in all the time she had been there this was the first time she had seen this room. Looking around she observed Master Yamatoya sitting at the head of the table then there were the other master's sat around it, her father was there and so was Jack; she noticed as she entered all eyes turned to her. She followed Tommy and stopped when they got to the table, tommy pulled a chair out for her sitting down she noticed that they were still looking at her, Tommy walked around and sat in the seat to the right of Master Yamatoya, once he was seated Master Yamatoya smiled he looked older his smile was weaker, and he looked much frailer suddenly.

"Sarah, myself and the other masters have been in conference for some time now. They want me to send you to the temple of the sun to complete your training, there you will be under the guidance of Master Tetsuko" Sarah jumped to her feet "No way! I am not going anywhere, if you are not going to train me then I will go home and follow the books that my mother left me." Master Tetsuko stood with determination "Young lady. You don't seem to understand the position you are putting us in, the law states that you must be trained at the temple of the sun." at this point Sarah stood with as much determination and anger as seemed to be emanating from Tetsuko. Raising her finger, she pointed "What law, whose law?" Master Tetsuko slowly moved around the table began to explain, "The law has been in place for over ten thousand years when the first Protector was born, and it has been that way ever since, when a new protector is born, they are raised by the guardians but when it is time to end their training they go to the temple of the sun, that is where they are put through the trials, that will help them so when the time of the awakening comes they are ready for it, you have been hidden from us for far too long, we knew that you were born and have made the preparations for you to come there to do the training you need." Sarah looked at them, "I don't care, Master Yamatoya has been training me for six months its only right that he finishes it" "I'm sorry but this we cannot allow, Master Yamatoya knows the laws, he has agreed to accompany you so that he can see your training through," "well if you are going to let him come with us. Why don't you just let me stay here and do my training, The Master of the Temple of the sun can remain here to see that it is done correctly," they are the ones who opened the door a crack and she was going to take full advantage of it.

They had been in conference for hours until she finally got them to agree, that she would stay there to do her training, once they finished, she got up to leave stopping for a moment. "And any way I trust Master Yamatoya, I don't know any of you" her words were directing a little cold, but she got her point across. How dare they try and tell her what she was going to do.

Looking at the clock it was almost five she had woken up before her alarm again but today was going to be different today she was going to be training with Master Tetsuko, for some reason she didn't like the idea she loved training with Master Yamatoya, but this guy she didn't even know him, true that until six months ago she didn't really know Master Yamatoya, but for some reason she liked him as soon as she met him. Groaning she turned over, what was she going to do master Tetsuko always seemed so cold, he was nothing like Master Yamatoya. The alarm brought her thought's back she might as well get up, god knows what he was going to make her do, climbing out of the bed she went and showered once she had finished getting ready she made her way down to breakfast, as she walked in all the guys looked at her and smiled, she was just about to take up her usual seat when Master Tetsuko stepped in "Not there, you will eat on your own from now on" she looked at him then to the others, "No I will not I have been sitting at this seat for months now and this is where I will sit," "Fine" replied Master Tetsuko turning to the men "you all take your food and leave" As they were about to get up Sarah jumped to her feet "I'm getting sick of this guy already, I've had Enough!" she shouted looking at Master Yamatoya, "I don't care what you say I'm not training with this guy!" With that she ran out of the room in tears with all the men looking after her Master Tetsuko went after her finding her in the Zen Garden. "Young lady?" "Sarah. My name is Sarah is that too hard to say!"

He fixed her with a blank stare, this was going to be hard she had not been raised the way Protectors were supposed to be raised, she had been in the outside world for far too long, bowing his head he had been trained on how to train protectors, but his training was how to deal with the normal situation. When a protector is born, they are given a guardian one who raises them often going into the home as a tutor, they were there to make sure that the protector was trained properly and had no connections with the outside world, that made it easy for them to accept the awakening, only after that are they introduced to the world in a coming out ceremony. However, this girl has lived the life of a normal girl for nineteen years, how could he possibly make her cut all attachment now, he was going to have to think of another way of doing this, the textbook so to speak were out of the window, he was going to have to attack this with a whole new angle. Sighing he looked at her then sat on the stone bench patting the seat next to him, "Sarah, come here, will you?" looking at him he had a different tone in his voice, gentler than the way he was before. Sarah walked over and sat next to him, he sat there for a while in quiet contemplation, how was he going to explain this. "Buddha helps us in all aspects of our lives, all we have to do to find the answer is to just look to his teachings." Great now he's starting to sound like Master Yamatoya, "I'm sorry I shouted" she said hanging her head, raising a hand he placed it gently on her shoulder. "There is a reason that protectors are raised the way they are, it is so when it comes time for the awakening they can accept it without any reservations, but you. You have already been out in the world you have made friends; I just wonder if you are going to be able to complete the training in time." he hung his head as he said the last part, Sarah stood and looked at him "Master Tetsuko. If Master Yamatoya has faith that I can, why is it that you can't" Master Tetsuko could hear the annoyance in her voice.

Master Tetsuko sat in quiet contemplating, in the meditation chamber what was he going to do she was back training with the men again and any objections he had made her more angry, sighing to himself how could she possibly complete her training this way, she hasn't even taken any of the steps that she was supposed to have and the date of her first trial was fast approaching, he was going to have to talk to Master Yamatoya see if he could make her see sense. Standing he left finding Master Yamatoya in the second meditation chamber, usually it was not right to interrupt someone who was in there, but this was an emergency, as he was about to walk into the room Master Yamatoya opened his eyes. "You wish to see me?" Master Tetsuko nodded, standing Master Yamatoya and he walked out to the Zen Garden, "Please tell me how I can get her to listen to me, she fights me on everything and nothing I try seems to work. How do you get her to listen to you?" Master Yamatoya laughed "You must be joking, listen to me no I always have to trick her into doing what I want her to do. If I out right tell her to do something then she basically tells me to get lost," "You what? she is so insolent no matter what I try she sees right through it and then goes back to training with the men." Master Yamatoya and Master Tetsuko both looked at each other. The answer had been staring them in the face all along, if she enjoyed training with the men then they had no choice they were going to have to put the men through the paces as well.

After that realisation they sat together that night and worked up a plan, on what she needed to do, and how they were going to accomplish it, they were going to tell all her group in the morning.

As they sat down for breakfast master Yamatoya stood. "OK, third years, you are going to start a new training regime in two weeks' time," no one argued they just nodded as did Sarah. Over the next two weeks Master Yamatoya and Master Tetsuko supervised the building of the new training area, Sarah and the others all looked at this new course it looked monstrous, "We thought the obstacle course was bad" Yestin said Sarah agreed with him, that place looked terrifying "It's got to be for the fifth years" one of the others had said, Mark chirped up "didn't master Yamatoya say we were going to start a new training regime next week?" they all looked at him them to the training grounds no way that couldn't be for them could it?

Finally, the day had come, and their worst fears were realised, the new training ground was for them. All were standing there a look of shock and horror was etched into their faces, Master Yamatoya and Master Tetsuko looked at them "Okay, men and lady this is your new training ground," "You've got to be kidding me" Sarah squeaked, "how the hell are we supposed to use these," luckily there were members of the temple of the sun there, even though this system was made to train Protectors, the monks had decided that letting them just rot until a protector was born to use them was a bad idea so they had implemented the use of it, so when the monks hit the third year they were placed on the training field; This took them all the way up until the fifth year.

The monks from the Temple of the sun fell in; the rest of that day was training on how to use the course, by the time they were finished they were so tired that the thought of keeping their eyes open and eating seemed like a chore. Once dinner was over, they made their way up to bed all wobbly and exhausted.

The alarm woke Sarah up she could tell from the moans and groans from the other room that she wasn't the only one feeling the burn, she hadn't felt this bad since the assault course; Sliding out of bed she made her way into the shower. Once she had finished, she walked out the others were also ready but sat on their beds, they looked at her and smiled weakly they were all still exhausted from the previous days training, getting up they walked down to breakfast Sarah was silently praying that they would be doing something easy, today; but her silent hopes were dashed when once again they were sent to the training grounds.

They had been training for some months, when it was finally time for her to take the first of three trials, these were set in place to open the mind, body and spirit, and there was no sidestepping them. Sarah knew that it was fast approaching and was getting more apprehensive as the time went on.

Chapter 5
The Trials

The alarm went off sitting up she looked at it, today was the day of her first trial getting up she looked at her bedside table five o'clock, showering she made her way from her room the others were still in their beds; it was unusual because usually she would come out of her room, and they would already be down in the breakfast room. As she walked past each of the beds, she noticed they were looking at her but not one of them said a word; they just looked at her she made her way down the stairs this place was usually a hive of activity, but it was now quiet not even the first years were around. Taking a deep breath she made her way into the Dining hall, both Master Yamatoya and Master Tetsuko were there. As she entered Yamatoya looked at her he was unsure of this test; was she ready for it. She had been training for a few months now they had even put the rest of the third year she was in through the training, and some were better than she was this was the test of mind,

Sarah sat down, master Yamatoya and master Tetsuko joined her you could have heard a pin drop that was how quiet it was, with that Jinn walked in with the food, Sarah really wasn't all that hungry but as she was about to refuse Yamatoya stepped in filling her plate. "You are going to need all the energy you can store; this test isn't any joking matter."

Sarah finished her food as did the two masters, once they finished, they led her to the large room that had been built, they walked in with her, but it was master Tetsuko who stepped forward to explain what she had to do, with that lights lit up the other end of the room there stood three glass cases and in each of them was someone she loved. In the first one was her father in the second was jack and in the third was Tim; he was someone she had grown really close to; even thinking of him as a brother and loving him as a brother, turning she looked at the two men standing in front of her. "What's going on here guys?"

Master Tetsuko stepped forward. This is your first challenge as you look out over this room you will see that at the top of each box is a colour now look around the room; you will see there are bowls matching the colour to each of the chambers all have to do is to declare which colour is first then collect the bowls of that colour once you have collected them. You see the pedestal situated next to each of the chambers, you must sit the bowls on top of them there are many things that will aid you in this. But know this you have thirty minutes to complete this challenge for every fifteen minutes after the original thirty the boxes will start to fill with water, if you have not completed it in that time…well you can guess what will happen."

The first chamber that her father was in was orange. "OK, I will choose orange for my first colour with that she noticed the tiles on the floor flip they were now different colours master Tetsuko stepped forward once again, "OK, now that you have chosen the colour you want to go as your first choice, look at the floor you will only be able to step on those colour tiles. If you step on the wrong colour, then what ever colour you step on water will start to flow into that chamber. The only way to stop that is to make three consecutive moves on the right colour on the fourth the water will empty is that understood." Sarah looked at him, there was no way that he would joke about something like this. Looking around the room she could see the orange bowls now all she had to do was to get them, then get them on that pedestal how the hell was she going to do that. With that there was a loud gong "Your time starts now."

Sarah didn't move for a moment there had to be a way of doing this, "If one only sees in a straight line then the path will be hidden from them…or something like that." Looking around "OK, don't look for the answer to be in a straight line…no that's not what he meant I'm sure of it…ummm there is always a way you just have to find it come on girl think." With that she looked at all the tiles then to the bowls "OK, so if I was to go this way" she stepped onto the first tile that was the same colour as the chamber with her father in, looking around she decided the best way to do this would be to get the equipment that she needed, before getting the bowls slowly she made her way to the left then as she was about to put her foot down the tile flipped turning it blue she wobbled slightly then balanced on the square she was on, "I knew it couldn't be this simple!. Master Tetsuko, you never told me the tiles change!!" Master Tetsuko looked at her, "If I was to tell you everything how are you going to learn to trust yourself?" "Gees great thanks" as she looked around she couldn't allow herself to get distracted by this setback, if she did then lord knows what could happen placing her foot down she closed her eyes taking a deep breath; she looked about her if she was going to have any chance then she was going to have to try going backwards turning she made her way back to the centre. It was then she noticed for every three steps she made the colours would change, so she decided to test the theory making three steps she should land on blue the next step, but as she moved her foot the colour changed to orange. "Right so every third step the blue changes to orange the orange changes to blue." That was her theory anyhow, but she found that it wasn't quite that simple she hadn't taken the third colour into the equation, she had gone through the mind-numbing process of counting her steps; she was at the edge to where she could almost grasp hold of the ladder. She only had to take two more steps then she would have it, without thinking that her theory was right; every three steps the blue would turn to orange on her final step. She put her foot down on to the blue as it changed but this time it didn't change to orange this time it changed to yellow. With that the water started to flow into Tim's chamber flustered she jumped to the edge grabbing the ladder she quickly jumped on the nearest orange that she could find, then to the next finally she was on the third once her foot hit the forth tile the water had completely stopped, what was she going to do looking around she noticed that the blues had all turned to yellow, the next orange would mean she would have to jump, she could do this just think of it like the balancing beams she had worked on balance throughout her training; but this time she had something with her, stopping she thought for a moment if she laid the ladder down she could walk across it, however if she did that there was no guarantee that it wouldn't set the others off, no she was going to have to jump, steadying herself she jumped she landed on the orange but part of her foot landed on the blue quickly she leaned herself forward, not to set off the trap she looked and the water that was in Tim's chamber was emptying. Finally, she made it to the pillar resting the ladder against it now all she had to do was get the orange bowls and place them atop the pillar, the first one was north it was then she realised that they were north southeast west. She decided to go for the north one first; looking at her watch she could see the time was counting down; slowly she made her way around the room collecting all four bowls then moved back to the ladder climbing she reached the top, looking at the pillar she noticed something wasn't quite right.

With that master Tetsuko stepped forward, "it's a combination lock if you turn the bowls over you will see the symbol for the temple of the sun, all you have to do is arrange it; if you get the combination correct then the chamber will open, but know this once you place the bowls on the surface you will have three tries to make it if on the third attempt you still haven't done it then water will start to fill the chamber, once the water starts you will have ten minutes to open the chamber before it is completely full. If you fail to do so you can only guess what will happen." Sarah froze three chances. Looking back at both her Masters "You've got to be kidding me! Why is it that you only let me know these things a piece at a time? Why can't you just tell me all the rules right from the start? This isn't fair" "Sarah! Stop whingeing like a child! You have been told we cannot give you all the answers the reason it is done this way is for you to understand your own strengths!" Sarah stands there and pouts for a moment; turning the bowls over she can see the banner of the temple of the sun placing them down in the right order she thought this is great, but as she was about to place the last bowl into position the lock shifts making the combination wrong. "This is not fair!" she screamed tears falling down her cheeks once again Yamatoya steps forward "Sarah! Stop acting like a petulant child they are placed now arrange them! Now you have three chances now concentrate!" Sarah looked at the combination grabbed the bowls she started arranging them she had used two attempts this was her last chance, and she knew if she didn't get it right that her father could die. Tears filled her eyes as she looked through the glass at him; he looked up at her and smiled. "Sarah listen to me, you can do this I know you can, believe in yourself, you already know the combination in your heart just let it guide your hands."

Tears stung her eyes but she fought them back, breathing she composed herself, looking at the combination she closed her eyes this time she used the visualisation technique that she had learned, visualising the bowls on top of the pillar and then arranging them into the banner. She hadn't realised but as she arranged them in her mind, they arranged on the top opening her eyes she looked down the lock was complete all she had to do was place her hand on it as she did, she heard a loud hiss, the chamber opened and her father stepped out climbing down she grabbed a hold of him in a grateful hug. Looking to Master Yamatoya and to Master Tetsuko she didn't understand they were just stood there smiling they had known that she was going to be able to do it, "Sarah this is no time for you to rest on your Loral's you still have two to get out remember, she just smiled for she knew exactly what to do she moved the ladder to Jacks chamber this time she didn't move off the spot. She closed her eyes and visualised the bowls assembling on the top of the chamber, opening her eyes she was right climbing up she placed her hand in the centre opening Jacks chamber. Climbing down as she landed on the floor the timer on her watch went off, looking at Tim as his chamber started to fill with water; she closed her eyes finally running up the ladder she pressed the centre the water emptied. Tim climbed out but he was holding something in his hand bowing slightly he handed her the temple of the sun banner turning she smiled. Yamatoya and Tetsuko walked across to where she was standing.

"We had every faith that you would be able to complete it" they said with a smile Sarah didn't know whether to be angry or relieved; it was then she realised just how tired she was it had taken a lot out of her, finally she collapsed into Conner's arms, gently he picked her up kissing her forehead "You now have the mind power my darling. Sleep gently he carried her from the room, the entire monastery was waiting in the large hall, as Conner carried her unconscious body through the door they all jumped to their feet but Master Yamatoya raised his hand, "Not a sound she passed the first test and has gained the mind powers, now she needs to rest, this will have taken a lot out of her and she is going to need her strength for the second test, I know how you must all be feeling but I implore you let her be until her body has had time to recover, Tim walked around Conner he was still holding the temple of the sun banner gently he tied it around the top of her arm bending he kissed her forehead, "Thank you" he said in a gentle whisper Conner carried her from the room placing her on her bed he removed the alarm clock so not to wake her.

Walking back into the great hall he smiled, "OK, I am only going to say this once, when the dorm goes to bed if any of you do anything to wake her you will have me to deal with. Is that understood?" All the men from her dorm looked at him and nodded not one of them wanted to get on the wrong side of Conner for they all knew that he was a guardian and probably stronger than ten of them together.

That night all of them went to bed they couldn't help themselves slowly they opened the door to her room it was only small, but they had to make sure she was okay she seemed to be in a dreamless sleep. They made their way back to their own room "Why did they choose you to take part in the test Tim?" one of them asked Tim looked at them, "to be honest I don't know?" he replied to Chen who was one of the third years, yeng looked at them all "Are you all completely stupid or something? Isn't it obvious to you all, out of all of us Tim was the first

68

one she met, and he is also the one she is closest to out of all of us, I know she will say she loves us all the same but it's different with Tim, she sees him like a big brother to her he will always be her number one?" They all looked around, but they knew that he was right even though she would see them all like brothers he is the one she would always go to first.

Conner, Master Yamatoya, Master Tetsuko, Jack and Tommy were all in the hall none of them spoke for the longest time, for they all knew that the mind test was the easiest the next would-be body, it would rely on her strength even though she had longer to complete it, it was still going to take its toll on her. She was going to have to do it all herself this time both Master Yamatoya and Master Tetsuko would not be allowed in the room, she would be given the instructions on what she was to do but this time she was going to have to figure it all out herself plus her mind powers would not be any use to her on this one. They were all deflated, once they realised that things were only going to get tougher from this point on, but the one that worried them the most was the final test the test of the soul this was the worst one because it would take part in the magical realm. This is the one that will figure out if she truly is the true protector, Yamatoya and Tetsuko knew what would happen if she failed but they could not tell Conner for they knew that if he was to find that out he would be frantic.

Sarah had slept for two days her body slowly healing from the exhaustion, finally it was early evening on the second day when she finally opened her eyes the last husky light of the evening streaming through the window, slowly she climbed from the bed the only thing on her mind was food she was hungry, she freshened herself up brushed her hair and made her way to the dining hall, as she walked through the door all eyes turned to her she still looked very pale, Conner stood and walked to meet her, her legs gave way slightly, Tim and two of the others grabbed her they walked her to where she normally sat. Conner walked behind her bending he kissed the top of her head she managed a weak smile; they could tell that she wasn't completely healed she needed more rest, but she was fighting it, "Sarah h.. Honey would you like me to bring some food up to you?" Conner asked gently master Yamatoya and Master Tetsuko both looked at each other they still couldn't believe that she was awake, not on day two no one usually woke up until the fifth day and they would look way worse than she did now.

Was it possible could she truly be that strong that in just two days even weakly she managed to make it to the dining hall, she had to be the one, both men thought but didn't say they never believed that they would witness something like this in their lifetime? Was this truly happening as they looked around, they could see all eyes were on Sarah, she had been there for over a year by this point but some of the guys still seemed to be a bit weary of her. They seemed not to know how to act but the one thing they had all learned and learned quickly one week of every month they all stayed well clear of her, the last person who upset her ended up with a broken nose and arm, plus they made sure that there was plenty of chocolate and cake on the premises as well, even Masters Yamatoya and Tetsuko learned that lesson.

Conner always laughed he always said, "Yip she's just like her mother," and walked away even as big as he was, he always stayed well clear of her only speaking when she spoke to him. Tim took him aside one day and asked why even he stayed away from her he just smiled and said, "you will learn that women go through changes like this, and when they do its best to just give them what they want when they want it or pay the price." With that he walked away Leaving Tim just as confused as before he asked.

Sarah finally finished her food standing she slowly wobbled from the dining hall and made her way back to her room collapsing onto the bed she fell back into a deep sleep, Tim walked in she hadn't even taken her shoes off or got on the bed properly; walking in he took her shoes off then gently lifting her he laid her on the bed, leaning over he kissed her forehead, lately he had been getting strange feelings. Every time he looked at her his heart would beat a little faster, he had never been in love, but he thought that this might actually be what he was feeling, he didn't know whether to talk to master Yamatoya about it or just keep it to himself.

Finally, he couldn't hold it in any longer every morning he would wake and look in on her and every evening he would do the same, he had to know what was going on with him, he found Master Yamatoya in the meditation chamber, walking in he knelt and waited finally Master Yamatoya spoke, "What is troubling you, Tim?" Tim could feel his cheeks burning slightly not sure how to approach the subject, Master Yamatoya opened his eyes and looked at him, but Tim could not meet his gaze, "Tim you have been with us a long-time you have graduated to third year, that is an achievement that you should be happy about. So why is it I can feel conflict in you?" Tim looked at him "Master you are right, and I am happy extremely; this isn't about that" he looked away before he had chance to say anything Yamatoya smiled "Is it Sarah?" Tim bowed his head slightly. "Master, every time I see her or even just hearing her voice, I don't know…My heart beats harder I get butterflies in my belly my knees feel weak, and I can't get her out of my mind for hours after…Is there something wrong with me?" Master Yamatoya laughed slightly, "Well you could say that it's called infatuation. She is someone that you find you have feelings for, and you are unsure whether your love struck or something else is going on. Well, let me assure you what you are feeling is a normal male response to a beautiful young woman. But Tim, I must caution you against getting the feelings mixed." With that he walked away leaving Tim looking after him, unsure what he was to do.

Finally, the time had come for the second test this time it was body, both Yamatoya and Tetsuko would take her in tell her what she had to do then leave, she would have to complete this test alone, as they walked to the room no one spoke this was one that was going to be hell for her; upon entering the room they explained what it was she had to do, master Yamatoya smiled and patted her on the hand, looking around the room she closed her eyes then mentally went through it; all she had to do was to get the temple symbols to the right place looking she could see the goal but getting there was another thing, she was going to have to rely completely on her own strength, there was no mental way of doing this. Slowly Sarah grabbed the symbol for the temple of the sun and made her way to the edge of the pool she was going to have to swim, but just as she was about to jump into the water a thought struck her, it was of the pool with all those stupid floats in it where she thought one way but found out it was wrong, so this time she looked around her and she noticed a track on the ceiling but where was it coming from turning she looked around and there it was it looked like a pedal machine no not one three and they all went to each of the symbols, she could do this she had used them on the assault course.

After she had worked out what she was going to do she put her plan into action, with the first symbol the temple of the sun, she chose the one she thought would lead her to it. As she made her way getting closer, she realised that the track she was taking was actually taking her to the temple of the frost not the sun, she was almost there the item she was taken had to go into the centre of the symbol. There was no way that this was going to fit it was of a different design, hanging there for a moment she knew she had no other choice than to go back, it was her second attempt she prayed that this one would be the right one, she made her way finally landing on the temple of the sun, she placed the symbol in the centre and it lit up, turning she made her way back to the other side slowly one by one she put them all in place as she placed the final one she noticed they started to pulse, slowly the floor started to open in front of her and there rising from it was a pedestal and in the centre was the temple of the frost insignia grabbing it, out of everything this was the one she was most proud of, leaving the room Sarah found that once again her body felt weak, stepping out she noticed that master Yamatoya and master Tetsuko were standing there waiting for her, she smiled weakly and held the frost temple insignia that she had received, both men smiled and followed her as she entered the dining hall a cheer went out; they had waited up none of them left until she had finished, it was only then she noticed how dark it was outside, it had taken her four hours to complete the task she had cut it close she had one hour left, she sat down and ate a little but her body needed rest, she looked at the stairs and slowly started to climb her arms felt as though they were going to fall off they were so heavy; she had thought the mind one was difficult but this one had taken every ounce of strength she had in her to complete.

She fell asleep as soon as her head hit the pillow, this time Tommy went to check on her she was still fully clothed once again she also still had her shoes on, gingerly he walked over to the bed not wanting to disturb Sarah, gently he leaned over removing her shoes he pulled the blanket over her bending over kissing her on the forehead before leaving,

As he entered the hall, he looked at both masters, who were looking solemn, as were the others that were still there, "What's wrong? She passed the test shouldn't we be happy about that?" Master Yamatoya stood walking over he told tommy to take a seat, they waited in silence until finally a man appeared he was from the magical realm; this was where she would face the final test. "Where is the girl?" Master Yamatoya stepped forward "She is resting, she completed the second trial earlier" the man looked about him then took up the seat to the side of Tommy, "She completed it in time?" "Yes, she had an hour left," "so you are telling me that she completed it in under five hours" "Yes" standing he walked to the window, "She is a strong one, I will give her that. The final trial as you know has no time limit, she will have three challenges" Tommy jumped to his feet "Three come on you are all treating her like a machine! She is a girl not yet Twenty and you are putting her through more than anyone her age should have to go through…it's not right. It's not fair how you can expect…" he was cut short by the man slamming his staff into the ground.

"Enough! These are not simple trials that just anyone can go through," he took a breath, and continued more gently "Son I am Gin I am almost ten thousand years old; I have heard the stories since I was a child about the great protector, I never thought one would be born in my time of reign. But she has, the fact that she has been hidden even from us for so many years meant that she never received the complete training she needed, you must understand that if she takes this task on and fails that will be it, she will never again be able to return to this place she will be trapped in the magical realm never growing old never dyeing. But she will also be without any magic for it will be stripped from her"

Conner and Jack both jumped to their feet. They hadn't been told that, they knew about the trials and everything else but this was different this time he was saying that she would leave their lives for good, Jack had listened to master Yamatoya and had kept silent about his feelings; but what was he going to do now, he didn't want to do anything that would make her lose focus but if he stayed silent and she failed, then he would never get the chance to tell her how he felt, he didn't know what to do.

Turning he looked at Conner he may be a guardian, but he was still her father surely there was a way for him to stop her from doing this before he had chance to say anything Gin spoke, "she finished the challenge today it is the twenty second, so I shall be back on the twenty eighth to collect her for the final trail," "But that's only six days!" Both Jack and Tommy yelled, but he ignored them, master Yamatoya bowed slightly "She will be ready" both men were now looking at Yamatoya then with a final thrust of his staff Gin was gone.

"Master Yamatoya you can't agree with this?" Yamatoya looked at them, "The final trial is administered by the magical realm we cannot interfere," with that he walked away. Jack, Tommy and Conner were all sat together in the Zen garden; they were all silent, they knew that no matter what they said she would say she would go through with it, she had already completed two of the trials and there was no way she was going to back out now, they wished there was a way that they could guarantee she would succeed; however it was impossible for none of them knew what this trial would comprise of, it was the only one that left them unsure, they knew that this was always considered to be the most difficult now they knew why, because unlike the others this one held the greatest risk, one that if she failed meant they would never see her again, finally Jack broke the silence, "We can't let her do it, there has to be another way." "If there was master Yamatoya would have told us." Conner replied solemnly getting up and walking away, he was having trouble with this but knew that it would be Sarah's choice in the end, it would all come down to what she would choose.

Chapter 6

The Magical Realm

The time was coming they had two days before Gin would turn up and demand an answer off Sarah, she had been in seclusion with Master Yamatoya and Master Tetsuko since she had woken up not even Conner was allowed to see her, they were preparing her for the decision, Conner and the others were sure they were trying to talk her into going, but the fact was they were doing the complete opposite, finally they emerged both men looking peaked they could not believe after everything they had told her she was still going through with it. They had explained the risk that she would never get to see her father or any of the others again, but she was determined she had come this far, and they had all worked so hard how could she back out now.

The two men looked at Conner and shook their heads, "She has made her decision," master Yamatoya spoke Horsley and with sorrow in his voice, "She has decided to take on the final trial, we have gone through everything with her explained what would happen if she fails but she is undeterred," with that Sarah emerged looking at them she smiled weakly, "Dad this is something I have to see through to the end, and I would hope that you will support my decision." Conner bent his head low he knew that she wanted him to give her his blessing, but she was his child how could he support something that might take her away from him forever, shaking his head he walked away with her looking after him, tears rolled down her cheeks she could not believe that they had such little faith in her first both her masters and now her father what was she supposed to do, "Dad! Why can't you of all people believe in me?"

Conner stopped and turned, "I do believe in you, it's just..." she looked at him "It's just what? Dad, I don't understand, you have always taught me that I could do anything, now I have the chance to follow my own path; you are unwilling to support that. Make up your mind do you want a daughter who will be her own person follow her own path, make her own decisions, or do you want a daughter who is afraid never doing what she knows is the right thing?"

Conner looked at her "But are you sure this is the right path for you, I know your mother left you the diaries and everything else so you knew who you were, but this is the first time I will not be there, I will be here and you will be out there on your own, that is the thing that scares me the most that I will not be there and if you should fail, I will never get to see you again," with the final words the tears that had been threatening were now flowing down his face, walking over she hugged him smiling she reached up and kissed his cheek.

"Dad you don't have to be there for I will always have you with me, and anyway I have no intention of failing this, I will go and I am coming back, Dad you always say that I have a lot of my mother in me, answer me truthfully if it was Mam standing here and not me, what would she be saying at this point in time?" Conner looked at her he knew exactly what his wife would do and that is exactly what Sarah had chosen, she would have gone to prove a point to herself as much as everyone else. He could not control what the outcome would be, but he could let her know that he loved her and would be waiting for her when she returned.

Sighing he looked at her and smiled "She would be saying the same things that you have said and doing exactly what you are doing now," he bent down and kissed her forehead she was his child, and the one thing a parent should do and that is to support their child even when it may be a decision that you might not have made or think they are wrong you have to allow them to make the mistakes.

"Well tomorrow is the day" a voice broke through the silence it was master Tetsuko, Master Yamatoya stood and looked at him, "We have taught her all she needs to pass this trial, but I fear that it may not be enough, this is the only trial that has no time limit she could be gone a day or forever we will not know the outcome until either she emerges or Gin comes to tell us she has failed, I just can't believe that she refuses to take these concerns seriously," Tetsuko looked at him and smiled "we knew when we undertook this that it would lead to this point." Walking over he stood at the base of the Buddha, "We have to trust that this is the right thing, we have taught her and even with the limited time we had she still surpassed our expectations, you said that the first day she came here you put her on the assault course, one with a four hour limit and even though technically she completed it in the allotted time, you failed her because she was on the wrong side, why did you fail her?" Master Yamatoya looked at him remembering it he couldn't help but giggle at the look on her face when he had failed her. "Because to have fully completed it she had to be on the other side, yes, she got around it in the time but because she was on the wrong side, I could have passed her, but it didn't seem right I would have failed the others for the same thing." Master Yamatoya looked at him and smiled, "Now tell me if this assignment had been given to a man would we be having this conversation?" It was only then that Yamatoya realised that if it had been one of the others then he would not be having the reservations, he was having now.

Finally, the time had come, today was the day Gin appeared at eleven standing there he waited for Sarah, as she walked into the room, he looked at this slip of a girl, he could not imagine she would look this way he wasn't sure what to expect but it was not the girl who now stood before him, bowing "Good morning my dear, have you made your choice?" Sarah suddenly felt nervous looking at all who had come to wish her well, this might be the last time she saw them, turning to Gin she nodded, "I will go," looking at her he smiled "You do realise what it will mean if you fail?" "Yes, I understand what it means…but it is something I have to do." Once again, he bowed "Take a hold of my robe" Looking at him she smiled quickly she ran to her father throwing her arms around him, "I love you Dad" she said kissing his cheek "I love you too my child." she went around them one by one hugging them as though it was the last time. She got to both Master Yamatoya and Master Tetsuko, she turned to Master Tetsuko first, "You and I have had our differences, and there are many things we disagreed on…but I want you to know that I appreciate everything that you have done for me," she gave him a quick hug then moved to master Yamatoya, "Master this is the hardest for me, you saw more in me.. pushed me further than I thought I could go…and when I was on the verge of giving up you are the one who helped me see what I was capable of…Master Yamatoya thank you for believing in me even when I didn't believe in myself, I will always be grateful for that."

Walking back to where Gin was, she looked at them smiled and bowed slightly, then in a moment she was gone, all who had been strong in the room while she was there found that they could no longer compose themselves, tears started flowing master Tetsuko and Master Yamatoya both left for they could never allow the others to see them cry, they went their separate ways master Yamatoya went to his chamber. Walking through the door he could no longer be strong finding his chair he sank down tears falling in torrents down his cheeks, it had been a short time, but he could not help but love her as a granddaughter, she was special to him and the thought of never seeing her again was crushing him.

Master Tetsuko went to his own room he also broke down, she was something special they all knew it, for him he was grieving the thought of not getting to know her better. In the time he had known her she had been like a belligerent child, sometimes pouted over the silliest of things but that was something he liked about her; she was stubborn to the last and to think that when they had first met, he had wanted nothing more than to put her across his knee the way you would a naughty child, but she had grown on him.

Sarah looked around her she saw green meadows full of unicorns and fairies, she was in awe by it the amount that she alone could see, with that Gin turned to her, "When a protector is born, they are shielded from the world, spending their time in quiet solitude only seeing those who were classed as their guardians, this is something you have never known, which makes me wonder if this is something you will be well equipped to handle. On saying that you are no mere protector you are classed as the great guardian protector it has been told that there have been three others before you, none of whom passed the third trial. After failing they were left with no power and doomed to walk the magical realm unprotected."

Sarah looked at him, feeling nervous "So you are saying that I too will fail?" he smiled "No, I am saying that because of the way you were brought up there is a stronger chance that you will succeed where others have failed. even though I cannot condone what your father has done, I understand you only have a short time and the only thing I can tell you is the first challenge is love the second compassion and the third is to face your greatest fear," with that he was gone no explanation no nothing at least masters Yamatoya and Tetsuko explained what she had to do before she undertook the trials, but this guy nothing.

She was brought out of her thoughts by a loud screech looking around she noticed there was a large red dragon flying her way she stood there just looking at it nothing in her told her to run. She watched as the monstrous beast came down to land in front of her, thinking that she was an idiot for not escaping while she had the chance, with that her stubborn streak kicked in there was no way she was running if she had been destined to make it this far then she was sure that, this beast would not harm her, standing there she just looked at his magnificent form, bowing his head he came to her eye line, "you did not flee from me why?"

he said in a low dangerous voice, but Sarah could see his eyes they did not look dangerous they looked kind and yet slightly sad, raising her hand she put it on his cheek, "Oh you poor creature why do you have such sadness in your eyes? No, I did not run from you when I could have that is because I didn't want to."

He raised his head and stood tall, "I am Caradog, the father of dragons I will be your guide until the final trial," Sarah looked at him and smiled nodding she started to walk "How do you know the path you must take?" "I don't know it's just a feeling," he let her continue they came to a fork in the road he looked at her not telling her where to go, she took three paces backwards and looked at the path, "Come on Sarah you can do this;" she told herself in quiet contemplation closing her eyes for a moment, she opened then and decided that they would go left, Caradog just followed behind her watching her every move, "Who is this girl? She hasn't once asked for my opinion the others once they got to this part took over an hour to choose the path then before making the final decision had asked for my advice," he had always taken them down the right because the left held more dangers but she had instinctively taken the left, he couldn't think to hope that this was the girl they had been waiting for no she didn't seem to have the attitude the others had, had he remembered the one being so full of herself that he wanted to eat her, but this girl seemed kind thoughtful even a bit considerate; she had seen straight into his soul when they had met seen the sadness that hid there, a sadness that seemed to have been there for an eternity ever since he had lost her she was the one he thought would be the great guardian protector, but when it came to facing her greatest fear found that it was to terrifying a prospect that she couldn't do it, she had used the old anointment dagger to take her own life, he remembered waking to find her lying at his feet blood had stopped spilling from the wound, it surrounded his one gigantic foot, he had loved her just being around her he found himself happier than he had ever been, then finding her body he remembered that day more vividly than anything time in the magical realm worked differently from the human world if you were in the magical realm for one month that would translate to the human realm you would have been gone for one day, time in the magic realm moved faster than the human realm.

They had been walking for some time, when she abruptly stopped Caradog stopped and looked at her and she was just looking down, as he allowed his eyes to focus in on such a tiny object he noticed that it was Marlwen he was the fairy prince of the western palace, what was he doing all the way over here he thought, gently Sarah bend down and picked him up he was injured but still breathing gently she cradled him in her hands looking at Caradog, "Is there anything we can do to help him?" he could see she was on the verge of tears, "Is he wounded?" Sarah looked him over but if there was an injury then it was too small for her to see, "The only hope he has is for us to take him to the western palace but walking will take you seven days," "can you carry us?" she asked Caradog looked at her and Marlwen he had never been told it was forbidden, he bent down as low as he could giving her time to climb on his back holding Marlwen, as they took off Sarah felt her arm begin to burn slightly, looking down she noticed a symbol starting to appear on it she said nothing but the pain got worse finally she could bear it no longer and let out a loud cry, Caradog looked back at her "Do you wish me to set you down?" "N...no please we have to continue." Replied Sarah,

As they came upon the castle Caradog landed Sarah climbed down still holding Marlwen, rushing to the entrance she looked about her "Please, we need help Marlwen has been injured and needs medical attention!" They were not there long when the king and queen emerged the queen glided up to her hands where she still cradled Marlwen, looking down at him she landed kneeling at his side, she brushed the hair away from his face, "My name is Myfanwy, I am his mother please set him down there," she pointed to an open window Sarah did not hesitate walking over she just managed to put her hand through the window looking she found what she assumed was a bed and gently laid him on it.

As she turned Caradog noticed the symbol on her arm, compassion, he looked at her and smiled "You have completed the compassion trial," Sarah looked at him "But I thought that Love was the first trial?" Once again Caradog looked at her "It doesn't matter the order of the first two trials, it is the last one that is the most important.... Sarah remember this; I can only take you to the location of the last trial, but I will not be able to enter with you. That is one that only you can face." Sarah looked at him and nodded her head, she wondered if that is why on her second trial both the masters left and she was there alone to succeed or fail by herself, and why is it that the other two trials have a time limit but this one did not, she didn't understand.

As they continued their journey night was falling and they needed somewhere to sleep, Caradog took her to the south where he knew of an old miller's cottage, as he came into land he noticed glints out of the corner of his eyes Sarah was about to climb down but Caradog stopped her. "Dark elves," he said in a hushed voice Sarah looked around but could only see what she thought were fairy lights, but that turned out to be the way their eyes shone in the night, Beren stepped forward bowing low he looked at Caradog, "My lord we did not know we would be having guests" Caradog long held a distrust of the dark elves, for they were the ones who ruled the dark magic, they had turned their faces away from the light. Long been known as out cast's even by their own kind.

"What are you doing here?" Caradog asked in a commanding voice Beren looked affronted "We own these lands; we have done for over five hundred years. We would have thought that you above all would have known this." Caradog just raised an eyebrow, "Last I heard it was the dwarves who owned this land, not the dark elves." Once again Beren looked angry "We took these lands from the dwarves centuries ago, it was during the Callaf battle, you have to have heard of that!" he shouted at Caradog, who once again just raised an eyebrow but before he could speak he heard a familiar voice coming from the back, he looked and just off to the side of Beren she was there, Eámané she was the mother to Beren and had known Caradog for many years they had walked together, when she was of the light but hadn't spoken in centuries since she fell.

"Caradog my friend, it has been many a year since we last spoke how have you been?" Caradog couldn't help but see her as the young girl who would ride on his back, they would talk about what the future had in store for them, he would never have thought back then that she would have turned her back on everything that was good, he remembered the time she started to change she became angry and bitter, it was after the great plague that had robbed her of two of her children and husband. It was then she had started spending time with Eó, he had convinced her that the dark was better for they had seemed immune to the strange plague that had struck, he had talked her into marrying him and converting to the dark elves, turning her back on her other two children when they refused, it was after that she had given birth to Beren son of Eó he had been raised in the dark he knew no other way, so Caradog was more patient with him than with Eámané.

For she had been raised in the light and had chosen the dark it had taken many years for the truth to be revealed that the dark elves were the ones that had caused the great plague, by that time Eó had her in his grasp, and refused to let her go, Beren knew he had a brother and sister who were with the light, and that his mother used to be, but every time he tried to ask her about it she would not speak, and would walk away he found as time went on it was better not to ask.

"Eámané, we were friends until you turned your back on everything you once stood for," "Come now Caradog, don't tell me you still hold a grudge over that, it was centuries ago can't we move past it and speak as we once did?" Caradog looked at her she hadn't changed over these many years, she was still a beauty even in the dark colours, "Eámané, you turned your back on our friendship the day you abandoned your children…who were still reeling over the shock of losing their brothers and their father. Instead, you went with Eó, who it turned out was the main cause of the great plague, and even after finding that out you stayed why?"

Walking forward she placed her hand on Beren's shoulder, "I could not abandon another child…you are right when I found out my husband and children died because of Eó, I wanted to leave but I knew that the light would never let me return. As far as they were concerned, I had fallen." She hung her head "There's no way back for me now," she said in a quiet whisper. Caradog looked at her; he could see her pain, *but she had brought it on herself,* he thought.

"What do you want Eámané, what do you want?" looking at him she stepped forward and smiled, "my dear friend you are the one who came here, should I not be the one asking that question" looking at him she could see Sarah on his back, "Who is that you have with you?" He looked at her and took a step back, Sarah climbed down and came to stand in front of him, "I am Sarah," Eámané looked her up and down then looked up at Caradog "she is a human, what is she doing here?" Caradog looked at her a bit surprised she was wise and old sure she knew exactly who Sarah was, everyone in the magical realm knew of her and that she was coming to take the final trial or was she testing him to see if he would lie to her.

Bringing a large foot up he placed it between Sarah and Eámané, "this is Sarah, she is the guardian she is here on her final trial," Eámané looked at him then to Sarah letting out a laugh "This is supposed to be the great guardian protector, I was expecting…well I'm not sure what I was expecting but it sure wasn't this, step forward child," she ordered Sarah gently put her hand on Caradog's leg.

"It's OK," she said as she walked past it coming to stand in front of Eámané.

"Yes, what can I do for you?" Eámané looked at her then to the others that were there. "Can you believe that this child is what they call the great guardian protector? Just look at her she doesn't even seem to be old enough or strong enough to take such a task on."

The others that were there let out a shout of agreeance with her Sarah stood tall, "I may be younger than you but who are you to say that I am not old enough or strong enough, you know nothing about me to be able to make such a statement." Eámané stopped and looked at her, smiling "you have some spirit, I will give you that, but come on do you really think you are ready for this," bending closer to her "Have they told you what happened to the others they believed were the great Guardian Protector?" Sarah looked at her "Yes I know what will happen if I were to fail, I have been fully informed, so you don't need to worry for I have no intention of failing." "My, my confidence but are you sure that this is the correct path for you?" "Yes, I am I was put on this path for a reason, and I must see it through"

"Oh really, even facing your worst fear does not scare you?"

"No, it does not."

"You do realise that the test is one that you may not be able to cope with, yet you are still willing to go through with it?" "Yes, I am, I am not afraid of what I may face, for only by facing that which scares you only then can you find who you truly are?"

Eámané stepped back and looked at her, "Is that so?" "Yes, you fear going back because of what they will do to you, which is your fear, but if you were to look past that and try?" Eámané stamped her foot, "How dare you presume to know what my greatest fear is! you are a child you know nothing of this world or of what I have been through?" It was Sarah's turn to stop her "am I wrong? Are you telling me the only reason you won't go back is because you don't want to or is it because, you are afraid of what will be said? You are afraid of their judgement?"

Eámané looked at this girl, one she had only just met and she seemed to see straight through her, she knew without being told what her greatest fear was, what Eámané could not understand was how, could she truly be that strong, with that Beren stepped forward and placed a hand on Sarah's shoulder, "Come, let us speak for a while" with that Caradog let out a mighty roar, making all in his presence jump, "If there is to be any speaking you will speak here!" They all looked at him but agreed, they made a camp Caradog lit the fire, quite an easy task for him, they spoke for the longest time, Caradog noticed that Eámané kept looking at Sarah, finally she stood and walked over to Caradog, "Can I speak with you, the way we used to?" Caradog looked from her to Sarah, "I promise you no harm will come to the girl, we all know what would happen if someone other than the guardian was to take their life."

Caradog walked with her out of ear shot of everyone else, once they were at a safe distance Eámané, an elf broke down looking at Caradog, "How is it a mere child can see into my heart, a child that I have only just met? Oh Caradog I want to go home I want to see my children, I hate what Eó has done to me, but most of all I hate that I fell for his lies," Caradog looked at her, there was no sign of deceit in her voice, she was being genuine she reminded him of the girl she was centuries ago, the girl that always went to him for advice, always looked to him for guidance.

"Eámané what do you want me to say? You didn't just turn your back on your kin you also turned from me, nothing I said back then seemed to get through to you why now?" She bowed her head, "I regretted my decision as soon as I made it, but there was no going back Eó was my husband what was I supposed to do?" "Eó was your husband?" "Yes, I wanted to leave him as soon as I had found out what he had done, but I was afraid I had abandoned two children and I just couldn't turn my back on Beren" she looked at him he could see the pain in her eyes, he wished more than anything there was something he could do.

Sarah appeared from the bushes, "Lady Eámané, you are wise and you are beautiful you know what it is you must do, you just need the courage to do it," with that Beren walked behind her coming to his mother's side, he knelt "I have asked you many times, but you have always refused to answer, ammé please what is the light like what is my brother and sister like?" Eámané looked at him and gently placed a hand on his cheek, "oh my son, the light is just that, there is no anger no hate, there is peace, your brother Huor and your sister Enelya, they are shining examples of good, I just wish there was a way for you to meet them."

Sarah looked at both, then to Caradog "Isn't there a way we can help them?" Caradog looked at her, but he didn't know any way of working it without her fully denouncing the dark and swearing her allegiance to the light once more, "Umm Caradog do you know where her children are?" "Yes of course I do" "Good will you take me there?" "Sarah what are you thinking, you do realise why you are here," "of course I do but I'm sorry the trial is just going to have to wait a little longer as I have been told there is no time limit remember," Caradog looked at her and could see she was serious, "Fine get on my back."

He took off leaving Eámané and Beren looking after them, Sarah fell asleep on his back as they flew over Phoenix valley, and the Cherub grove they made their way to Tíwele the largest light Elven city, slowly he landed leaving her sleep, he was so tired himself that slowly he drifted off. They were both woken by the sound of an elven horn Caradog jumped to his feet causing Sarah to slide from the back but before she hit the floor she was caught by a very handsome man with the bluest of eyes and hair the colour of snow, she was still in his arms and he was looking into her eyes, "Umm would you mind putting me down." she seemed to bring him back to reality in one fluid motion he put her on her feet, Caradog looked at him thankful that he had caught her, for if she had landed on the floor from that distance then she could have really been hurt, Sarah looked at the man who had caught her, and the first thing that came to mind was how handsome he was.

Caradog finally finding his voice "Huor Melwasúl," Huor looked at him and bowed, Sarah noticed all who addressed him always bowed something she had never done was he royal or something? She thought to herself "my lord Caradog so nice to see you again," he looked from Caradog to Sarah and stopped dead, "Umm my lord please excuse my bluntness but is this?" he asked pointing to Sarah, "My name is Sarah thank you very much and please stop pointing at me." Caradog looked at her then to Huor "Yes this is the girl you have all heard about, this is Sarah Daily she is here on her final trial."

Huor looked at her and smiled, "you are so young," Sarah was fed up of hearing that and any way he looked just a young as she was, "Well excuse me, but you don't look much older than myself" this caused both Huor and Caradog to laugh, Caradog turned to Sarah, "This is prince Huor he is over two hundred, so even though he may not seem it to the eye he is a lot older than you."

Sarah stood there aghast for a moment she could not believe that he was that old he only looked in his early twenties; they stayed for a moment talking then Caradog asked him to take them to his uncle who was the current ruler.

As they came to the door of a large grand building Sarah looked it was amazing as were all the homes she had passed they were tall and elegant built into the trees, on the side of the mountain looking around the long winding trails that were there they had passed many elves both men and women who the moment Caradog walked passed bowed low, they had all eyed her but none spoke, they just smiled sweetly they were so different from the dark elves that she had met even down to the way they dressed they wore long flowing robes and in all shades, whereas the dark elves wore mainly dark browns and black their clothes were more fitted than the light the light were more loose and flowing.

There was a short wait before the doors finally opened and the king walked out, he like all the others bowed low before Caradog standing he smiled, "My lord it has been too long, what brings you here?" Caradog moved his leg to reveal Sarah, Mablung looked at her for a moment then stepped forward, "Hello my dear, I presume that you are the protector that we have all heard so much of?" Sarah unable to speak just nodded.

Mablung took her by the elbow and led her with him, he seated her on one of the many seats that were around once they were both seated and comfortable, he turned to her with curiosity. "So why have you come here?" Sarah looked at him "Well it's about Eámané," with that Mablung moved from her, "That name has not been mentioned in this place for many a year," as he was about to walk off Sarah jumped to her feet, "Please she just wants to see her children again she knows she made a mistake, but can't you show a bit of compassion for her, she has lost so much." Mablung raised his hand, he didn't raise his voice but spoke very deliberately, "She turned her back on her family a long time ago, and why would she care to know them now after all this time? No, it's out of the question" Sarah couldn't believe what she was hearing, "You are supposed to be light elves, you walk in the light, but to me you don't even know what that means."

Mablung looked at her, "You are a child and a human one at that what could you possibly know about the lives we live?" "But" "Enough my sister turned her back on everything she stood for, and for what to go with Eó who was the cause of the great plague, she wouldn't listen to anyone, not even me her own brother, she chose her life and we were left to pick up after her, she had no idea what it did to her family. Now she says she wants to know them again. No if she had really felt that way then it would be her standing here instead of you."

Sarah bowed her head and put her hand on his arm, "Where I come from, people make mistakes and some really big ones, but we show compassion we allow them time to show they have changed, we don't just condemn them being a family means forgiving when they have done wrong, being there when they fall so you can help them up." Mablung looked into the eyes of innocence, he knew that she meant well but for him to do as she was asking was to go against everything he believed, when a person went from the light to the dark there is a memorial held for too them that person has died.

Now she was asking him to look past everything that had happened, the only way for a person to be redeemed is for them to kneel at their memorial and ask for forgiveness, and as far as he knew there were only ever two instances of that happening and they were both in the history books it had never happened in his lifetime.

Standing in front of Sarah he knew this child was something special you could just feel it when you were near her, but what she was asking a man walked to where they were, Mablung turned to him smiling he put a hand on his shoulder, turning to Sarah "This is Huor, he is Eámané's son." Sarah smiled and nodded her head Huor looked at his uncle, "Who is this?" he didn't even acknowledge the fact that his uncle had said his mother's name, or the fact that they had already met, for he was the one who had caught her, Sarah stepped forward and smiled but before she had the chance to say anything Mablung continued, "This is the protector that you have been told about, but she is here on a different matter, she wishes us to give your mother an audience so she can see you and your sister," Huor pulled away from his uncle and looked at Sarah, "Why would we give that woman anything? She turned her back on us when she left, she is dead to me."

Sarah listened to what he had said, she understood that he may hold anger and resentment towards his mother, but she was his mother, "She realises that she has done wrong, but she really wants to see both of her children and for you to meet your brother." Huor stepped forward he didn't know that his mother had another child, "Brother? No, it doesn't matter he has obviously been raised in the dark, I will have nothing to do with either of them." "But she is your mother, and he is your brother can't you look from the past, yes, she left and turned her back on you, but it is a decision that she has regretted for many years. She didn't know that it was Eó who had caused the great plague, when she found out she had already given birth to your brother and could not face turning her back on another child. Can't you understand that your mother loves you? What she did she did out of anger."

Huor looked at her, he had a brother well half-brother but his father was the plague bringer, he had wiped out many of the light elves in a bid to rule, but had failed when a cure was found and administered, but by the time everything had gotten back to normal he was short a father brother and sister, and his mother had turned her back on everything she had known and was taught, how could he forgive her? "I will have to speak with my sister and if we agree to this it will be on our terms not hers."

Sarah smiled and nodded, "OK, when can we expect your decision?" Huor once again looked at her then to his uncle "I will speak with my sister and then we will talk to the council, if all is in agreement then you will have your answer in a couple of days," Sarah smiled and nodded, Huor stepped forward, "You shall stay here while the deliberations go on," he pointed to the castle "This will be your home for the next few days so feel free to go where ever you wish," with that he turned his attention to Caradog, "My lord, as always you may stay where ever you wish, we will take great care of Sarah you have my word," Caradog bowed his head slightly as a sign of respect, "My lord I will stay in the grove but Sarah is to come with me, being her guide means that she has to stay with me at all times."

Huor smiled and nodded, "I understand but don't you think that she would be more comfortable here?" "That may be, I'm sorry but I will feel much better if she was with me" Sarah looked at Caradog and smiled then turning to Huor she bowed slightly, "I agree with you and yes it would be nice to sleep in a bed, but Caradog is right, he is my guide and I do believe that I should stay with him." Huor smiled and bowed before taking his leave.

Sarah and Caradog went to the grove as they landed Sarah could not help but admire the sight of it, filled with cherry blossom trees, willow trees and many other species of tree, it was a sight to behold magnificent, as she climbed down she walked over to one of the grandest trees there it was a very large very old willow tree, reaching out she touched its bark "Oh my, what a lovely tree" with that she heard "Why thank you" she looked around but saw nothing the voice spoke again, once again she looked around by this point Caradog started to laugh "Sarah this is Gem Whisperwood he is the oldest and wisest of the trees in this realm" with that she noticed a face emerging from a nook in the tree, the old face smiled at her, "Hello my dear, so you are the one we have heard so much of? Stand back and let me take a good look at you."

Sarah still quite shocked stepped back with that she could hear chattering going on, she looked around was it coming from the trees were they all talking, with that Gem Whisperwood cleared his throat, "Silence!" his voice rumbled through the ground causing her to lose her balance, as she tumbled to the ground she noticed that all the chattering had stopped she looked around then looked at Gem who was looking at her he smiled "Are you OK?" Sarah nodded she was just a bit dumb struck at everything that was happening around her, she was not used to trees talking but then again there was a lot that happened in the magical realm that she was not used to, one was finding out that elves truly existed and the other was meeting Caradog an actual dragon.

Finally she found her footing and stood up she brushed herself off, taking a deep breath she laughed "OK, I can honestly say that is the first time any man has taken me off my feet," with those words both gem and Caradog started to laugh and once again the grove came alive, as it all settled she walked to Gem and sat in front of him, "Hi, so are you older than Caradog?" Gem laughed "there are few that are older than Caradog and I have to say yes but only by three hundred years," "oh only three hundred not long then" she said laughing slightly.

"You have to understand there are some creatures who are immortal and other who are not I was born Immortal as was Caradog, he is called the father of Dragons for that fact, I am called the tree father because of it, being a protector you understand, it's a little bit like you not all trees or dragons fairies elves and other mythical creatures are born with total immortality, by that there is nothing that can kill us, as when you pass the final test after the awakening there will be nothing that can kill you. We are classed as the true immortals, ones who cannot be killed by the hand of others, we will never age the way others age we will remain looking young for thousands of years only starting to look old when a new Immortal is born to take our place, but then we do not die, we retire so to speak many choosing a life of solitude away from the world, there are times that an immortal will seek the company of others instead of going into solitude," "Gem, why do they go into solitude?" he closed his eyes, he knew that she would have to be told many times immortals are born and go through the transformation without understanding what it will entail, he could see that Caradog was watching him closely, but how many times would he get the chance to help shape someone, at least this way she will understand what she will go through.

"Sarah many choose seclusion because they see so much death that they cannot cope any longer with the sadness, they live a life out of the world one can say, no longer being part of anything. But there are those few who don't do this they choose to live with people the reason for that is because no matter what happens, they love being a part of this world, you will never grow old and you will never die, but you will have to watch those around you die."

Sarah stood and looked at him then to Caradog, she hadn't thought of that she hadn't thought that she was going to have to watch all she loved die, Caradog looked at her raising a mighty foot he gently placed it upon her head that looked tiny in comparison to it, "Sarah are you OK?" She looked at him but she didn't know herself, was she really okay with knowing that all the people she loved would die out of her life would she forget them over time, or would she always remember those who touched her life, a tear ran down her cheek at the thought of her father master Yamatoya Jack even Tommy dyeing from her life, was she truly ready for this, she knew that if she failed that she would never be able to see them again but the prospect of her passing going back, just to watch them die she wasn't sure that she wanted to do that, bending her head she walked away from them she needed time to think, what she was going to do as she walked she noticed a path, it caught her eye because of the colour it was purple with pink edges.

As she followed the path, she could hear singing coming from the distance, she could not understand it, but the voice was what she would class as angelic, as she drew closer to the voice, she could see a woman in the glen just gliding as she sung, she was beautiful with copper skin and sun kissed hair. Sarah stopped and just watched her she was there for the longest time, just watching and listening all thoughts and worries washed away.

She knew just standing there listening that she was going to go through these trials and then return to her family, this woman's voice washed over her taking the cares away she was enchanted by her.

All of a sudden, the woman stopped and looked straight at her she bowed her head and made her way over to where Sarah was standing, stretching out her hands she grasped hold of Sarah's and pulled her into the glen, then once again started to sing Sarah didn't care about anything all of a sudden she forgot everything the trials Caradog, why she had come to the elven city all she could see was this woman and her singing.

Finally, she came to a stop sitting she guided Sarah down kneeling there looking at her was like looking into the face of Aphrodite herself, she smiles at Sarah "Why are you worried about your path?" Sarah looked at her and all the thoughts came back, "Because, if I complete this and go back to my world then all I know will change in time, I will watch those I love and who love me die," "Yes, this is true but you will also have the joy of living with them, when someone dies they are never truly gone, you are afraid that you will never see them again is that right?"

"Yes Gem Whisperwood said that they will die and I will have to continue my life without them, that is why a lot who are like me choose a life of solitude when their replacement is born so they no longer have to deal with loosing anyone else," the woman smiled, "this is true, but I am an immortal and I still see those who I have lost over the centuries" "But how, if they have passed on how do you see them?" With that the woman pulled what looked like a piece of glass from her pocket, sitting there she held it out slowly letting it go it floated closing her eyes she held her hands either side of it, Sarah watched as it began to spin.

Slowly a head started to form, it was no one that she knew as it finally emerged the eyes opened the woman looked at the face, "Ellendiel my dear husband how are you?" the face looked at her and smiled, "Frayer it has been a while since you have called me, I am well what about you?" Frayer looked at him and smiled then turned to Sarah, "This is the Tranprant it allows the owner to speak with those they have lost, for we never really die we just ascend to a different plain, those who do not go into seclusion usually own one of these, so that no matter what they will always be able to converse with the ones they have lost, true that they are rare, but you will be able to get one you just have to prove you're worthy of it to the Gensin, for only they can create them," "what do I have to do to prove myself?" Sarah asked, "Well it's different for everyone, the way I proved myself would be different to the way you will have to prove yourself; it is up to them they will decide how you will prove yourself, no one else."

Sarah smiled and thought about it for a while she wanted one of those and now that she knew they existed she was going to have to find a way, but first, she must complete this trial. She smiled said her goodbyes then walked away with a newfound determination. She was going to bring this family back together and then set out on finishing the last of the trials, this was something she had to do. She knew that the only way of getting through this was to let everyone know that she was unafraid of the final trial; she didn't care what it was she would face it head-on.

As she returned to the grove she could hear Caradog and Gem talking, they were having quite the debate, she hated to interrupt so she stood back and listened to them, they talked about many things what was right what was wrong who was the better judge of character, "Man when you live so long there must be something interesting to talk about?" so far she had been bored out of her mind, finally she could not take it any longer she walked into the middle of "The best way to tell if a bat is evil is?" When she walked over both stopped talking Caradog came to her side, "Sarah, Gem has something he would like to tell you?" Sarah walked over and sat under his long branches and waited, he cleared his throat and finally looked at her. "My dear I am truly sorry if I upset you, that was not my intention but before I had a chance to say any more you left, I do feel regret that I caused you to become solemn." Sarah patted his bark, "It's okay I understand why you told me what was going to happen, but honestly, I am fine," she smiled but Caradog and Gem looked at her earlier she looked so defeated why is it that now she seems at ease with herself and the choices she must make, neither asked her about it they just changed the conversation. Both watched her as she wandered around the grove smiling.

Caradog recognised the tune, "You have seen Frayer haven't you?" He asked with trepidation in his voice he was hoping that she would say no but she nodded, "Oh Sarah, she is of the light, but she is also very tricky. She can make whoever hears her sing believe or see anything, she is a mystic blessed with immortality, she will only show you the truth but it's not always your truth, she has the power to see into the future, please what is it she told you?"

Sarah looked at him "She didn't tell me anything about my quest but she knew that I was worried, when she asked why I told her but she already seemed to know what I was about to say," "That is because she can read your desire and fears," "but she didn't tell me anything really, except about the Tranprant and the Gensin," At the shear mention of the name made both Gem and Caradog's blood run cold, they knew all too well about the Gensin and what they could do, not many people who dealt with them returned the same.

The Gensin were neither light or dark they were what you would call truly neutral, but they would only deal with people who they deemed worthy, someone like Sarah a young innocent girl they would deem unworthy for she will not have lived long enough, "Sarah, The Gensin are not something you should consider, you have seen the way Frayer is…she was not always like that…It happened about six hundred years ago after the death of her husband she was so grief stricken that she sought them out to get one of the Tranprant, she has never said what they asked her to do but she has never been the same since."

Sarah listened to them speak and warn her about the Gensin and what they were like, but she knew once she passed the final test then she was going to seek out the Gensin and ask for them to create a Tranprant for her, she didn't say to Caradog or Gem what she was planning on doing, she just let them believe that she had heeded their advice.

It had been a few days and still no decision had been made, Sarah found herself wandering down a path she had not seen before as she walked she heard a voice softly calling her name, she looked about her but there was nothing that she could see she continued on her way, every so often the voice would float in, once again Sarah looked around but could not find where the voice was coming from she stopped for a moment and listened, she heard it again but this time she focused on where it was coming from, she noticed that it was coming from the glen.

As she came to stop at the edge of the glen she hoped to see someone but it was empty, she noticed that in the distance was what looked like a pool, as she drew near she noticed that it was not a pool at all, it was a well a very large well, she could see a fountain in the centre of it there were also steps leading up walking over she removed her shoes and as she was about to step into the water she heard the voice again, this time it told her to stop, not to enter the water standing there she did not understand but did as advised, instead sitting on the wall surrounding it. She had heard that voice many times now but why had it stopped suddenly is this where it was leading her and if so, why?

It soon became apparent why the voice had led her here when she saw Huor coming down the large tree at the edge of the clearing, she watched him until he placed both feet on the ground, he turned seeing her he headed in her direction finally coming to stop in front of her, "why are you here?" Sarah looked, was she going to tell him the truth that a strange voice had led her or something else she pondered on the decision for a moment, then decided the truth would be best after she told him what had happened and that she had been led there by some strange voice but it had stopped her when she was about to step into the well, he smiled there was no doubt in his mind he knew exactly who had called her there.

"That would have been the voice if Atherial, she is the guardian of these lands, if she was the one who called to you then there must be a meaning behind it, can you tell me what she said?" "She just called my name, I followed it to this well, but when I was about to step in she told me to stop and that was the last time I heard her voice," Huor held his hand out "Come with me" he said, leading her away they spoke as they walked not about the voice or anything to important, it was mainly making sure that she was okay and that she was comfortable.

Finally they came to stop at the large building they had first come to when they arrived, Huor walked her inside the grand entrance was the size if her house, even though from the outside it didn't look like much when you walked in the high arched windows that looked like stained glass, the furniture was all carved wood and stone, very beautiful the one piece that caught her eye was a wooden seat, it was large and magnificently crafted with white ash and oak married together to make such a beautiful seat, it was the only odd one out, all the others were either oak, ash or beach but this one she didn't know what it was about it but she fell in love with the elegance of it, she hadn't moved when Huor came back with his uncle they stood there for a time just looking at her, finally Mablung stepped forward "Sarah" at the sound of her name being called it brought her out of her trance that she was in smiling he stepped forward, "Beautiful isn't it?" "Oh yes, it's magnificent what is it?" "It is a piece that was given to me when my reign started it was crafted by the wood elves, they apparently took two years to complete, but like you sometimes I like to come in here and look at it."

Sarah smiled walking over to the seat, "What does this mean?" both Huor and Mablung looked at her then came closer to the seat and there in the upmost Corner was an inscription that none of them had noticed before, and being elves with their eyesight they should have noticed it, a Picture on one of the windows drew her attention as she moved away and closer to the window both Huor and Mablung notice the writing begin to fade, Huor caught hold of her arm and brought her back once again the writing was there, Huor looked at her then to the chair, "Sarah would you do me the kindness of sitting in the seat please," she looked at him a bit mystified but did as he asked as she sat down the once dull engravings started to glow, with that Sarah jumped up "wow what was that?" Mablung said nothing just guided her back into the seat sending Huor to fetch the elders, he did as his uncle said while he was gone Sarah was bombarded with questions on her family line questions about her mother her father her grandparents, she answered all she could but there was much she didn't know because her father had taken her into hiding after her mother had died she was only young when her mother had passed but she knew her from the books and dvd she had left.

Finally Huor was back with the elder who the moment they saw the seat said nothing they all gathered around her, with that the heavy door opened and in walked Featherstrike, he was one of the woodland elves, he wasn't the one who created it but maybe he would understand it, as he entered he noticed all were gathered around the seat walking over he spoke not a word when he noticed what the seat was doing he stood there in shock, Mablung and Huor spoke to him but he said nothing it wasn't until Mablung put a hand upon his shoulder he seemed you come back to reality.

"Featherstrike is there anything you can tell us about this?" Mablung asked pointing to Sarah and the seat that none of them would let her get up from, he looked at Huor "I have to call my father, this should not be happening, there is no way a mere human even if she is the guardian she is still human this is impossible," with that he left Sarah was finally permitted to move after one of the elders had marked down all the writing that had appeared in the carvings, once again when she moved away, all the writing and light disappeared with that Caradog was called, Sarah waited outside until his monstrous form landed in front of them, she had been gone for so long he was starting to get worried if it hadn't been for Tellen coming to let him know where she was he was about to start looking.

As he landed Sarah ran to him "pick me up please" Caradog did as she asked Mablung and Huor came to his side, they looked up at Sarah who was now way out of their reach, and she knew if she asked he would not let any of them get near her, "What is going on?" it was Mablung who offered up the explanation once he had finished Sarah chimed in "and if you think I'm getting back down your out of your minds, I have never been treated like a guinea pig before and it won't be happening again, Caradog and I are going back to the glen, please inform us when a decision has been made," Huor tried to argue but she was having none of it in the end asking Caradog to take her back to the glen to which he happily obliged.

They had been back at the glen for over an hour when Mablung, Huor and some of the other elders escorted Featherstrike and some of the other wood elves to where they were, as soon as she saw them coming she quickly climb up onto Caradog's back they came to stop in front of him, one of the woodland elves someone that Sarah did not recognise bowed to Caradog then walking around he bowed to Sarah, this was a new one on her, he was the first to do that she was used to seeing people bow before Caradog but that's where it usually ended with that the familiar voice of Gem chimed in. "Well bless my soul, Fern is that you?" the elf smiled and walked around Caradog and stopped in front of Gem, "It has been a long time my lord," his voice was warm and tender there was no harshness it was like listening to the wind in the trees, Gem and the elf talked for a while when the subject of Sarah came up with that he turned from Gem to Caradog, "Would you bring her back to the Calfal please?" Caradog looked at him and in his most authoritative voice asked why, Fern stood there for a moment then walked so he was standing in front of Caradog, "My lord what happened today should only happen if the Woodland princess sat on the throne, It may look like an ordinary seat but it was crafted by the royal guard of high lord Mythindranda, the runes that were inscribed on it are from the old language a language that has not been used in over two thousand years, and can only be activated by a member of the royal family, now I am looking at the young lady, and I see no elf in her so it leaves us a most unusual question why is it that she activated the throne."

Sarah was sat on his back and had no intention of coming down she had been through enough with that stupid seat as it was, and wanted no more to do with it, but Caradog agreed with Fern that this should be inspected further, "Sarah I am sorry but this goes far beyond likes and dislikes, the fact that you activated a dormant throne needs to be looked into further," Sarah crossed her arms and pouted "I'm supposed to be here on a trial not to be some stupid lab rat, it's not my fault the throne or whatever it is started acting up, why do I have to go they wrote everything that showed up down, can't they just work off that?" "Sarah remember this it was your decision to come here in the first place, if you had done as I suggested then none of this would be happening right now, so the least that you can do is help out." "humph fine take me to the stupid throne," she said in a rather unflattering and some would say childlike tone, Caradog just shook his head but followed behind the procession as they led the way back, finally they were outside but there was no sign of Sarah disembarking, finally Huor with great skill climbed up grabbing her "You better hold on wouldn't want you to fall," he said with a wicked grin as he jumped somersaulted and landed on his feet with Sarah screaming all the way down.

As they landed, she hit him in the chest pushing herself out of his arms she stumbled slightly, but soon found her footing not caring who was there she up and slapped him so hard he lost his balance for a moment, all who were there gasped, but she didn't care, "What in the hell do you think you were doing? Anything could have happened," Huor rubbed his cheek and looked at her, "for a human girl you sure can hit," he seemed unfazed by what had just happened but offered no explanation or apologies for it, instead walking past he turned to his uncle, "There you go she's down and unharmed," Sarah looked at him what the hell nothing, he had nothing to say well she had plenty she wanted to say.

But before she had a chance to say any of it he walked off still rubbing his cheek, Sarah turned crimson not with fear but pure rage, she hadn't noticed but she started illuminating her own light, not like the other guardians or protectors they had seen, this was pure blue but around her was a brilliant white something that in all his years Caradog had never seen and he was next to Gem the oldest one there, she closed her eyes only for a second but when she reopened them they had also changed, "Huor how dare you walk away?" The voice that was coming out was also different from the girl they had spoken to earlier, all who were there quickly moved aside leaving a clear space between her and Huor.

Huor stopped hearing the voice and turned to look at Sarah he could not help but be surprised for standing in front of him was not the girl he had plucked off Caradog's back, she was looking at him and he noticed that her hair had changed she and the light emanating from her was brilliant he could see that it seemed to form a shape the shape was that of the mythical blue dragon, at this even Caradog took a few steps back, he was having trouble believing what he was seeing himself, the blue dragon died out over a millennia ago. But she had not finished, stepping forward all that was there giving her more space, Huor looked at her the light stung his eyes, but he could not look away finally she came to stop in front of him,

"You don't just pluck someone off the back of a dragon especially when that dragon stands over a hundred feet high and just take off with them, I am not a bloody doll I have a mind of my own and would have gotten down when I was ready, not when you decided it am I understood." Huor stood there and nodded but she had more she wanted to say this time she started to pace,

"And furthermore, has any decision been made on seeing your mother we have been waiting for more than a few days now, and I do have trials that I have to undertake, I know they said there was no time limit to this trial, but I would like to get them finished before my father dies of old age." Taking a deep breath, she looked at all who were in her company, they were just staring at her not saying a word, she didn't understand what was going on but since she seemed to still have the floor, she decided that it would be best to say everything to try and make him understand what his mother was going through.

Taking a steadying breath, she looked at him and this time more gently and from the heart she started to speak once again, "Umm can we sit please?" by the time the please had come out she noticed that all that was there was sitting,

Walking over to Huor she placed a hand gently on his shoulder, she looked down at him and couldn't help but understand in her own way what he was going through, "When my mother died I was angry I felt that she had abandoned me even though I know your mother actually turned her back to you, she is trying to reach out where I come from we call it giving an olive branch one that is meant for peace, you have to understand the time that she did that it came from a place of rage, she was angry, heartbroken she had just lost her husband and two of her children. She could not see that there were others there that needed her; all she was thinking was the lies that Eó had told her. Please even if it is for a short time can't you find it in your heart just to meet with her?"

Huor looked at her he noticed that she seemed to not realise that she no longer looked like herself; she could feel a burning start on her arm again Huor looked at her and nodded he agreed that he and his sister would meet with her if Sarah came with them. Sarah had agreed and as she and Caradog walked away they noticed that the light was starting to fade, she was returning back to herself. By the time they got back to the glen she was back to her usual upbeat self, looking at Caradog she smiled and then run over to where gem was jumping up and down, she was finding it difficult to compose herself, smiling she shouted "I did it! They are going to meet with their mother" she was laughing and jumping up and down Caradog was still trying to wrap his head around what he had just seen, if Sarah was a dragon then she had no idea that she was, could it be that she was? but how could it be the only way that it could happen, gasping he looked at Sarah no it was not possible, could this be true he knew that he could not leave her but there again gem would know the lore better than any scroll, clearing his throat "Sarah, why don't you go and explore, you have had an eventful day. There again there is a babbling brook just on the other side of the glen I'm sure that you would like to get freshened up." Sarah looked at him and smiled she would love nothing more than that, so off she jogged stopping "what direction do I have to go in?" she asked he smiled just follow the green road and it will lead you there, but I will caution you to stay on the path."

Sarah smiled and jogged off once more he knew that if he had told her to stay on the path that there was no way she would, curiosity would get the better of her, and he knew that she would wander off and when she did, he knew that she would be safe. Because the path he set her on was the unicorn path and he knew that once she saw them that she would have to stay because unicorns due to misguided beliefs could speak, he knew that once mamma Morwen saw her then she would keep her there for a while just talking, he was sure of it.

As she faded from his sight, he came to stop in front of Gem looking about him once he was sure that no one was around he began, "Gem do you remember the old prophecy about the return of the blue dragon?" Gem looked at him and smiled "Of course I do I was the one who wrote it why do you ask?" "Gem please explain to me what the prophecy says?" Gem looked at him a bit bewildered but he knew that there was a reason he was asking clearing his throat he began, "it is said that when dark and light combine and the phoenix awakens that on the third month that the blue dragon would be revealed but only on the night of grate conflict when her dormant powers are awakened, it is said that the one who is chosen to be the host of the blue dragon is one who is pure of heart, and as strong as Orodreth Ar-Feiniel he was the oldest dragon he lives today but to find him you would have to go to the black mountain's, over the forbidden valley to the north of llandrangor river of fire, it is one journey that I would not wish on anyone, know this Caradog even being a true immortal even you would be at risk there, for even though it is true that we cannot die there is a legends as old as the immortals themselves, like you I had to undergo trials but if I failed that would have meant the end for my kind for I am the last tree immortal in all the thousands of life times I have lived, there has not been one yet to take my place, however there is a legend that goes as far back as time its self. That on the night of the awakening an immortal can be killed by the Ashanti dagger, the dagger was lost many years ago no one knows where it is, but as the legend goes, when the sun and moon share the sky on the night of the blood moon, as the chosen stands on the altar of blood at the moment the awakening ends he who possesses the Ashanti dagger can plunge it into the heart of the chosen and all the powers of the immortal will pass to that person, and the immortal that had the powers will die."

The Ashanti dagger is the only thing that can kill a true immortal but there is only a short window it has to be done on the night of the awakening,
The blue dragon prophecy is one that was written by gem for he had read all the signs and knew that it would happen.

Caradog looked at him this was the first time that he had ever heard of the Ashanti dagger, but there again there are many things that would have to fall into place for this to happen.

Sarah had been walking down the path for about an hour when she noticed that there were horses to the left of her, remembering what Caradog had said she thought for a moment he had said that she should not leave the path, but she loved horses, as she drew nearer, she noticed that these were not mere horses they were in fact unicorns. She could not believe her eyes she had noticed them when she had first arrived with Gin, but had not had the chance to go and see them, "oh come on how many chances in life are you going to be able to say that you have seen a real unicorn" she thought to herself.

"Hello there my dear," came a sweet voice from behind her it sounded the way you would imagine a kind grandmother to speak, turning around she saw no one there then the voice spoke again, once again it was that sweet elderly voice but looking around she could not see anyone, with that she felt a slight nudge on her arm looking around it was a unicorn it stood taller than her and was as white as the driven snow but she noticed that on her forehead just around the horn emitted a pale blue light, for a moment Sarah was mesmerised by it, she could see different colours swirling inside the light, she was brought back to her senses by the sweet voice she had heard previously looking around she was trying to see where the voice was coming from it was then that the unicorn started to speak in that very same voice, "Hello my child I am Mamma Morwen the queen of the unicorns and you must be the one that this place has been buzzing about," Sarah just stood there looking a bit befuddled that a unicorn was speaking to her, Mamma Morwen could not help but let out a slight laugh, "Don't take this the wrong way my dear but you would swear that this was the first time you had conversed with a unicorn," Sarah found her voice at that moment and laughed, "Umm you could say that, you see it is not common practice for people to speak to animals, where I come from." Mamma Morwen looked at her a bit puzzled "But how do you know when the animal is happy or sad or needs help? Sarah looked at her and smiled, "Mamma Morwen is it, you see where I come from animals are pets that you love and look after they are more companion's than anything." Mamma Morwen looked at her "But they are free to come and go?" "Well, no they are usually kept at your home or in a kennel" she had not managed to finish Mamma Morwen was stamping her large hoof on the ground; "You mean to say that they are prisoners where you come from? And you think that this is OK," Sarah raised her hands to calm her down, "Mamma Morwen where I come from yes, they may seem to be prisoners, but they are also free, I used to go riding and all the horses were always well looked after and cared for they had the freedom of the fields to run around in and they actually enjoy their lives." Mamma Morwen looked at her, "But if they do not speak how do you know that they are happy?" Sarah looked at her and smiled, "Because even though they do not speak like you and I are at this time, they speak using body language so you will always know if they are happy or not in that way." This seemed to satisfy her for the moment, they carried on speaking for a while then Sarah remembered that she was on her way to the Babbling brook to bathe but she noticed that they were far away from the path, she had not realised that they had gone so far, and after Caradog telling her not to wander she had once again not heeded his warning, turning to Mamma Morwen she smiled, "Mamma Morwen could you tell me how to get back to the path? You see I was on my way to the babbling Brook to bathe and freshen up, I did not realise that we had walked so far from the path," Morwen looked at her and smiled, "The babbling brook is to the south not the north it's the dragons brook to the north the water there is warmer than the babbling brook, who told you to come this way?" "Caradog said that this was the way to the babbling brook, but he also told me not to leave the path I was on." Mamma Morwen laughed gently "Well I see that he has still not changed still pulling pranks and at his age, he should know better," Sarah looked at her "Caradog plays pranks?" she could not believe it he always seemed like such a stiff to coin the phrase, "Yes Caradog is well known to us old ones I knew him when he was a hatchling, and even as a young dragon he always would find ways of pulling pranks, I remember the time that he nicked king Othiren's staff and hid it in the cherry grove, the king searched for over a month looking for it then one day it was back in its rightful place, when they looked into it they found out that they had been struck by the Caradog, we all got used to it then over time as he grew he would still pull them but nothing like the Ophilias scandal," Sarah looked at her "The Ophilias scandal? Please do tell." She sat there as Morwen divulged everything about the time that he had flown of with Ophelia's first born daughter, "he had thought it funny but it was during the great riots of Meredic and the king believed that Morenden the king of the north had kidnapped her, he had flown into a rage and without thinking had demanded that Morenden return his daughter and for every day that she was missing he would take one of Morenden's children, no doubting if Caradog had known what was going to happen he would have returned her straight away, but he had taken her to the chasms of chaos, there he left her for a time while he went back to see what was happening and it was at that time he had found out, she had been missing for four days and in her father's dungeon was four of Morenden's children, once he realised what had happened he quickly explained everything, to the king but the damage had been done, he returned Athrina and everything was settled with minimal bloodshed, it was not long after that he underwent his trials, and when he came back he was different no one knew what he went through and he never spoke of it, and until this point I believed that the old Caradog was lost to us for he no longer played pranks in fact he stayed away from everyone only paying a visit when he was called upon." Sarah looked at her and a thought came to her if he was pulling pranks then could it be that he was returning to his old self, she smiled at that it was nice to hear stories of him from people who knew him, once again she sat looking at Mamma Morwen "could you tell me more about him? He is my guide, but I feel like he knows more about me than I do him." Mamma Morwen sighed "There are many stories I could tell you about many people for I am one of the oldest in this realm and I know everything you see my horn, it's not for stabbing or anything like that it collect's the stories that are yet to be told" bending over she placed her horn in Sarah's hand "Now think hard, what you truly wish to know then close your eyes, Sarah did as she was told she wanted nothing more than to know what Caradog was like thinking hard she cleared her mind of everything except Caradog, then slowly she closed her eyes and it was as if she was transported back in time to when Caradog was young she watched him as he went through his phases the pranks the anger the sadness, then she seemed to settle with one image of him talking to a young woman she watched as they went on their way, as time went on she could see that the woman was becoming sad and then the memory shifted slightly to him waking finding her body at his feet, he let out a mighty roar bending down he raised her lifeless body taking flight he had taken her to the chasm of fire, there he landed laying her down he slumped to the floor overcome with grief she could see him crying, could hear his sobs after a time he calmed himself taking a giant claw he raked at the ground there he placed the body of the woman covering her over he breathed fire leaving a mark on the soil around the grave site. Sarah opened her eyes tears streaming down her cheeks, he had gone through so much that she felt sorry for him. Morwen looked at her "now you know why he is so weary about letting you go off on your own, you see an immortal can die if they take their own life, before they finish the trials she was the second that he was guiding and he had loved her like his own child the day she died I remember it vividly the sky had turned a crimson red and rain began to fall all about us, it smelt of molten rocks, but that is because she was buried there, only the other unicorns and he knew where she was placed he has never told anyone else opting instead to let them believe that he had eaten her corpse to stop anyone interfering with it, so now you know too but let me tell you something that no one else knows, Caradog is one of the gentlest creatures that you will ever meet, he may seem ferocious but those who know him know that he would rip out his own heart if he could so that you will survive, so promise me this that no matter what happens you will see this through to the end," Sarah looked at her and smiled, "I have every intention of completing the trials so that I can go and see my father again" Morwen smiled "Then come I will take you to Dragons brook, you will find the water there more desirable than the babbling brook."

Standing she walked by the side of Mamma Morwen as they made their way back to the path they talked the whole way there Mamma Morwen enjoyed the time that they spent together she could tell that there was something different about Sarah she didn't seem as cold as the other protectors, she had met she seemed warmer more human one would say, as they entered a clearing Sarah noticed a large rock formation that was in the shape of a dragon she understood in an instant why it was given the name. mamma Morwen said her goodbyes and left, Sarah walked over to the brook kneeling she placed her hand into the brook the water was warm standing she undressed, slowly she slipped into the water it was fantastic the feel of it on her skin she could feel the heat permeating her body relaxing her muscles as she swam, coming to the surface she laid on her back just floating there with her eyes closed, not once thinking that she was out in the open, all she thought was how nice this was finally having the bath she most defiantly needed, why could Caradog not have told her about this place a few days ago, but she didn't care she knew where it was now and was going to take full advantage of it while she was there.

Huor had been out walking he had agreed to meet his mother and he was having reservations about it, he knew that he could not go back on his word but also knew that she was one of the last people he wanted to see at this time, there again at least he would get to meet the brother he never knew he had, even if he was the son of Eó he was still his brother and he had lost too much during the great plague, he could not turn his back on him not knowing that he was his blood, for the light elves always believed that family was important there were many times that elves would be with different people, they lived for so long that even with their soul mate they would often father or give birth to other children from different fathers to different mothers.

It was accepted in their society Huor had been promised to one of the daughters of the woodland elves they had not yet met but it would be their choice if they wished to form a union, as he walked he found himself walking the unicorn trail that led to the Dragons brook he loved going there it was one place that he could think while cleansing himself, as he walked past the unicorns he noticed that Mamma Morwen was not there, it was rare to pass this place at this time and not see her he had wanted to speak with her, instead he continued down the path finally coming to the clearing where the brook was as he stepped out he noticed Sarah was there well her clothes were, without thinking he made his way to the edge of the brook standing there he gazed upon the water, it was so clear you could see all the way to the bottom, as he focused his eyes he noticed that there was someone swimming it took a moment for it to sink in that the naked form he was looking at was Sarah, her body was toned and beautiful slowly she rose out of the water her back to him, he looked at her hair was down it stopped just before her bottom he looked at her, as he gazed upon her naked form he noticed that there were many scars on her as well, the one that caught his eye was the one just up passed her thigh it seemed angry it hadn't healed well, he stood there just gazing at her not for a moment thinking that it was wrong, Sarah settled back into the water and started to swim again not realising that she was not alone, once again she lay on her back her body on display for him to see, he just stood there looking at her this time he saw the scar that was just below her right breast, finally she decided it was time to get out as she stood up she opened her eyes and came face to face with Huor, letting out a blood curdling scream she covered herself and lowered herself quickly back into the water, her scream was heard through the glen and within moments there were elves unicorns and Caradog surrounding them, Huor's uncle looked at him then to her, her face was scarlet looking about her she realized she was surrounded by men it was Mamma Morwen who quickly started ushering them away.

Finally, she was alone with Mamma Morwen who waited with her until she dressed, this time she was angry at Huor for a completely different reason, "How dare he stand there and watch her" she thought angrily once she was dressed Mamma Morwen let them all know it was safe to come back as they all surrounded her she waited patiently for Huor to come back as he emerged from the tree with his uncle she threw a killer right, this time when she hit him he actually lost his balance and fell to the ground, "How dare you spy on me you peeping tom!" she yelled at him as he got to his feet she wanted to hit him again but decided to walk over to where Caradog was, standing there seething with anger Mablung looked at her then to Huor, "OK could someone let me know what is going on?" Sarah couldn't believe her ears, "don't tell me that this is normal to spy on a girl while she is naked?" Mablung looked at her then to Huor who stood there just looking at her his face still bore the mark where she had struck him. "Huor have you anything to say?" Mablung asked Huor looking at him and then to Sarah "Yes, can I ask where you got those scars from?" Sarah stood there for a moment aghast at the question when she noticed all who were there had turned a quizzical eye on her.

Turning she stormed off not wanting to explain herself she could not believe it he was the one in the wrong, but they all seemed to be more interested in the scars she had on her body, the accident had happened over a year ago now even though she sometimes felt the pain from the various injuries she had sustained she still did not like to think about that night or her recovery. She sat on the rock that was by the whispering woods, there she looked at her hand it still stung slightly from the right she had given Huor earlier, she couldn't help but see the funny side of it now thinking about the look on his face when she screamed, but there again how on earth did everyone get there so fast was one thing that she was wondering now, as she sat there trying to arrange her thoughts she heard the familiar sounds of Caradog's wings as he came into land she stood up, "Before you say anything he deserved that right I gave him and there is nothing you can say that will make me apologise." Caradog looked at her for a moment he was more interested in the scars that Huor had said he had seen on her body. They had spoken after she left, and he told them of the many scars he had observed on her, he said he didn't mean to spy on her but when he saw the marks on her body and the fact that she was so young made him continue to watch her, he hadn't realised until she screamed that he had been there for so long.

Caradog paced back and forth for a while finally stopping he turned to Sarah he had to know what was going on, why did someone so young have so many scars on her body, he was led to believe that the human realm was one of the safest realms to live in, but after hearing Huor he thought about it could it really be that she has had to fight all her life or was there another reason, he had to know; clearing his throat he came to stop in front of her. "Sarah please I must know, what did Huor mean when he said that you were covered in scars? Is it true?" Sarah looked at him, even he was more interested in the scars on her body nobody seemed to care that she had been spied on.

Heaving a hefty sigh of both anger and annoyance she looked at him, "I was in a car accident a while ago I almost died that is where the scars came from," she could see the look of concern on his face, making it harder for her to stay angry it was her turn to start pacing, "Listen I'm fine honestly, it was over a year ago now and the wounds have completely healed I am fine" Caradog looked at her wondering if it was normal for a human to heal so fast, even being a protector until she received her powers she was human after all. He was sure that he heard it took them a lot longer to heal than other immortals, he thought about it for a while and then decided that he wanted to see at least one of the scars she had, that way he would know how severely she had been injured but how was he supposed to ask her to show him her body. Especially after the way she had reacted when she found Huor watching her, but this was different he was not asking to see her naked body just some of the scars she had on it.

He thought on how to approach the subject for the moment, then decided the best way would be just to come out and ask her straight if he could see them, looking at her he thought about the best way to ask her but nothing he was coming up with seemed right, finally he decided that the direct approach would be the best. Taking a deep breath, he turned to her "Sarah could I please see the scars that Huor was talking about?" She looked at him for a moment but didn't see him as a man she saw him as an animal, so she decided that there was not a problem with it slowly she took her top then her trousers off and stood before him in her underwear, he looked at the marks on her body but the one that he saw that seemed a lot older than all the others was the one she bore just below her right breast, raising his foot he pointed at it, "That one is a lot older than any of the others. Where did it come from?" Sarah looked down slowly she traced the scar with her finger, "That one has been there since I was a child; I have no idea where it came from. Whenever I ask about it my father brushes it off saying I was in an accident when I was a child," Caradog looked at her and smiled he didn't want to push her if she didn't remember it was probably because she had blanked it out. However, that also posed a problem for the final trial facing your worst fear.

Finally, she got dressed and they changed the subject moreover he could not shake the feeling that there was something she was not telling him. However, he decided that he would not push the subject until she was ready.

Finally, the day had arrived for Huor and his sister along with Mablung to go and see Eámané as they walked along the path, they had agreed they would meet at the edge of the white elven border, as they approached Sarah once again felt the burning on her arm looking down at it, she noticed that there was nothing there, where was the burning coming from. Finally, they were there on the border they stood there looking slowly they saw Eámané and some of the others approaching them Beren was next to her they came to a stop in front of Huor and the others.

Huor looked at his mother and the man who stood next to her Eámané was the first to break the silence "Brother it has been too long," then turning to her children, "I am so sorry that I abandoned you, and left it is a decision that I have regretted these many years not seeing the people you have turned into," Huor had done as asked and come to see her he turned and was about to walk away when she grasped hold of his arm, "My son I know you are angry and have every right to be; but please hear me out." For a moment they all thought her pleas had fallen on deaf ears but this time when Huor turned to face his mother it was with anger, pulling his arm away. "Let you explain, please as if there is any excuse for what you did. Yes, you lost a husband and two children; but you didn't think for once that we also lost them as well; we are taught that feelings and emotions should never drive our actions, and I have never let them drive mine. But you the one who was supposed to be there the one who was supposed to stay strong for the remainder of your family allowed your anger to consume you to the point that you allowed Eó into your life, the very person we should have been fighting all along, you went to the marriage bed with, that is not the actions that comes from a mother; that is the actions you would expect from a child who hasn't yet chosen what path they wished to choose.

You had already made your choice a choice that is given to every elf on their Lúinwé the day they come of age, with the right to choose it is the one day that you can choose the dark without fear of being judged, if you choose the dark you even have the time of fasting to fully commit to the side you have chosen, you get the chance to say Fair well to your family, before the ceremony is held, but you chose the light on that day as did I when it came my time."

Pointing to his sister he steadied himself, "she has not said a word since you left, we have tried everything to get her to speak all she does is sit in her tower and look at the pictures of our family, then you come along and say you have seen the light that you wished to see us again? Mother, there is only one way for us to accept you back and you know what it is you must go to your memorial and ask for forgiveness, are you prepared to do that?" Eámané looked at him then to her daughter, then turning she placed a hand on Beren's arm, turning back to her other children, "this is my other son, Beren your brother at that Enelya looked up the girl who had not spoken in over a hundred years began to speak.

107

"Beren, our brother?" All eyes turned to her Huor could not believe his ears she was speaking; he did not say a word nor did anyone else who was there they allowed her to continue. "You turned your back on us, I remember running after you mother, can you remember the words you said to me that day because they have been etched into my mind, you told me you would always love me and Huor and that you wished we would change our minds and follow you, when I said that I was a light elf and would die that; your words were just a few, then please think that I died in the plague. Do you realise what those words did to me I could never bring myself to tell Huor so I decided the best thing to do was not to speak at all that way I could never slip up. Do you realise how many times I wanted to speak to someone how many times I cried over it, and now you have decided that you want us back in your life, well mother it is not that easy. You can't just abandon your children then when it's convenient for you decide you want us back."

With that she stormed past them, as she walked into the forest Sarah ran after her leaving Huor and the others talking if there was anyone that she could get through to it should be Enelya, as she followed her Enelya continued walking not once looking back she had sheer determination in her stride, Sarah decided to put the years of training into action she picked up her pace. As she drew closer to Enelya she called out, finally, Enelya stopped and looked at her Sarah could see her eyes were brimming with unshod tears, causing Sarah to stop for a moment but she knew that she had to bring this family back together if there was even the slightest of hopes. "Enelya please, she is trying to reach out to you. Can't you just give her a chance?" Enelya looked at Sarah she could not believe what she was hearing had this child not heard what she had said, shaking her head she turned away, "Enelya if your mother meant nothing to you then you would not be this upset" Enelya once again looked at her this child someone that she had only just met could tell this from just one meeting.

After they spoke for a while Sarah managed to get her to come back and speak with her mother this was going to have to be resolved one way or the other, there was no way that she could just leave it like this. Finally, they re-joined the others, Beren and Huor were off to the side talking and Eámané stood speaking with her brother and Caradog, as Enelya emerged with Sarah they all stopped talking and looked in her direction. Stopping she looked in her mother's direction walking over she looked at her "The only reason I have come back is that I made Sarah a promise that I would listen to what you have to say."

They sat for the longest time just listening to Eámané talk of her life after she left and finding out that Eó was the one who had set the plague on them in the first place; she explained everything and begged for their forgiveness. With that a loud eruption startled them all standing they turned in the direction of the noise, slowly emerging was one of the elven guards he was injured badly and collapsed just before he got to them Eámané and the others rushed to his side it was then that they learned that the one threat they all believed dead, Eó was still alive and searching for Eámané and Beren, he was angered at the fact they had run away from him, the story of his demise was greatly exaggerated.

It was at this point that Eámané pleaded for them to take her to her memorial so that she may plead for forgiveness, they would know if she were truthful that she truly wanted forgiveness for if she were to kneel there and lie, she would be struck down by Ainarél Númenessé the great spirit who watched over the light elven lands.

They travelled for three days all the time the pain in Sarah's arm was worsening, but once again there was nothing there, as they came upon her memorial she noticed that there were guards around it some she had never seen before but she would remember Longléssan anywhere they had grown as children together, as they drew near to it he stepped forward looking at Eámané he stopped he had not seen her since she had left yet there she was standing in front of him just as beautiful as she was the day she left.

Walking past him she knelt at her memorial sight, closing her eyes drawing on the power of the light, she unsheathed the Lúthorien dagger the ceremony called for the blood of the fallen that was her, dragging the dagger across the palm of her hand she laid it upon the urn slowly a light started to surround her it was the light of Ainarél Númenessé, they watched as it engulfed her this was the first time any of them witnessed this they had read about it happening in the history books but none of them had ever truly witnessed it, they watched in awe as the light brightened as she was raised off her feet light surrounding her slowly it started to fade by the time her feet touched the ground the light was completely gone, gone were the dark colours once again she was clothed in pale blue her hair that had been tied up was now flowing around her, stepping out of the memorial she walked towards where the others were standing, the closer she got they noticed that the ground around her was rejuvenating.

As they looked at her they noticed that she had changed, gone were the pale blue eyes instead they were a deep violet, her once beautiful raven hair was now the colour of the cherry blossom the more she walked they noticed that there were differences about her finally she came to stop in front of Sarah, raising her arm she placed it just below Sarah's left breast, "to know the truth can sometimes mean more heartache," with those words she collapsed to the floor. Caradog looked at Sarah's arm and noticed that the crest for love was there, she had passed the second trial. Caradog smiled to himself, but it was tinged with sadness for he knew that he would only have three weeks to get her ready for the final trial. After what Eámané had just said he was even more nervous could it mean that it was something that her mind had blocked out.

Finally Eámané awoke, she had slept for two days, getting out of bed she made her way to the large elegant window she passed the eye of Ellendda the large mirror on the wall as she passed she stopped for a moment it was then she noticed the dramatic change in her appearance; gone were the dark colours even her hair and eyes had changed, finally she pulled herself away she made the short distance that was left to the window, throwing them open she walked onto the balcony holding the rail she took in the site of the land she had grown up in, it was mostly the same.

"Hello," came a voice from below looking down she saw Drallen stood there smiling up at her, he was one of the guys that she had not seen in many a year, smiling she looked down at him then taking the steps to the left she made her way down coming to stop in front of him, "Drallen it has been too long, it is nice to see you" he looked at her for a moment and realised that even though there were a few differences she was still the girl he had grown up with.

After they had finished speaking, she made her way to the great hall to see her brother, Beren was standing there with his uncle and brother none were speaking there was a tension in the air, before Eámané had chance to let her presence be known Enelya bound into the room grasping a hold of Beren and Huor. She pulled them with her they could not help laughing Huor had not seen his sister like this for many years, and it was nice to hear her sing once more she had the most beautiful voice. Eámané smiled and let out a cough to let them know she was there, all came to a stop and watched as she fully entered the room Enelya ran across she smiled at her mother then hugged her.

Sarah entered the building, but this time was a sadder occasion this time it was to say goodbye for she had completed the task that she had to do, and it was time for her and Caradog to leave for the misty mountains the place she would train for her final trial.

As she entered the room, they all smiled at Sarah, Enelya was the first to speak and greet her, then came the others they talked and laughed but they noticed that she seemed quite solemn "What is wrong?" Eámané asked as she stepped closer to her, Sarah smiled "I have done everything that I set out to do here so my time has come to leave, I go now to the misty mountains to train for the final trial," all who were there were talking and frustrated at the thought that the girl who had reunited them was about to walk out of their lives, they knew that if she passed they may never see her again, for she would go back to the human realm, Beren turned to his mother and uncle "Can't we find a way so that she can stay?" Sarah looked at him and smiled there was no way of doing it she knew that but the thought of having to leave so soon after reuniting them was quite saddening as well, finally they all went out to where Caradog was standing.

A long discussion ensued but Caradog had the last word and that was no there was no way that she would be able to stay there any longer, due to her having received the second crest she had three weeks until her final test that meant journeying to the misty mountains which was three days travel, so there was no way that she could stay,

Finally, after the discussion they decided that she was going to have one last night and they were going to make it a night to remember, a night of festivity and thanks to the one who united them all, Sarah smiled but these things just weren't for her so she planned with Caradog that they would leave in secret. Her plans were thrown off course when Huor decided to stop by before it was all due to kick off, he found himself becoming enchanted with this human, before he had the chance to think of anything else the voice of his sister broke through his thoughts, "why brother what are you doing all the way over here?" she said through a broad smile, Huor looked at her, "I was just coming to get the guest of honour." He smiled back not realizing that his sister could see straight through his heart and knew that he was falling in love with a human, but even she had to admit the specialty of this human she was warm caring followed her heart as much as her head and always seemed to be able to read people, for only she had noticed that even through her silence she still loved her mother and wanted her back.

The festivities started with a few speeches first from lord Mablung he stood there very proud taking a deep breath he smiled "For the first time in a hundred years my family is once again whole, but not just that I have another nephew Beren," he pointed in his direction, as he ended his speech he turned to the one

111

who had saved them, everyone knew to whom he was speaking finally he smiled and beckoned everyone to raise their glasses to Sarah, everyone had wanted Sarah to give a speech, but she knew that if she had she would have cried so politely refused all offers, until they finally got the message.

Sarah found herself wandering close to the old foundry she had always wondered what it was, as she walked she knew this was her final night, she was glad in a way that Huor had messed up her plans; but she was sad at the thought of saying goodbye to them all, she had loved her time there and had wished she could remain but she knew that she would have three weeks before her final trial, she had been told that there was no time limit and there yet she had three weeks to complete her training before her final trial, but when the trial started she had as much time as needed to complete it, for it was as everyone kept reminding her the hardest and worst of the trials because unlike the others this time she had to face her greatest fear, she knew what that was the thought of losing her father was her greatest fear but how were they going to test her on it. Was she going to have to watch her father die repeatedly or were they going to do something else, the more she thought the more tense she got.

Huor interrupted her thoughts "so this is where you got to" he said smiling, seeing the look on her face he came to stop in front of her, "What is it?" he asked she smiled and looked down, "I leave in the morning and that thought scares me, because I know what it means, I have completed two of the trials so in total, I have completed four two in the human realm and two here so in total I will have completed five trials not three as I was led to believe, and just like the trials back home they get harder but these are like nothing I have ever faced before, what if I fail?" Huor smiled stepping forward he placed his hands on her shoulders. "From what I have seen of you, I have every faith that you will pass the final trial, but will you do something for me?"

"Anything" "Before you leave to go home will you come and see us first, so we know that everything is, OK?" Smiling she nodded her head "If I succeed then I will come in person to let you know that I am safe," he brought her close holding her as a lover would he didn't want this night to end he wanted her to stay but knew she had to leave. They stayed like that for the longest time Sarah could feel the hardness of his body beneath her hands, yes he may be a lot older than her but being held like this by him just felt right, slowly she tilted her head to look up at him, her eyes pleading for him to kiss her to feel his mouth on hers, Huor could feel his body reacting to her slowly he moved his head claiming her mouth with his, she felt a shudder run through her body as he deepened the kiss, he stepped forward making her back arch slightly raising his hand he encircled her bread feeling her nipple hardening beneath his fingers, she let out a low groan, he kept massaging her breast making her move against him, she had never felt like this before the feel of him setting her body on fire, she run her hands in his hair grabbing hold deepened the kiss one that she wished would never end, picking her up he moved them both to the grove lying her one the soft earth he came to join her, he did not know that this was her first time, before now she had never know the touch of a man.

He slowly undid the top then with one quick motion released her breasts form the confines of her bra, looking down at her he could feel the fire burning inside him, moving his head he took her breast in his mouth softly he bit at her nipple causing her to moan out loud, her back arched against him, he moved his hands down the flat plain of her stomach to where the top of her trousers, with a flick of his finger he popped the button open then sliding his hand inside to the damp curls of her woman hood, slowly he run his fingers over her she could feel the arousal rising the more he moved his hand he started to quicken the pace her hips started to move against his hand the more he moved the faster her breath became ragged, she could feel everything it was as though every nerve ending in her body was crying out for this until finally she could not hold her voice back anymore letting out a cry of pure ecstasy, raising his head he looked down at her smiling gently he freed her from the trousers, suddenly she felt a little apprehension as he was about to take her she pressed her hands onto his bare chest, her voice almost a whisper, "please be gentle" he looked at her a moment then the realisation dawned on him, covering her body with his he came close to her ear, "Sarah is this your first time?" he asked his voice hoarse he looked at her, her eyes flickered for a moment then she nodded, in one motion he had rolled off her and was lying at her side the thought of what his was about to do flooding his mind, sitting up she pulled her knees to her chest, "did I do something wrong?" looking at her he gently caressed her back, "I want you to be sure before we do anything" coming to his side she kissed his chest making him move beneath her, "I'm sure" she said gently tugging at his nipple with her teeth, a groan escaped him what was he doing she was truly innocent, it was her turn to move her hands down his body grabbing him in her hand she started to arouse him he could feel himself hardening under her smooth strokes, he could feel it building he couldn't take much more he had to have her, grabbing her hand he pushed her back onto the earth, "are you sure, because I don't know if I can stop if you're not," he said his voice ragged and hoarse, Sarah looked at him and smiled "I am sure," pushing her back onto the ground he started to kiss her claiming her mouth he moved kissing her neck then down to her breasts, once again he took it in his mouth teasing her nipple with his tongue and teeth, she could feel herself getting hot again the feeling was getting intense as he moved down her body, finally coming to stop between her thighs, opening her he moved his hand over her then slowly his mouth his tongue encircling her she could feel herself harden against him slowly her hips started to move pumping against him, he sucked her taking her into his mouth, a groan escaped her, gently he pushed his finger into her the pain was slight and made her catch her breath slightly, raising his head he looked at her "Sorry, did I hurt you?" looking down at him she shook her head, he stopped for a moment kneeling up but keeping his hand on her moving it back and forth he came to her side.

"You know the first time will be painful?" she looked at him and nodded, "Sarah are you sure?" he asked as his fingers flicked over her once more, "Oh, yes I want this" she said breathlessly, he moved once again between her legs his mouth finding her once more this time move feverish, pushing his finger into her a little deeper this time, moving it around until he found the right spot, he pushed his finger into her then out over and over as his tongue continued its assault on her, then moving his hands he grabbed a hold of her legs raising them so her could see her face as he continued his delicious enticement of her she had a beautiful glow about her, her eyes were closed she was near the edge and he knew it, of all the women he had taken in his life there was something about her a lust in him that would not be sated until he made her his, she could not take anymore the feeling was too powerful too much she could feel her body arch and stiffen against him as a cry broke from her slowly he positioned himself between her legs, kissing her he gently pushed himself inside her the pain was searing for a moment he began to move, it was painful to start, but she could feel the pain ebbing as a new feeling took over he started moving faster thrusting deeper into her, she could feel the arousal moving through her body again, her body moving under him her hips meeting his every thrust, both of them started to breath heavily Sarah flung her arms around his shoulders raising to him she kissed him just where the neck and shoulder joined softly biting him, her hands that were around his shoulders now moved down his back he could feel her nails biting into his skin to the firm round buttock grabbing him she pushed him in deeper her body writhing beneath his as she did, "Oh, Huor" she managed with a strangled breath, he didn't know how much longer he could go before exploding in her, raising he looked down at her "Sarah, look at me" his voice as soft as silk, slowly she opened her eyes the pressure building, "What do you want me to do?" he asked in earnest, Sarah looked at him as though she did not understand the question, "Do you want all of me?" he asked through gritted teeth, "Yes, I want all of you" she moaned not realising what he meant, once again he found her mouth this time his kiss invaded her, her every sense was heightened, the feeling growing more intense until finally she could not take any more her hands grabbing around his back nails biting into his skin, she cried out, the ground around her was moving her head felt light as though a thousand fireworks were surrounding them finally it was his turn to finish, she could feel him inside her the warm sensation as he exploded inside her she could feel it moving, his body went limp on top of her, it was only then that she had thought she had no protection, slowly he raised his head looking down at her he smiled kissing her gently he rolled off to the side, lying there she could still feel her body tremble slightly. Moving she placed her head on his chest, hugging her he held her tight.

Slowly Sarah sat up she needed to go clean herself wash him away how could she have been so foolish as to let him ejaculate in her, looking at him was that what he meant by her wanting all of him, she had said yes putting her head in her hand she stood and walked away over to the hot springs as she slipped into the warm water she looked about her, she didn't regret it not one bit she had wanted him there was no shame in that.

"Sarah," he spoke softly looking up he was there he had not dressed she took in the sight of him his toned and muscular chest down to the firmness of his legs and thighs she could see he was still aroused.

How was he supposed to let her go now, the feeling ate at him, he knew that he could not ask her to stay even though he wanted to plead with her not to leave him just stay there, they could have a life together, she started thinking of everything he had done to her and she started to feel the still slightly unfamiliar feeling between her thighs, she was starting to feel aroused again and looking at him only made it worse her face flushed slightly, she blamed it on the water but knew that it was not, she wanted him to take her again, as she was about to move away from him he lowered his body into the water beside her, grabbing her hand he pulled her to him, her breasts crushed against the hard wall of his chest as his mouth once again found hers, she tried to push him away but he could not let her go he had to have her again here and now, slowly with one arm around her waist her moved the other down her body her protests in vain he turned her so her back was against the warm rock, raising his head he looked deep into her eyes, she knew resistance was futile but she had to try, he seductively ran his finger up the inside of her leg gently tapping on her causing her to catch her breath, this time he brought his mouth down heavily on hers she could feel her lips plumping under the assault grabbing her legs he wrapped them around him this time he wasn't as gentle ramming into her the pain pierced her like a hot skewer, she cried out in pain but he did not stop, this was not like the first time this time he was more demanding as he thrust into her gabbing at his shoulders she tried to push him away crying out "Huor please your hurting me," at those words he went ridged, that was the last thing he wanted to do, looking at her he kissed her tenderly, "I'm sorry" he panted in her ear, this time when he moved he was much slower entering her it didn't hurt, slowly the momentum built she could feel her self-coming close to climaxing, her breathing heavier fisting her hands in his hair she pulled his mouth to hers kissing him deeply, she tightened around him, as she was getting ready to climax as she did he started to kiss her neck feeling himself getting closer, this was heaven he thought pure heaven, finally he finished his body feeling spent he lowered her down, looking at him she put her arms around his neck kissing him, she had never felt this way before her heart felt as though it might burst it hurt so much, tomorrow she would be leaving and may never see him again the thought tugged at her.

Huor moved back slightly so he could see her the swell of her breasts the toned body, the scars that still held a lot of wonder to him, slowly he traced the one under her right breast, "this looks angry, how did it happen?" she looked at him then away, it was the one scar she had no memory of she didn't know when it happened or how, gently lifting her chin to him he looked into her eyes, "how?" was all he said shaking her head she looked away, "I've have had that since I can remember, my father always says it was due to an accident when I was a child but refused to tell me anymore about it."

He nodded "what about the others?" she had many scars due to the car accident, some had healed well and could barely be seen but others she was not so lucky, "I was in a car accident, just over a year ago, I almost died," he caught his breath hearing those words almost died, if she had then they would never have met she would never have reunited his family, pulling her into his arms he held her close, he could never imagine a world without her but he knew this

116

could never last because she was after all a mortal, even if she did pass all the trials and gained the immortality of the protector then she would have more realms than this one to govern and how could he ask her to leave the realm she grew up in, but it was nice to dream.

Turning her back to him he started to wash her rubbing her shoulders then down to her buttocks, kissing her gently on the neck as he did, finally he turned her to face him her eyes alight with want, he could see it there raising his hand he traced her face him finger moving across her lips that were still bruised from his earlier assault on them, grabbing his hand she gently nipped at his finger, "aah Sarah stop," he groaned as he could feel himself becoming aroused once more, but she didn't this time she was the one to take command moving closer to him she kissed his neck, gently grazing her teeth on his shoulder, grabbing her by the shoulders he pushed her away, they could not do it again it would only make it harder on both of them, but she wouldn't stop slowly she stroked her hand down his body moving in she kissed his nipple taking it between her teeth she mirrored his movements from earlier grabbing his hand she lead him into the shallow water where the water lapped around his knees, kissing down his body until she came to his pubic bone she nipped as she went lower, slowly she grabbed his shaft in her hand and started long slow stroked at first then more rapid movements, throwing his head back he moaned aloud, finally she took him in her mouth, sucking him then she stopped looking up at him she smiled then just sucking the top she licked around the tip causing him to bite down hard on his lip to stop himself crying out, he didn't know how much more of this he could take before he released himself in her, grabbing her hands he pulled her to her feet, "do you realise what you are doing to me?" he almost growled at her, she lowered her eyes in mocked coyness looking up lustfully into his eyes, "is it wrong for me to never want this night to end?" he spoke softly; grabbing around her waist he raised her out of the water walking to the bank he laid her on the soft earth, kissing her gently, he positioned himself so he was situated between her legs grabbing her knees he raised them higher to have more penetration, slowly he pushed into her this time he was not just satisfying a need he wanted to make love to her, he thrust into her making her arch against him, lowering his head he claimed her breast sucking on it grazing her nipple with his teeth, he was going to take it slow let her feel every inch of him, and there was a lot of inches; she could feel him deep inside her the feeling the sensation was blissful, moving her hands up to his shoulders she clung to him, "Huor" she said his name in a moan, that quickened his pulse he wanted her to say it again, moving faster thrusting deeper into her, her nails were biting into his flesh only making him want more. This time when they climaxed, they did at the same time, their bodies going limp.

Once she had finished cleaning herself she came to his side lying there next to him she leant over kissing him, "If you want any more I'm afraid I will have to disappoint you, you have left me quite depleted" smiling she kissed him again then lowered her head down so it was on his chest, she grew heavier and he knew she was asleep he didn't want to move he wanted to stay there like that with her for eternity. His eyes grew heavy and before he knew it, he had fallen asleep.

A familiar voice broke the silence rousing them both from their slumber, "my my... what would mother say," Enelya said with a giggle Huor and Sarah jumped apart as though an electric current had just run through them, "Enelya we were just" she cut them short it was then they realised they were both lying there naked, Huor looked a little flustered as though he was finding it hard to breathe, grabbing his clothes he quickly dressed as did Sarah, they both just stood there faces slightly flushed "Enelya, please can we talk about this" Enelya smiled coughing slightly, "I believe that the words you are looking for, is heat of the moment, you both have to know that this could never go anywhere." Sarah looked at her a little bemused what did she mean could never go anywhere, "I know, I was just so taken with her I knew when it happened that it would only be this once, for she leaves in the morning," Sarah gasped at the bluntness, only once never again how could he, she thought anger started to build in her she had been used, "What! Wanted to know what would be like with a human is that it nothing more!?" He lowered his head she took that to mean she was right.

Tears stung at her eyes to think that she had allowed him to do this to her to use her then throw her away like this. "You. You monster!" at this even Enelya looked at her but she wasn't finished, "You knew I had never been with a man before you took me, I told you and you acted as though you loved me, oh how stupid could I have been!" Huor came close to touching her, but she hit his hand away, "Don't you dare touch me; you say you're good and that you walk in the light how can that be when you can use someone in this way? I hate you Huor and never want to see you again! The worst thing I ever did was to come here I wished I had listened to Caradog and left well enough alone!" she ran past Enelya into the darkness of the grove tears streaming down her face, why didn't she leave like she was going to why had she let him talk her into joining the party

118

what type of man was he, that he would do this to a girl make her feel so special only to reveal his true colours. Her arm started to burn once more when she looked under the symbol of love there was a mark. Finding Caradog and Mablung deep in conversation she did not wish to disturb them so made her way to the grove there was Gem she knew that she could talk to him the way she did with Caradog.

As she entered the grove she noticed the Eámané was there talking to him, a little flustered she turned to walk away "Sarah you wish to speak with me," It was the voice of Caradog turning she noticed that all the chatter had stopped Caradog, Mablung, Eámané and Gem were all looking at her, she could feel the tears even more threatening to fall, turning she ran from them, she needed to get away from them she could not allow them to see her cry, but she found running did nothing for Caradog caught up with her with just a few beats of is enormous wings, landing in front of her she stopped sharply causing her to fall she could not hold it in anymore the tears fell, raising her knees she clutched them tightly to her chest, the tears also took her ability to speak she just sat there crying she had not noticed Caradog shooing the others away slowly he came to her side sitting down he looked down at her, wondering what he could tell her how could he help when there was no way of understanding what she was going through, looking down at her arm he noticed the mark, it was altered slightly he had heard of it but to think that it was actually true was another thing.

"Sarah, what happened, that mark only changes like that when your heart changes, is there something you wish to talk about?" Sarah didn't know what to say she had felt the burn and had noticed the change, but her heart hadn't changed she felt sad and angry sad at the thought of saying goodbye and angry at the way Huor had treated her; he had taken her virginity and not cared about it. She knew as soon as she got the final trial out of the way then she would be able to go back home back to her father as well as jack and tommy, along with all the other friends she had made while at the monastery. That thought made her heart even heavier because if she was to go back then she would not be able to see Huor again or any of the others, Caradog gently nuzzled her face with his snout, "Sarah you know that I am here for you, you can ask me anything that you like, and I will answer all your questions without riddles or anything." For a moment Sarah sat there just looking at him, she wanted to tell him what had happened between her and Huor, but she wasn't sure how he would react, there were many things she wanted to know but the only thing that kept coming to her was never seeing any of the friends she had made again with the exception of Huor she could not care less what happened to him he could rot for all she cared, finally taking a steadying breath she decided to put it out of her mind as though it had not even happened, but it was hard getting the thought of that hard body against her own, once again the emotions started coming to the surface his body moving on top of her and what more the way he had softly asked her if she was sure, she had been such a fool tears once again started to fall this time at what she had lost she could never get that back throwing her arms around Caradog's leg she held on for comfort more than anything the tears refused to stop even Caradog was taken aback by this emotional outburst bringing his other foot up he covered her with it, "Sarah what's wrong is it the final trial are you worried about it," he asked in a very soft tone she just shook her head, she couldn't tell him she could never tell anyone what had happened slowly she stopped crying looking at Caradog there was only one thing she wanted to know more than anything else. "Caradog when I complete my trials and go home when I have the awakening does it mean that I will never be able to see any of you again?" Caradog looked at her, "Sarah once you have the awakening you will be able to go anywhere you choose if you wish to see us there will be nothing stopping you, for being a protector of the realms means you will be able to enter all of them, how are you meant to protect something if you are unable to go there,"

Sarah hugged him best she could with everything that had gone on she had forgotten that, it made her happy knowing that even after all this she would be able to see them all when she wanted to, "Caradog would I be able to bring anyone with me?" he eyed her for a moment "there is away but you have to understand that the realms are separate and different for a reason a human in this realm if left unchecked could cause a great deal of trouble like a magical being in the human realm could wreak havoc. You must be careful." Sarah smiled at him "Why?" the question popped out before he had the chance to stop it, "Because I would love for my father to see this," she said without stretched arms "To see you and the others that I have met even though I could tell him I would really love for him to be able to see it for himself one day."

The time had finally come the sun was just peeking over the horizon, Caradog had been awake for hours just sitting there watching her sleep in her usual place a small patch under Gem, but he had noticed this time she seemed to be having a night of very restless sleep, he was unsure but she kept calling Huor's name, but then some of the noises she made he would never like to guess where they were coming from, she had finally settled as dawn slowly approached, Gem had woken not long after Caradog and they had talked for the longest time the talk eventually turned to the restless sleeper and why she kept calling Huor's name out as though something terrible had happened, they were thankful when she finally settled.

It was time for them to leave, taking a deep breath he gently called her name, Sarah opened her eyes and looked about her it was a glorious morning but tinged with sadness the realisation that they were leaving left her feeling a little deflated, stretching she did her usual routine that was go down to the water's edge and wash, the water was cool on her skin as she slowly stripped the clothes from her body, as she washed the thoughts of Huor came into her mind and the last time she was in water, the thought made her shudder, she had to remember that she meant nothing to him that, that night meant nothing he was just using her so that he could say that she was one of his conquests; a notch on his belt so to speak. The thought of it made her angry and she dove under the water, swimming around trying not to think about that night, the night that had meant so much to her, his touch his gentleness had all been an act, rising out of the water she dried herself, looking at the clothes that were there ready for her; she had not worried about clothing for Enelya had supplied her with many different outfits and last night just before she went to the grove, she had picked out the clothes that she would be leaving in, she had loved the dress light fabric and beautiful colour it was like the autumn leaves just before they turned that crispy brown, but instead had settled for the trouser suit that was there it was usually worn in battle not really suited for anything else, but Sarah had thought that it would be better for her to have something that she didn't have to worry about at least in trousers if anything were to happen you did not have to worry about anyone seeing anything.

Finally she was ready walking back to where Caradog and Gem were she noticed that they were not alone for it seemed everyone had come to see them off, all that was except Huor he was nowhere in sight, she came to stop next to Eámané who turned and smiled at her, Sarah smiled back but before she had chance to speak Mablung walked over grasping hold of her hand he smiled sweetly, "You are the one I will always think of as the one who reunited my family, to everyone else you will be the great guardian protector but to me you will forever be known as the one who healed what I once thought was a wound that was going to fester until my death, I know that I have said this many times but I will say it once more, from the depth of my soul, thank you for coming and if by any chance you do not pass this final trial know that there will always be a place for you here with us, don't forget about us Sarah for you will be etched into the collective minds of the elves and will be talked about long after I have gone." Sarah felt tears sting her eyes but refused to let them fall she just smiled rising slightly she kissed him on the cheek and walked on, Enelya stepped forward it was unusual to see an elf cry but the tears were there she hugged Sarah tightly and whispered "Thank you for reuniting my mother and me, I am sorry for what happened but know that I am sure that my brother did not intend on using you, Sarah please find it in your heart to forgive him." Then stood up Sarah looked at her and smiled, with a slight nod moved past her Beren stood there tall and handsome she could still remember being plucked off Caradog by his brother and that thought made her smile, he placed his hand on her shoulder, "You will pass this trial for I see something in you that will assure it, and that is a heart of pure intent, you will not pass with strength you will pass because you are worthy of it." He looked at all who were around them and Sarah noticed that they all seemed to agree.

As she was about to climb upon to Caradog's back she heard her name being called looking around she noticed Huor he was running at full speed and came to stop dead in front of her for a moment she thought that he might actually collide with her, gently he put a hand on her shoulder "Will you walk with me for a moment," She looked at Caradog who nodded slowly they walked past further into the grove where they could not be seen. He came to stop by one of the fur trees, turning he looked at her, "I know you have to go and you have promised that you will return once you have completed your final trial, but I ask you now please stay with me," Sarah was taken aback after last night she was sure that he had used her, but he said this with such earnestly that she actually believed him, smiling she looked at him she knew what he asked was impossible, for if she stayed with him that would mean not completing the trial and never seeing her father again, Huor could see the look on her face he knew what he asked was unfair but the thought of her completing the trials and leaving was even more fearful to him, for if she did then he would lose her forever.

"Huor, you are handsome funny smart, and kind, you have your uncles heart, and I know that even though you are asking me to turn my back on everything to stay with you, you know it could never be, for if I were to do as you asked I would be a mortal in an unfamiliar world and moreover you are asking me to turn my back on all those I hold dear, and whom are waiting for my return, I am sorry but what you ask is impossible and I believe you know that. But thank you up until this moment I believed that you had used me for my body." Walking over to him she placed her hand gently on his cheek, "But now I know that was not the case, and for that I thank you."

He looked at her the hurt was evident in his eyes, but he knew she was right what he was asking was something that she could never do, walking over he embraced her, the thought of letting her go was tearing him apart; finally he released her and she made her way back to where the other were, Beren looked at her this was the girl who had reunited them all, he was getting used to the way the light worked, he still didn't understand how the light were the ones that found emotions to be a problem the dark embraced the emotions yes they let them sway them on many occasions especially when It came to hate, she was the one who had in a short time given him a family, one that he was truly looking forward to knowing, his father had been an evil man, when he was born he give him the name Beren for no other reason than to hurt his mother for that was the name of the husband she had lost, so every time she said the name she would automatically think of him and that made her suffer greatly, he had not been aware of it as a child it wasn't until much later that he learned that his mother was actually born of the light, he assumed that was why he never wanted to see anyone hurt and was always thoughtful of others emotions.

When his father had found out he was furious at the thought his son and heir was like this, he remembered one day being called to his father's side, someone had broken the rules and he had wanted Beren to punish them for it he knew that he wanted him to hand down something severe to them but Beren simply ask for the persons oath that it would never happen again, and was about to let them go when his father had flown into a rage, calling him some awful things, but he argued that the rule that had been broken was only a miner thing and didn't require any more than that, he watched that day his father sucked the life out of a man in front of his children and because the father had done this then the family were to pay; Beren tried to intervene tried to stop it from happening but one by one his father slaughtered the entire family except one daughter who's beauty is what saved her, Grabbing Beren he thrust him on the girl. He knew what his father had wanted him to do but it was against his very nature, elves were above such depraved methods.

But his father had learned from the human realm that this was one way to truly show ones dominance over the female, plus it would break her spirit, once again Beren refused saying that it was something that was barbaric and beneath an elven lord, to take a woman by force was an archaic and barbaric practice and it was something that he would have no part of, this time his father's rage was not turned to the daughter of the family he had slaughtered but to his own son, Beren had a scar that was hidden from most it was the one that had turned him forever against his father, and it was also the turning point of his mother that was the day that he was very near death.

The night they had fled believing that his father slain, they did not realise that he still lived and that he was looking for them. Caradog's voice brought him back to reality Beren bowed low and kissed her hand then guided her upon to Caradog's back, sitting there she looked at them and smiled,

"I will return once my trial is complete, before I go back to the human realm, I will see you all again." With that Caradog with one giant swoop of his wing lifted them high in the air looking down she could see them all smiling and waving at her; she waved back but soon they were out of sight she could feel the heaviness in her heart but smiled, besides that soon she would complete the final of her trials and would be able to go home.

She must have fallen asleep on Caradog's back because when she opened her eyes she could see the sun just disappearing behind the mountains, Caradog was just coming into land Sarah climbed down off his back, looking about her the area seemed desolate devoid of the lush greenery that she was used to seeing in this place, under her feet was drab grey ash and the smell of fire filtered into her nose, turning she looked at Caradog, "Don't wander too far here" was all he said as he strode towards what looked like a mound of rocks, a bit puzzled she followed behind him, but to her amazement it was not rocks it was a giant rock monster, he had heard Caradog approach, moving what looks like a pile of rocks turned out to be a giant hand, the ground beneath her shook as he sat up, "Well it has been a long time since you have come to my home Caradog" his voice was low and gravelly but it sounded gentle as well he looked monstrous but for some reason Sarah did not feel fear, "Llangord I have to speak with you" Llangord looked at him and nodded, "I thought you would be stopping by, Caradog there has been a lot of talk about the Protector being here and a female one at that which can only mean that the prophecy seems to be coming true, is this why you have come?"

Sarah looked from Caradog to Llangord prophecy what prophecy this was the first time of her hearing about this, stepping forward she noticed a giant hand heading in her direction it was Llangord's hand, gently he lifted her up, "Let's have a look at you," he said in his gravelled voice his breath smelled like earth and moss, he raised her so he could see her properly his head coming close, she didn't know whether to be afraid or not, He let out a loud laugh "This slight thing is supposed to be the one to unite all come on Caradog look at her, she is no more than a child," he eyed her his eyes looked like burning embers of a fire that had died down to a smoulder, "Tell me child how old are you," Sarah just sat there for a moment not knowing what to say, "come, come how old are you?" he asked once more she took a deep breath I am 19" the elemental looked at her and then to Caradog then laughed out loud, "you are a baby how is it that you are able to walk and talk nineteen and you think you are the great guardian protector, don't make me laugh."

There it was again she was getting fed up with being called a baby she was a woman, not a child, looking at him in defiance "I am a woman, not a baby why does everyone see just my age why do they not see me?" Llangord could see that she was offended by his remark and chuckled lightly, "you have to forgive me, child, it's just in this realm someone of just nineteen years old is nothing more than a babe in arms, we see them as a child needing to be protected not one that is destined to be the protector, but I'm sorry if I upset you, it was not meant in that way I just don't understand." With that, he placed her back by the side of Caradog.

Llangord: the giant in the mountain there are many rock giants and much like the elves they can be either good or bad Llangord is one of the oldest rock elementals on the good side.

Darnesell: is the oldest rock elemental on the dark side he answers to no one except Eó whom he has forged an alliance with.

Theo the last great elven prince had gone missing during the great plague believed to have died in the battle between dark and light. He was half-elf half Kenda his mother was Elena his father bu,

"Llangord I really have urgent needs to speak with you in private is there somewhere that Sarah can wait until we have finished?" Llangord looked at him raising his hand, if you go just past those rocks you will come to Shantee canyon there you will find Thistlewick. She has control over the fire elements and works quite well with them," Sarah looked at him for a moment did he mean that she was made of fire?

Sarah did as she was told and made her way to Shantee canyon, as she got there she notices a young child she was about three and a half feet tall, with hair that was white with just the hint of pink and red as she turned Sarah noticed that she had a cherub esk face with eyes as red as the reddest ruby you ever did see she had a light complexion with high cheek bones, she was dressed in a red and amber, her top and trousers were the same material it was not unlike the light elves flowing and beautiful, she stood there for a time just watching her as she danced about merrily in her own little world as though not a care in the world, Sarah wondered if she should interrupt her after all Llangord had sent her, but she felt it wrong somehow.

Looking up she noticed that the child she had been watching was gone from sight she looked around "Hello," came a small voice that made Sarah jump looking up she noticed that the girl was standing on the rock just above her, Sarah raised her hand and put it over her chest. The young girl jumped down and came to stand in front of her, "you know when someone says hello, the polite thing to do is say it back," she said in a voice that sounded like it belonged to cherubs, Sarah smiled for a moment then kneeling so that she was in eye line with the child, "Hello there my name is Sarah, what's yours little one?" the girl didn't seem to like being called that and crossing her arms she swung her head to the side "Humph whom do you think you are calling little one, you are the only child I see," came her reply Sarah stood up and laughed slightly more to herself than anyone else at the thought of someone so young calling her a child, "Sorry I didn't mean to offend you." She said as earnestly as possible the girl looked at her and smiled, "that's okay I'm Thistlewick, what's your name?"

Sarah was taken aback slightly this was the person that Llangord had sent her to see, but why a child she wondered then remembering she had been asked a question quickly answered, "My name is Sarah, pleased to meet you Thistlewick," she said with a smile, Thistlewick looked her up and down for a moment then smiling she grabbed her arm, "Come want to see something cool?" Sarah smiled and allowed Thistlewick to guide her where she wanted to go. They came to a stop just outside what looked like a large cavern, "This is my home," Thistlewick squeaked Sarah looked about her and couldn't help in a way feeling sorry for the child sleeping in such a dreary drab place, Thistlewick pulled at her arm "come on this way" she said Sarah followed and noticed she was being led to a small gap in the rock, as she walked through the narrow doorway the room seemed to open up revealing a beautiful room it was filled with everything anyone could need.

She stood there for a while then turned to Thistlewick "Oh Thistlewick this is lovely," Thistlewick giggled "but of course it is you know when you've lived as long as I have you get a lot of things," stretching her hand out "All that I got when I was still young but the rest of it I acquired over the years, oh the adventures I have been on the people I have met, some kind others horrible, but all teaching me how to refine my craft, how to control my anger," She sighed for a moment looking at a picture, "This was my brother, he was tall handsome and everyone who met him loved and adored him," "what happened?" Sarah asked Thistlewick looked at her then back to the picture she was holding, this time when she spoke Sarah could hear the pain in her voice, "it was during the time of the great plague the one that killed a lot of the light elves, my brother heard about what was happening and decided to try and help, being only part elf he wasn't sure if the plague would have any effect on him, I remember begging him not to go, it was too dangerous, but being the man he was would not listen. I remember the day he left I shouted after him that he was selfish and that if he left then he would not be allowed to return, he just turned to me smiled and bowed slightly. That was the last I saw of him, the news came from the trees who spoke to the rocks it was a time of great morning for us, they never even found his body so there was nothing for us to retrieve or bury" she broke off a tear sliding down her now ashen face.

Sarah reached for the photo as she looked down at it she gasped "Granddad?" looking at Thistlewick and then back to the picture she could not help but make the comparison for he looked exactly like her grandfather Theo even down to the strange colour of his eyes after some pondering and realising that she must have been mistaken, as it was unlikely that he was the man she had grown up knowing and lovingly called Grandpa Theo could not possibly be the same man.

The moment had passed and before she knew it they were talking about many things, but Sarah was still unclear on why Llangord had said she controlled fire that was until a shiver went through her she was starting to feel a little cold. Thistlewick as quick as a flash noticed it and walking over to what looked like one of those really old fireplaces clicked her fingers then with an outstretched hand lit the fire as the heat permeated the room it felt warm and comfortable.

Sarah awoke to the sound of her name being called, when she opened her eyes she jumped slightly Thistlewick was standing over her a smile on her face, "my you must have been sleepy, you've slept most of the day away," she said with slight laughter in her voice, Sarah sat up apologising for nodding off but Thistlewick was fine, "Come on its time to eat" was all she said as she skipped across the room to a large dining table, Sarah rubbed her eyes and looked there was loads of food and it wasn't until that moment she realised just how hungry she was, sitting down she helped herself to the various types of meat and vegetables that were on offer.

Caradog and Llangord had been talking for some time when he finally realised that the sky had grown dark. They had been there for an entire day when they landed dusk was just setting in and now it was night again, Llangord and he had spoken about many things including the legend of the blue dragon Llangord had pointed out the fact that she even being a protector was human with no magical heritage, so for her to be the dragon was quite impossible for it was said that one with ties to the magical realm could be the blue dragon and as she had no such ties then it would be quite impossible for it to have been her, however, Caradog knew what he had seen was true, he could not explain it but he had to find out for himself.

Time was getting on and Caradog thought it best that they stay there another night and leave in the morning, taking the path that Llangord had sent Sarah on he came to the canyon but there was no sign of her there, looking about him, he called her name, but nothing he called again once again nothing, finally with urgency in his voice he called again this time so loud that the rocks around him trembled.

"Are you trying to kill someone?" A small voice shouted at him looking around he saw nothing it was then he felt a slight tap on his leg looking down there stood Thistlewick her face red with anger, "of all the stupid things to do, well I'm telling you Mr big dragon if you have my home crumbling down around me I will be very cross," Caradog watched as Thistlewick paced back and forth going on about her home and how she would be very cross with him if his big mouth caused any damage. With that Sarah emerged from inside the cavern that was just to the right of him Caradog looked a sigh of relief escaped him.

Waving his foot in the air he tried to calm Thistlewick down but she was still pacing back and forth her little face glowing with annoyance, Sarah walked across and gently put a hand on her shoulder, Thistlewick looked at her and smiled slightly, then turning to Caradog sighed heavily, "OK, Lord Caradog father of dragons, just because you are big enough to squash little old me as well as most things around here does not mean that you have to. Sarah was quite safe." Then turning to Sarah she smiled, "he never has been one for patience this one," Caradog laughed "Well Lady Thistlewick it's nice to meet you again," Thistlewick laughed at being addressed so formally looking up she tutted "why do you always address me as Lady Thistlewick, it's just Thistlewick silly," Caradog looked at her he knew she hated being addressed in such a formal way but it was only right, after all, she was soon to be the queen of the west even if she didn't want it, it was something that would have been handed down to her brother, being the eldest male but she has had to step in since his disappearance, even though she had refused to leave her home and move to the family residence. They had been trying for years to get her to take her responsibility more serious, but Thistlewick was part Kenda, although looking at her you would have thought she was pure Kenda, and they were a race that never really liked anything too serious.

Caradog looked at her he remembered when Thoriadin Had disappeared it weighed heavy on her, in a way she had blamed herself if she hadn't told him he would never be allowed to return then maybe there was a chance that even if injured he would have sought them out.

Caradog smiled and shook his head slightly turning to Sarah, "We shall spend the night here and head out in the morning," Thistlewick jumped up and down "Oh boy overnight guests," she said the excitement clearly visible on her face, "I haven't had overnight guests in a long time, well except for last night when Sarah stayed here but she also slept most of it and the day away so we didn't really do anything fun," she turned a smiling face to both of them Caradog hated it when she acted all cute, it usually meant that they were in for one of her hide and seek games that no one other than her won due to her small size; and that she would be able to get into such small spaces that no one could find her. "No, Thistlewick" was all he said. Looking at him she lowered her head she pouted that was her favourite trick because someone always fell for it, Sarah looked at her then at Caradog, "Oh Caradog you've upset her now" Sarah said with annoyance in her voice walking over she put her arm around Thistlewick shoulder, "Don't mind him he's just being grumpy," she said Thistlewick sniffed "He's always grumpy when it comes to me," Caradog looked at her oh she was good before long she would have Sarah eating out of her hand and him in the wrong, as only she could, "what is it?" Sarah asked gently "I just wanted to play hide and seek, but he's such a Meany just because he's too big to hide, he never wants to play," Sarah turned a stern eye to Caradog, and there it was.

Smiling she said, "Why don't you and I play and Caradog can keep score?" shaking his head "Hook line and sinker," he thought to himself but did not say out loud, Thistlewick jumped up and down then turning to Caradog, "see Sarah wants to play, you can just keep count on how many time she can find me Hehe." Sarah wasn't sure but she knew there was something not quite right with that statement before she had time to dwell on it Thistlewick was explaining the rules. "OK, so Sarah the rules are simple I go and hide and see how many times you can find me, if you get to five then it's your turn to hide and I have to try and find you OK?" Sarah smiled. "OK, so if I find you five times, then I have to hide five times for you to find me, am I right?" Thistlewick jumped up and down squealing with delight, "Look Caradog and I only had to tell her once and she gets it," turning to Sarah "Hehe it took over five hours for him to understand the rules and in the end, he still didn't get it hahaha."

Sarah couldn't help but find that a little funny herself, once they were ready Thistlewick told her to close her eyes and count to ten, then all she had to do was find her, and so she didn't cheat Caradog had to close his eyes also, that way he couldn't give her any clues.

Sarah stood there and counted to ten, upon opening her eyes she saw no sign of Thistlewick, but she applied a trick she had learned in school when they played, hide and seek which was to call the person's name and stand completely still, they always tended to give themselves away with a small sound or slight giggle. "Thistlewick" she shouted then stayed silent closing her eyes and concentrating, there it was the slightest giggle, that most would have passed off as the wind but she knew better, walking over the rock she came to a very small crevice, reaching her hand in she found the hand of Thistlewick, "Ah I found you," Caradog just looked in amazement she hadn't even been hiding five minutes before Sarah had found her, jumping out of the crevice she looked around then up at Caradog, "Are you sure your eyes were closed, Caradog?" she said accusingly Caradog looked at her and raised his foot, "Hey don't look at me all I'm doing is keeping score remember," putting her hands on her hips, "OK, that's one."

Sarah closed her eyes again and waited the allotted time, then once again "Thistlewick" closing her eyes she waited, just the slight sound of a rock falling, walking over "There you are." Thistlewick jumped out, "OK, Caradog you have to go away when I hide next time, there's some funny business going on here," Sarah couldn't help but stifle a giggle that was rising, "OK, that's two, but this time you won't have Caradog cheating with you telling you where I am," she said very childlike that Sarah covered her laugh for a cough, then once again she hid and once again Sarah found her, this time she couldn't accuse her of cheating because not only had she sent Caradog away but she had made Sarah count with her hands firmly over her eyes, she hid for her fifth time and once again Sarah found her, jumping up this time demanding on one final go but this time Sarah had to go and count by Caradog while she hid, and if she still found her then Thistlewick would know for definite that she wasn't cheating somehow, Sarah giggled but did as she was told and went next to Caradog who was finding it very fascinating on how she was able to find her, once again she counted and Thistlewick hid and once again on returning took no time in finding her.

Thistlewick conceded defeat but Sarah had ruined her favourite game no one was ever able to find her once let alone six times, once the game was concluded and was deemed a draw due to Thistlewick using her ability with fire to aluminate everything so she could find her, Sarah thought it quite funny when Caradog claimed that they both had one, while they were all sat around the fire Caradog asked her how she was able to find Thistlewick so easily, Sarah explained to an outburst from Thistlewick that it wasn't fair she didn't know that Sarah had played the game before so that meant she was cheating to which Sarah laughed and pointed out that she only found her using sound whereas Thistlewick used her abilities, to which she conceded and said fine it was a draw, pouting slightly that she had been bested in her favourite game.

Sarah woke early the sun still hadn't risen fully but she was awake, so decided that she would find somewhere to wash up before they left. Stretching she stood up looking around, where was she supposed to find water in such a desolate place? She hadn't taken five steps when "Sarah I thought I told you not to wander off around here?" Caradog stretched his long body arching his back as he sat up, "I was only going to find somewhere I could wash up," she protested, he looked at her "Climb on, there is a place just over the next mountain that you can use." He was never this protective in the elven lands she had free reign there, but for some reason here he was quite strict on where she was or was not to go, deciding it best not to argue as to wake Thistlewick she bent down kissing the Little one on the head walked over and climbed onto his back.

As they landed she noticed a small pond it looked okay not as nice as the elven ones but it would do, as she stepped away from Caradog he looked down at her, and without thinking she started to strip off her clothes, Caradog was not human but he was male, she had done it once before when he had asked her about the scars she had on her body, but this time she was totally naked, as she walked away the warm wind swept around her blowing her hair over her right shoulder, the scars there for all to see, Caradog couldn't help but feel sympathy for her the pain she must have endured in her short life was much.

Slowly she sank into the water without warning she let out a scream Caradog spun around just in time to see fizzle jump into the water next to her, Caradog made his way over looking down at the blue-grey creature he shook his head, "I see you still enjoy sneaking up on people fizzle," Sarah clambered for the rock looking at Caradog "What the hell is that?" she squeaked Fizzle jumped up onto the rock beside her making her recoil slightly from him, she could see him clearly now, he was small almost like a little cat, his colour was sapphire with just the hint of gold around his bat-like ears, walking close to her he nuzzled her cheek he felt like silk, his fur had a gentleness to it that almost relaxed every bone and muscle in your body, it was as though you had just gone through a deep tissue massage and an alignment.

Sarah didn't want to move just being near to him made her feel that everything bad in the world was gone, Caradog cleared his throat causing Sarah to look up at him, shaking his head slightly, "Sarah this is Fizzle he's a Heldregord, they are a species of animal that feeds on pain and anguish taking it away so to speak, he's not dangerous just has the habit of turning up where he shouldn't be," he turned to Fizzle who was making himself quite comfortable on Sarah's shoulder, "Fizzle aren't you supposed to be in the west with Markumbie," Fizzle stretched and jumped on to a nearby rock, and proceeded to clean himself seeming to totally ignore the question he was being asked, then standing up he swanned off walking past Caradog he simply replied, "I go where I please." Then without another word he was gone.

Sarah finished cleaning herself, getting out she wandered over to where Caradog was sitting, "I'm all ready," she said he eyed her suspiciously she had not asked once about Fizzle, who he was or any of her usual annoying questions, that only led him to believe that she was trying to trick him into telling her all about his race, what were they how did they make everything feel better, these were normal questions that anyone new here would have, and on top of that the fact that he had spoken, now he knew that animals in the human realm did not speak so this would have had to be something she was curious about but nothing, it was as though she just accepted it, and knowing her the way he did he knew that there was no way she would just accept something without checking about it first. "Um Sarah is there anything you would like to ask me, anything at all?" looking at him she just shook her head, "are you sure that there is nothing picking at you? I may be able to help you with. I mean you can ask me anything you like?" but once again she just shook her head.

"Are you telling me that you are not a bit curious about who Fizzle is?" with that she spun around, he was right she was goading him into this, smiling "Well since you asked, there are one or two things that you may be able to help me with?" She said with a smile, Caradog knew that once he had opened the door there would be no stopping her and he was right, she asked about Fizzle's race and what it meant and how he could feed off the anguish of others and yet remain unaffected by it, they sat and spoke for hours on what Fizzle actually was, and the best way Caradog could explain it was while he was in his docile phase one would call him, he stopped for a moment, well in the human realm they were sort of like a house cat, the humble cat thinking nothing more than sleeping eating and finding a nice place to curl up, but he explained when he had to be there was a different side to him a side that held great majesty.

For when he needed to be he could be the size of an elephant, but that was mainly while fighting or wanting to play jokes then he could be a fantastical and frightening beast, but none the less there was never any hatred or malice or act of malcontent, as for a species they had evolved into quite the lovable characters, they were a neutral faction as they didn't like fighting, so you would see them on both sides, usually as a companion to an elf or some other type of magical creature, "I remember oh it would have had to have been over three thousand years ago now, there was a Heldregord by the name of Banthum, he was one of the most revered of all the race for he unlike most had partaken in the battles of the great war, he came back battered and bloodied with many scars from the battles he was in, never once did he regale any of the stories, but they were found out and so that made him legendary amongst the race. Then about five hundred years ago he disappeared nobody knows where he has gone or if he will ever return. Do you remember the wall hanging in the great hall, that depicted Mablung on the back of a ferocious beast, that beast was Banthum, and Mablung has searched all over the magical realm for him, his dearest friend that even in his darkest hour, kept watching over him?"

Sarah sat there intently listening to Caradog tell the tale of the mighty Banthum and a lone tear slid down her cheek at hearing that he was lost to this realm maybe forever. Caradog lifted them off it was time for her to finish her training, as they came to land on the shores of the misty mountain there was something that had been puzzling her for the longest time. "Caradog, they say that this trial has no time limit, but if I am to receive the awakening when I turn twenty-one how can this be?" Caradog had been waiting for this question, "Sarah the way these realms work is different from anything you will have seen, for if one year were to pass in this realm then only twelve days will have passed in the human world so if you were to take three years, here then you would have only been gone from there thirty-six days, so that is why it is said that there is no time limit for time moves at a much faster rate here than it does there." "So, you are saying that everything I have gone through over here in the human realm I would have only been gone six days. Not even a full week" Caradog smiled and nodded.

"This way," he said as he walked towards an old arch made of stone, Sarah followed still a little bemused at how the time is so different when the days seemed to be just as long, "this is where we will complete the last of your training before you go to the forbidden lands." It looked nothing special the drab greys surrounded by large pools of water, she had expected something breath-taking given its name, "what a let-down" she thought but said nothing. 'Come on let's get this part of the journey over" he said with slight annoyance he always loved and hated coming here for this very reason, you had the stone arch then you had to cross the valley of thorns, there was so much you had to do to get to the training ground that he wished he would be able to fly, but that was forbidden on this sacred ground, there were many rules and you only had to break one to have the full power of Athurwen come down on you, the protector of these lands and everything on it, once he had landed he knew that they were in her domain, everyone knew the rules even though they were not set in stone or anything, there were things that she would allow and others that would go against her very nature, as they walked Sarah noticed that she could hear laughter coming from one of the pools but as she drew near to it Caradog shouted, "Stop!".

Sarah jumped then froze where she was turning, she looked at Caradog who seemed to be holding his breath for a moment then continued more gently, "You must not go near the forbidden pools, no matter what you hear." Sarah gulped slightly then moved back coming to stop at his side, "Why?"

"These are Athurwen's lands all that dwell here are under her protection," Sarah nodded not quite understanding the problem, she only wanted to see where the laughter was coming from, but she also did not want to incur the wrath of whatever deity was on this land. This time she did not move from his side.

As they came up over the ridge she looked out and all she could see for miles were densely wooded areas of thick tangled thorns, looking at Caradog she wondered why he didn't just fly her over there, but she knew if he was walking then there must have been a reason behind it. As they came to confront the start of this vast labyrinth the thorn weaving in a tangle knotted array of thick undergrowth, *these were no ordinary thorns*, she thought, *I doubt you would even find one blackberry amongst this mess*, her thoughts had gone to food because she was becoming increasingly hungry, slowly the thorns began to move creaking and groaning like an old man that hadn't moved for a while, to reveal a path, Sarah looked about her then to Caradog who walked tentatively through the opening. Sarah close behind noticed that the path was not made of earth as you would have thought but there were large paving stones leading their way, as they walked both remained silent, Sarah too frightened to speak and Caradog to busy making sure he didn't catch his great wings on some of the hanging thorns, their progress was slow, and every so often Caradog would stop and look up, then continue down the path, as they came to a sharp turn Caradog stopped breathing deeply the path seemed to open up at this point; where as in the first part was slow and cumbersome this part Caradog could stand tall, no stoop of the head and the groan every so often that was all gone.

Sarah heard a noise to the right of her, looking through the thorns she saw a pair of pale grey eyes looking back, she didn't move the sound drew near to her and slowly out of the thick haze of bushes came a man he had short cropped black hair his face was chiselled with a strong jaw line and high cheek bones he wore a dark green tunic with what looked like leather trousers, he had a dirty brown cape that came down to his knees, he stood about six foot seven to look at him very tall, he bowed slightly then stood back up, moving past her he came to stop in front of Caradog, "My lord, I haven't seen you in an age" his tone was light but with some huskiness to it. Caradog bowed his head and greeted the man calling him Shane, it was unusual to hear a human name in this land it was usually and elven or Kenda or some type of elemental name.

The man and Caradog talked for the longest time until he seemed to realise she was there, at one point she wondered if she should dig a hole in the ground and jump in, turning to her he apologised "Shane, this is Sarah" he didn't have the chance to say anything else when Shane was holding up is hand, "I know who she is, the one that's supposed to be the true grand guardian protector, here on her quest, I see by the markings she already possesses that she has completed two of the trials which can only mean that you are here to complete her training before she undergoes the final trial, the one that will truly show if she is meant to be the great guardian protector or if like the others one who believes it but didn't deserve it," he looked at Caradog for a moment as though he was trying to find the right words, "I have to say that's she has come further than the ones before her, wasn't one of them almost to this point when she took her own life," he said more as a jeer through his teeth than as a passing comment.

Sarah stood tall looking him in the face how dare he bring her up and in front of Caradog of all people; she remembered when mamma Morwen had shown her a glimpse into his life, she had never told him because she knew it was a source of great pain for him, squaring her shoulders she came to stop in front of Shane, "I don't know if I am the right person or even if I will have the ability to pass this test but I know that I will die trying if the need arose;" Shane looked at her for a moment then to Caradog "she has spirit I will give her that," he said with a smile, Caradog was no longer smiling he looked crest fallen at the Meer mention of her, Sarah could see how much even after this amount of time it still affected him, raising her hand without thinking she slapped Shane across the face then walked to where Caradog his head hung like a fallen statue, his eyes were full of sadness and pain, pain she knew she could never take away.

Shane grabbed her arm pulling her into his rock hard frame, "How dare you strike me!" he bit out his face twisted into a snarl, Sarah pulled away from him with a thump against his chest that hurt her hand slightly, man was he firm, "I slapped you because you were being a complete and total jerk, so what I'm the only one to have gotten to this stage, do you have to rub that fact in, can't you see what you have done?" she said as she pointed in Caradog's direction, Shane looked at him for a moment then away seeing the complete and utter devastation in his face, he knew he had gone too far but without saying another word strode off into the thicket from where he had come.

Walking over she placed a tender hand on Caradog's snout leaning her head into his, "My dear friend, what weighs heavy on your heart, such sorrow I see

136

deep in your eyes, talk to me let me lift some of the burden from you." A large tear dropped onto her she knew why but said nothing just stood there giving comfort to him, that was all she could think of doing.

Finally they were on the move again this time she rode on his back, as they came out of the tangles web of thorns she saw a view that was breath taking rolling green hills over a landscape that seemed out of a fairy story, the trees stood tall in the majestic light of day the shimming off the water looking like a thousand stars danced over the surface, in the distance she could see more unicorns and what looked like elves and dwarves she knew when she saw Thorn that he was a Kenda there was no mistaking that childlike quality just as she had seen in, Thistlewick, they walked along the lush green meadow, as they walked they could see they were being followed, Caradog came to rest near one of the old trees its gnarled bark and crooks and nooks made her feel happy, looking at it she couldn't help but think of gem climbing down off Caradog she walked to the large tree touching it, she brought her head in so that she could feel the rough bark on her cheek, she stood there for a moment just thinking of the time she had spent with gem in the elven lands, a sigh broke the feel was the same the same roughness the same texture the only difference was that this tree seemed slightly cooler than the warmth of Gem.

It had been a long journey and she knew that it was nearing its end she would be here three weeks and then she would undertake the final of the trials, this seemed to weigh heavy on her, to the point that she thought only for a moment that she would like to stay here forever with the people she had grown to care deeply for, as for her even though she had been there for a relatively short amount of time, she had grown fond of them all and Caradog had become such a dear friend, that the thought of leaving and not knowing when she would be able to return grieved her; for it was like having a long holiday and finding it was coming to an end, knowing that you were leaving; you want to go to the travel agents and just see if you can stay a little longer, but realise there are others awaiting your return.

Standing she looked at Caradog walking over with, outstretched hands she embraced him, a tear run down her face for the realisation finally hit that it was almost over. The end was insight, and he would have to remain there for there was no place for him in the human realm.

They had been there for a couple of hours when a familiar figure came slinking across the meadow towards them, Sarah could not help but smile she would know that sapphire coloured coat anywhere. It was Fizzle, there was a playful shriek from one of the Kenda's who was charging towards Fizzle whom had stopped and was looking at this small form running towards him, he seemed to embraced the inevitable when the Kenda reached him he claps hold with both hands and raised him high in the air, then embraced him in a hug; Sarah could not help giggling slightly at the sight, the thought that this small animal could if he had wanted to change into a magnificent large beast, that would have undoubtedly scared the wits out of the Kenda, but he did not instead he just let him do as he had wanted, finally the Kenda released him and he continued towards Sarah and Caradog.

Finally coming to stop at her feet, "Hello" was all he said before jumping into her lap and curling up, it wasn't long before his rhythmic breathing showed he was asleep, Sarah stroked his silky fur, breathing deep as she did, after a while Caradog decided it was time for them to move after all how was she supposed to do her training if she didn't move, Fizzle reluctantly got down as Caradog led her away to where she would undoubtedly be spending the remainder of her time before the final trial.

The weeks went by quickly and she found herself thankful that Fizzle had been there for each night, after a long day training it was nice to have someone she could snuggle up to. It was the last day of training before she was due to leave and take the last trial of all, Caradog came to her "you have done well, I have taught you everything you are going to need to complete the task that lies ahead of you," Sarah smiled and nodded "Then it is time for me to return home to my family, it's hard to believe that something like this could happen to someone like me, I am nothing special, I'm just a girl when it all comes down to it. How am I meant to protect the realms? What does it mean to be a protector? Am I always going to be fighting what will my abilities be?" Caradog had no answer that he could give her for as with all Guardians and protectors alike the trials are different, same in some respects but delivered in a unique way to the one who undergoes them.

Chapter 7
The Final Trial

Sarah woke to the soft tone of Caradog calling her name, it was time for them to leave, the sun was just cresting over the mountains, it looked even more beautiful she slowly climbed to her feet trying not to wake Fizzle, but with only the slightest movement he stirred, he knew as she did that today she left for the ancient grove to meet with Gin. Who would administer the final test, she had not known this and it would come as a slight shock to her, but both Caradog and Fizzle knew that they were not allowed to tell her anything.

As she mounted Caradog she smiled down at Fizzle who had been her constant companion these last three weeks, "Goodbye Fizzle, see you around sometime," Fizzle could feel the emotion rise in him at these words, "Sarah," as he said the words he transformed into a magnificent animal, "May I carry you to the border," Sarah smiled and dismounted Caradog slowly she climbed onto Fizzles back, lying her head on his furry main she laid there for a time, finally they were off they made their way back through the valley of thorns back to where Caradog had landed that first day. With a quick hug she climbed down once again mounting Caradog, as they flew off, she could see Fizzle still in his large form slump down, letting out a giant roar that almost broke her heart.

Finally they landed at the ancient grove, and there standing in front of her was Gin he bowed slightly and moved to greet her, "Sarah you have passed both tests and have done so in a most enlightening way, I must commend you for that, this trial is nothing like anything that you would have faced in your short life, I will have to have your complete trust, I know I ask a lot but if this is to go as smoothly as possible then I will need it."

Sarah looked at him for a moment then to Caradog, this is where they would have to say goodbye she knew that, but she had found it more difficult over the last couple of weeks, wondering how she was going to be able to succeed without him he has guided her over the past months she knew that no matter what it was she could go to him, he would always have some wisdom that would help her. However, this time she was leaving and going with someone she had only met once who had not really interacted with her much and yet he stood before her asking for her complete trust.

"How long do I have to decide?" she needed a little more time to gage who this guy was she couldn't just accept it, as she made her way over to Caradog Gin waved his hand and she was whisked away, there was dense fog surrounding her, "Caradog! Caradog where are you? I can't see anything" but it was Gin who answered her, "You are in the valley of mist on the ancient isle Caradog is not here. Now you are to make all decisions alone for there is no one here who can aid you, feel it know it and speak it, for all the answers lay before you. And only you can decide them." "No! How can you ask me to trust you when you pull stuff like this, please I need to speak with Caradog take me back to him?" "No for he has no part to play in your final trial, all decisions have to come from you, Sarah look deep inside use what you have been taught feel the answer with your heart and mind, you can do this you have to do this."

Sarah stood there in silence breathing deeply she closed her eyes she had to do this for everyone who put their faith in her and who believed in her. Standing there she could see a path in her mind she followed it, not knowing where it would lead, there lay many things before her, boxes and door on either side but she pushed forward without stopping, slowly a form began to appear in front of her it was Caradog running to his side, "Oh Caradog I thought you were gone, what should I do? Should I put my faith and trust in this man?" but Caradog said nothing just smiled and bowed his head then he was gone, as she continued she noticed her father coming into view, running she called his name but he too turned away and disappeared, it was then she heard a voice that she knew it was the voice of her mother calling to her, she looked about but saw nothing, it was then she noticed that it was coming from one of the doors slowly she walked to the door swinging it open wide she stepped inside, she was transported to a room it was her nursery when she was a child, with her mother standing over her.

"My darling, you are loved and precious to me, but I hide you from those who would want to take you away," with that her mother, pushed something into her, Sarah noticed that it was in the same place as the scar she had but never knew where it came from, her mother had given it to her not out of hate but out of love.

Then it seemed to switch her mother had the headscarf she wore when she was going through the chemo, the door opened and a woman she had never met walked in, "Sister you look pale, are you sure you are OK?" she walked over to Sarah's bed where she was sleeping, she had opened her eyes to see the woman give her mother a drink, which she graciously took, once she had finished it she slumped into the chair, the woman came to her side kneeling down "Tokagine sends his best."

Sarah caught her breath as the woman came to her side, "you will be in his hands before the awakening, and he will have the power that coursed through your veins," Sarah let out a cry she could not believe that she could have forgotten this, why had this woman done this why she couldn't wrap her head around it, but before she had a chance to think any more on it the vision switched again, this time to her mother's funeral and that woman was there morning the woman she had killed. She walked to Conner's side, "My sister loved you both dearly, why don't you let me take Sarah with me for a few days so that you can sort everything out, she will have a wonderful time with her aunt meg's" but her father had shook his head, "No, she is all I have left of her she will stay with me but thank you for your concern."

Then it shifted a final time this time her father was packing them up, this must have been just before they moved to Wales, he turned to her, "Always remember Sarah, not all who seem nice have your best interest at heart. A time will come for you to rely on your own knowledge" he placed a hand over her heart, "As long as you follow this you will always be led down the right path. Remember these words my darling, never fear who you are fear who they want you to become," with that her eyes flew open, "Gin, where are you?" she asked in a loud voice for she knew what the answer to the question was, slowly he appeared before her, clasping a hold of his staff she thrust it into him, My worst fear has always been someone pretending to be my friend and leading me astray, so the answer to your question. No I will not put my complete faith in you, for you are not Gin this I know for his staff had the red ember on top and yours is blue," with that she felt a sharp pain under her breast the pain took her breath away and she fell to the floor lying there she looked around her she could see Caradog and many of the others she had met on her journey through this place, she must have passed out for her next memory was seeing Gin and Caradog talking,

As she composed herself she sat up looking about her Caradog and gin were both smiling at her, shaking her head she wondered what it all meant, finally clearing her throat "Caradog what happened,?" but before he had chance to say anything she heard her name being called softly from behind her turning she looked into the darkness of the trees, standing she moved towards the voice Caradog or gin didn't try to stop her they let her continue on her path she came to a door carved into the tree it looked like a mirror for she could see her own reflection, slowly hers faded and her mother's took its place, Sarah just stood there and looked at her mother she hadn't seen her since she was a child and for a moment she thought that she was still dreaming until her mother spoke to her. "Sarah my darling child you have finally come to where you needed to be, darling listen to me we don't have long, and do you remember everything?" Sarah thought back nodding, "Yes, Mum, I do,"

"Good you are still here, you still have your powers meaning that you have passed the final test that was laid before you, this is part of your reward seeing me again for one last time so I can tell you this. Darling, you have to find the blue dragon look deep inside you will know when you find it."

With that, she disappeared without Sarah being able to ask or tell her anything. With that, she once again found herself alone making her way back to where Caradog and gin were, she smiled weakly how had she passed the test what was this great fear that she was to face her eyes started to feel heavy again she heard gin counting backwards Five Four Three and she was asleep.

Gin laughed and looked at Caradog "now, she is a true immortal, she will have the pain and Burdon to go with it once she receives her full powers" "Gin, what was her greatest fear I know that you have knowledge of it?" Gin looked at him "have you ever told anyone your greatest fear, beyond the tester?" Caradog looked at him and shook his head, "Then why do you wish for me to break her confidence and tell you?"

Caradog knew that he was right and what he was asking was out of the question, there was no way that he could tell him and Caradog was okay with that after all if she wanted him to know then she would tell him herself, standing he gently lifted Sarah onto his back. "Caradog, where are you going?" "She has a promise to keep?" he could see the question forming in Gin's mind smiling "She said that she would say farewell to the elves before she left."

With a beat of his wings, he was off he knew she would sleep through the journey this was the toughest of all trials it wasn't just mentally taxing, but it took a toll on the body also. And he was right she slept for five days they had landed in the elven village and all had gathered to see her wondering if she had passed or failed, Caradog had taken her into the glen and laid her at Gem's feet he was the first to discover the truth for there on her body was the final crest, Gem was so happy but made no sound he knew how these trial taxes the body it may have been thousands of years since he went through it but it's something you never forget, finally she awoke looking up at Gem, jumping to her feet she wondered for a moment if it was true had she undertaken the final trial or had it just been an elaborate dream she thought no she was sure that she had gone through it looking at her arm she saw the final crest that proved she had done it so how was she back here? Caradog broke through her thoughts, "I brought you back so you could say farewell Gin will be here tomorrow to take you home," Sarah was happy but also sad she had been with Caradog for so long that the thought of leaving was a sad thought, she was happy she would get to see everyone again but she knew that the awakening would not take place until the night of her twenty-first birthday, that was almost two years away for even though she had been there for so long in her world she had only been gone a matter of days. With that, she heard the familiar voices of Huor and his mother coming closer as they entered the glen Sarah looked at Huor the thought of that night came to her, and she felt a shudder run through her body, walking over he bent his head to kiss her on the cheek, but that night was still strong in her mind. The thought of what he had done when he had taken her innocence and she had thought he felt nothing doing it, walking across to where Eámané was standing she clasped hold of her hands and smiled but the shun had not escaped them, Huor knew he had no right to be angry after what he had done. The thought of her actually coming back was slim after all he had asked her to stay with him but she had said no, how could he have thought that she had just forgotten, there was no way he had to realise that but he needed her to know the truth about that night and that she had been wrong, thinking that it meant nothing to him for he had not stopped thinking about her all the time, she was gone he wanted nothing more than to go and find her to tell her everything. He thought she had forgiven him; the day she had left after their discussion he had asked her to stay. Was that not evident to her he did not understand this? Enelya was right he had no right to confuse her this was, he was a lot older than her that should have made him wiser also, but he could only see her. If only there was a way that he could be with her in her world but that also was not an option.

Slowly all the others started filtering to where Sarah and Caradog were, by the time they finished the grove was full of elves congratulating her on a job well done. Some said that they knew all along that she would pass the final trial, the sun was beginning to set on the day and she knew that Gin would be coming to get her in the morning so she was going to have an early night, as she said her farewells to everyone she walked over to where Gem was she wanted to talk to him before she left it felt nice being under the shade of his branches once more she felt safe, "Sarah" a voice broke through, looking around there standing at the edge was Huor, "What do you want?" she tried to leave the anger out but failed slightly, letting him know that she still remembered everything. Walking over there was nothing for it he was going to make her listen to him if it was the last thing he did.

Grabbing her by the shoulders he turned her to face him, he knew that he was stronger than her for the moment, "Sarah I need you to listen to me, I need you to understand" she pulled away "Understand you think that that talk we had before I left meant nothing, Huor I understand and I know what you would ask if you could; but you have to understand that I cannot stay here with you, it's impossible." He raised his hand "I know it is but what if there was a way that we could be together." It was her time to stop him, what she was about to do tore at her insides, but she knew that this was going to be the only way. "Huor I'm sorry but I don't want to be with you, yes, we had a fantastic night, we were caught in a moment of passion, me knowing that I was going to take the last trial and you knowing I was leaving. We just let the mood take us, but Enelya was right that night was all it could be."

Huor looked at her in disbelief for the words she had just used were the same words he thought of himself, walking over she gently laid her hand on his cheek, "You are a dear friend, and I would never do anything to hurt you, but I have a life back in my world and its one that I can never turn my back on."

Huor put his hand over hers and smiled he knew that she was right and that what he was asking was a lot, standing he pulled her into him holding her the way he had that night, the night of unbridled passion that she would always remember, but they both knew that there would be too much in the way for it to be anything else.

She looked up at him his eyes were hooded she could not see what he was thinking, Caradog cleared his throat letting them know they were not alone, he was not the only; one they had forgotten that they were next to gem who had

144

heard everything. Sarah looked at Huor then to Caradog then to Gem, Huor did the same then they both looked at each other and flushed a lovely shade of scarlet that even Caradog would be jealous of, but all Gem did was laugh, Caradog looked at him then to the two very embarrassed people who were standing before him, but it was lost on him he had no idea what was going on but knew that Gem did clearing his throat, "Gem my old friend is there something that I should be aware of?" both Sarah and Huor looked at Gem with pleading in their eyes he just laughed slightly, "I'm sorry Caradog but this is one story that is not mine to tell," Caradog looked at him then to Huor and Sarah who seemed to breathe a sigh of relief but now his interest was piqued he needed to know what was going on, but he could wait he knew that one of them would spill eventually he just had to be patient.

Finally, the tension was cut by Mablung who joined them he had been looking for Huor and this had been the one place he thought of "Huor," they all turned at the sound of his name, Mablung smiled and walked over bending close he kissed Sarah on the cheek, "OK, so I was thinking that if it wasn't too much trouble to pull you away that we might have a word I know that Sarah leaves tomorrow and you want to spend time with her but this is something that cannot wait,"

Sarah looked at Mablung then to Huor, no way had he told his uncle, had he? "Huor" he looked at her and smiled weakly, she had a thousand thoughts running rampant in her head, she was sure that if he knew anything then he would have said something, before she had the chance to say anything they walked off Caradog looked at her and cleared his throat, "Umm Sarah is there something that you would like to tell me?" she looked at him a little puzzled well if Mablung knew then there was no harm in telling Caradog, sitting down she told him everything, he just nodded and walked away she thought no more of it until Huor came charging through the glen with not only Caradog but uncle in pursuit running over he gripped her, "How could you tell him what happened?" he asked breathlessly and flushed, "But I thought you had already told your uncle," "are you kidding me why on earth would I tell anyone,?" "Oh, I see so you are saying you're embarrassed that you slept with a mortal, but there again it wasn't that big a deal for you, you had done it plenty of times before on the other hand, it was a big deal for me! You Jerk! It was my first time!"

By this point Caradog and Mablung were standing there the look of shock evident on their faces they could not believe what they were hearing, so he had not only slept with someone not of that realm which was forbidden he had taken her innocence as well, Caradog let out a mighty roar, Sarah jumped in front of Huor "and anyway so what, what's wrong with us sleeping together?" both Mablung and Caradog looked at each other wondering which of them was going to have the chat with her; on the reasons that it is forbidden for them to be involved that way, before either of them had the chance to say anything gem chimed in, "Sarah come sit by me please, there is something that you need to understand and I think that being the oldest here it would be better if it were to come from me."

Sarah walked over and took shelter under his branches as Huor was about to leave his uncle pushed him next to Sarah, "But Uncle I already know what he's about to say I have heard the stories a thousand times?" Gem looked at him and continued to speak waiting for a moment for him to get the point that there was no way that Caradog or Mablung were about to let him leave, finally, he slumped next to Sarah looking ashamed of his outburst.

"OK, first off Huor you would never have heard this story before for it was one that happened thousands of years ago when I was a young tree myself, and Caradog was just hatched, I remember it because it indirectly involved me OK, it was when the first Great guardian protector was undergoing her trials in this land she found herself separated from her guide this is why it is said that guides are not too be far away from their charges, so it could never happen again, anyway the young woman found her way here and hid under my tree for shelter, it had rained heavily that night and by morning she was soaked that was when Maldwen appeared, he was a light elf and much like you had never really seen a mortal before, he was captivated with her, and she with him, by the time that her guide had found her they had fallen in love, and she no longer wanted to be the great guardian protector but her guide would not hear of it, the reason she was there was to undertake the last of the trials, she like you had completed the first two trials and only had the training and the last trial to take, so she was not given the choice, it was complete the training or he would take her far away so they would never lay eyes on each other again. After she had made her choice to complete the training she believed that she knew what her greatest fear was but she had been wrong and failed, stripped of her powers and now just a mere mortal with no magic stuck in this realm forever she wanted to be reunited with Maldwen but her guide was so infuriated at the thought that she had failed on his watch, took her away no one ever knew where she was taken to, but Sarah I believe you have met Shaun,?" Sarah looked at him and nodded, well it is said that he is the child of Maldwen and the other protector, although he has not said who his mother is or father just by looking at him you can see that he is part mortal part elf, he has been here for many years living more the life of a ranger never choosing a side to be on, he chooses to live as an outcast with no home no family, nothing this is why it is forbidden for you to have that type of relationship. It is not written in stone or anything it's more an unspoken rule one that Huor knows all too well."

Sarah looked at Huor, "Is that true, you knew that there could never be anything between us?" Huor looked at her then away it was at this point she knew that he had known all along and had not told her, tears stung her eyes, but she refused to let them fall instead standing she walked away from them, she needed time to digest everything that she had just been told.

Mamma Morwen was stood atop the hill as she walked down the path, when she saw her she made her way down, Sarah didn't really wish to talk to anyone at this time, but she knew that mamma Morwen already knew everything, due to her horn, thousands of untold stories was the way that she had described it to Sarah, they were there for the longest time talking about everything she had learned from both Gem and Huor the thought that he could have done this knowing that there could never be anything between them, she felt crushed wishing nothing more than to go home and forget this place even if it was only for a time, she knew that once she had the awakening then she wanted to return but to see Caradog and some of the others, and maybe she would have been able to forgive Huor's betrayal.

Sarah awoke back at the Glen she must have fallen asleep while talking to Mamma Morwen, stretching she looked Caradog was still asleep the sun had not yet risen sitting there she thought about her time here everything she had gone through, the trials the reunion of a family and the final part that she had passed, yes, she was ready to return home now.

Caradog stirred and opened his eyes it was almost time Gin would soon be here to ferry her away, he didn't know when or if he would ever see her again that thought made him sad at the thought of her leaving never to return, he wished there was a way that he could, he knew that he had to remain behind while she left.

The sun was high in the sky when Gin turned up everyone was looking sad as they knew when he arrived that she would be going, stepping forward, "Sarah you have passed all the tests it is now time for you to return to your realm to train for the awakening," Sarah smiled hugging all one at a time saying goodbye then she turned to Caradog the one who had been with her through it all, grasping hold of his giant leg a sob broke from her throat, "My dearest friend you have taught me so much, been with me through so much now I have to say goodbye I don't want too" the tears were free-flowing now and she knew that there was no way of stopping them, Caradog himself was having trouble keeping the wobble out of his voice while he said goodbye.

It was time Gin walked over and placed a hand on her arm and they were gone in a flash, to Sarah it was as though she had blinked looking around at the empty room there was no one there to greet her, Gin smiled said goodbye then he was gone.

Sarah ran from the room to the dining hall where she was sure that they would all be, and she was correct when she ran through the door first there was an audible gasp, then they all shouted in unison for they knew for her to be there then she would have had to past master Yamatoya and master Tetsuko stood and walked to her side they said nothing just bowed low,

"Where is my father?" they looked at each other no one knew that she had passed; and that she would be returning today so Conner and jack were both at work, they had decided it better than to wait around there and worry plus it had only been just over a week in their time that she had been gone.

Evening was just coming upon them when Conner and Jack turned up jumping out of the car, he didn't even wait for Jack he just run through the doors shouting her name. Sarah hearing her father's voice went running to him throwing herself into his arms it had been months for her but barely a week for them even so he hugged her as though he hadn't seen her in years, "Oh my precious girl I knew you would come back to me," he said breathlessly kissing the top of her head, as he did jack had finally caught up with them and was also making a fuss of her, the boys had already made a fuss of her and everything, so it was just the guys. With that master Yamatoya interrupted as he did, "So Sarah you passed the tests now starts the training for you to be able to width stand the awakening, it is not just as simple as standing on a rock and being surrounded by pretty white lights as the movies may suggest, no there is a lot more that actually goes into it, Sarah looked at him and rolled her eyes she hadn't been back more than five minutes and he was on at her about more training, "Master Yamatoya, I have just got back and I would like to relax I don't have to do the awakening until my twenty first birthday I am not quite twenty so I have a while to relax first, don't I?" Master Yamatoya looked at her and he wanted more than anything to tell her yes, but he knew that they had thirteen months not a moment more, taking a deep breath he looked at her, "OK, you can have two days on the third your training starts," he didn't wait for the protests that he was sure that were about to come; he just bowed and made his exit.

Conner and Jack just wanted to know everything that she had gone through, looking at her father she wondered if he knew that her mother's sister was the one whom had killed her; walking into the hall with them to where the others were they were all sat in the same position not one of them had moved since she had left to meet her father, it was obvious that they all wanted to know what had happened over there as well, she spent the next few hours telling them of the months that had past as the time in that realm was different, she told them of Caradog and gem and the elves and even the Kenda she had met she went through the trials showing them the emblems she had received on her body each time she passed the trial, by the time she was finished she wasn't just tired but hungry as well, looking at her father there was one thing she had wanted for months and that had been taco's but they had nothing like them in the magic realm, "Dad? Is it possible that you could cook; I know its late but for months now all I have wanted was taco's" her father held his hand up she didn't need to ask him twice, even though to them it hadn't been that long he had missed her as though she had been gone that long.

She fell asleep on the seat she had been on with the guys all looking at her they all knew how special she was, but none of them really wanted to move her in fear that they might wake her, it was then that master Tetsu walked in, seeing her asleep he called for Ludwig, he was one of the biggest there, he wasn't fat he was over seven foot five and built like a small mountain, walking over he easily cradled her in his arms as though carrying a small child he walked up the back stairs and into her room, the boys who had gone up the front stairs were already in the room, Ludwig placed her gently on the bed, as he came out of the room after making sure that she was settled he looked about him, warning the others that if they woke her they would have him to deal with then leaving the boys looked at each other even though they had spent some time with her they still wanted to look in on her just to make sure she was OK, they agreed that they would go in two at a time just to make sure she was fine, as the first two opened the door they froze to the spot, Sarah wasn't on the bed but floating above it. It was then they decided they would leave her be until she woke up.

Chapter 8
Jack

There are many things that happen in a man's life the one thing Jack was thankful for was Sarah had been brought into his, the accident had opened his eyes to his true feelings for her and he knew that one day he was going to have to face those feelings even if it meant heartache. He was unsure what would happen after she received the awakening, would she still be the same girl as now or would she be different, he knew that no matter what happened he had to be there for her; she was above all the one he wanted to be with. Master Yamatoya had forbidden him telling her his true feelings; he was now questioning those commands. If he were to stay silent what would happen when she received her full powers, would she be able to love him with the responsibility that came with them. Or would it put a permanent divide between them.

Two days had passed since Sarah's returned, jack was hoping to spend some time with her, silently praying it would be before Master Yamatoya had her back training. However, for the moment he and Conner were still in the middle of an investigation into the accident; they had heard the news Mike was out of intensive care and would be allowed home in a few days, it had been a bit touch and go for a while, they had managed to stabilize him. The swelling on the brain that they had been concerned about had gone back to normal, they were thankful that there were no lasting effects due to it, they had been warned there was a possibility he would not remember anything that happened the night of the accident. Today was the first time they would be able to talk with him, and see exactly what he remembered, as Jack arrived at the hospital his phone rang it was Conner asking where he was, he knew he was running slightly behind and agreed to meet Conner at the hospital.

Finally, both were walking through the entrance, they were greeted by Mikes oldest son Aaron "Jack, Conner hi; how's everything going?" Jack stretched out his hand and took Aaron's "hi yeah everything is going great, we are just on our way up to see your dad," Aaron stopped for a moment, "you do know that even though they say that he has no lasting effects, he is still having problems with his memory;" "what type of problems?" Conner asked "Well when he first came around he wasn't sure where he was or who he was; his memory is coming back he recognises who we are now but it is still a bit sketchy there are some people who he doesn't remember one of those is his old school mate Barry Williams, when he came to see him the other day, Dad had no idea who he was, he did try to jog his memory but as we told him it may take some time before he remembers him," "did you say Barry Williams?" Aaron nodded, Conner and jack looked at each other they both knew that Barry Williams had died more than ten years ago in a skiing accident while he was on holiday; there had been a large funeral held for him, not wanting to alarm his son they just smiled and said goodbye.

"OK, so if it wasn't Barry who came to see Mike then who was it?" As they stepped out of the elevator Jack collided with captain Davies, "Captain, just the man… we were talking to Mike's son at the entrance, he informed us of his father's memory also of the man claiming to be Barry Williams;" captain Davies nodded, "I came to check on mike's progress he is indeed having problems with his memory, he remembers something's but anything to do with the accident is completely gone, he doesn't even remember being in the car that night or anything to do with Sarah, sorry guys but anything you were hoping to find out is going to have to wait, for now we need to find whomever it was that was impersonating Barry."

As Conner and jack got into the car a call came over the radio an emergency call had come through dispatch for someone to go to Tir Gwenu house, Jack froze that was Megan's house. Conner put his foot down, as they raced to the house a thousand thoughts went through Jacks head. He and Megan had married not long after they had finished school because she was pregnant, their son James was born six months later. They stayed together for the first three years of his life, however due to complications they decided it would be better if they divorced, it had taken sometime however they managed to build a friendship both agreeing Jack needed to be in James's life, they had made a plan that would benefit both the last thing he remembered was telling her that he would be unable to have his son on the coming weekend, she smiled and said it was fine because she knew Sarah and her father.

As they pulled up to the house Jack jumped from the car before it stopped racing through the door, he froze his blood ran cold, the house was in a total chaos, there was blood on the walls ceiling and floor, looking towards the stairs he noticed blood smears as though someone had been dragged. Clasping hold of the banister he raced up the stairs stopping when he saw three officers there, they looked pale one officer turned and looked at Jack then to James's door it was open he walked past them; knowing the sight that awaited him they grabbed him, Jake with a quiver in his voice said "jack you don't need to go in there," jack being as strong as he was easily shook them off made his way into the room; there on the bed were two bodies covered by a sheet blood had seeped through still weeping wounds and stained the white sheet, looking he noticed his sons feet protruding through the bottom, there was something on his ankle. As he reached to pull the sheet off Conner was there pulling him back, "No I need to see!" "Jack come on son let the team do their job here come on" pulling hard Jack fought ferociously causing them to fall to the floor, Jack was inconsolable fighting screaming trying everything in his power to get into his son's room.

It had taken Conner almost an hour to get Jack outside; the coroner waited until he had vacated the premises to enter out of respect. The force knew Megan and his son, he had been to many of the police social football and rugby matches with his father, and uncle he was known for his funny voices and kicking ability.

Jack sat in the car outside turning to Conner "Is there anything she can do?" "Anything who can do?" "Sarah come on Conner they say that she has all this power, do you think she could bring my son back?" "Jack, do you realise what you're asking, there are things in this world that no one can rectify I believe this is one of those times." "Conner what would you do if it was Sarah lying in there and James with all this new power? You would be asking me the same thing... please Conner can't I just ask her if there is nothing, she can do fine but at least let me try?" Lifting his phone Conner rang through to master Yamatoya he knew that they were going to need a heads up on this.

As they entered the monastery, master Yamatoya met them. "I am sorry for your loss; but you must realise what you are asking for is impossible, she cannot mess with the order of life, death is a part of living, sometimes life isn't what we want it to be, we lose people we love. There is nothing that can replace the death of a loved one, but to do what you want goes against the order of the universe."

Jack looked at him tears in his eyes, "You say that she is this powerful person that she looks after all the realms, and you are saying that she doesn't have the power to undo this?" "Jack she doesn't have that power she has not yet gone through the Awakening, if you go to her now and ask her she will want to do anything in her power to help and the outcome will be the same, your child will still be dead and she will feel as though she has failed you; and to be honest even if she had gone through the Awakening I'm still unsure if she would be able to break that sacred law, nature has her own agenda as does Buddha the one thing that happens to all living thing is death,"

At those words Jacks knees buckled beneath him he felt as though someone hit him hard in the heart, letting out a scream of anguish the tears that he had managed to keep at bay were falling. He could not believe it his child was gone he knew that Yamatoya was right, he was going to ask was for her to do the impossible; he just wanted his son back.

Jack got to his feet and asked Conner to take him to see his son, he didn't want Sarah to see him like this, Conner did as he asked getting behind the wheel, he made his way back to the morgue as they drove Conner looked at him he wished there was something he could say but knew there was nothing. He knew what it felt like to have to travel to the hospital, but this was different he knew there was a chance that Sarah would die whereas in Jack's case he knew his son was gone and nothing could bring him back. The journey was done in complete silence they pulled up outside the hospital Conner climbed out of the car but Jack stayed seated, Conner looked at him closing his door he walked around the car opening the door, "Jack you don't have to go in if you don't want too;" Jack looked at him a face of stone no show of emotion what so ever, slowly he climbed out of the car turning he looked at the hospital the one that Sarah had been in a little more than a year ago, but this time he was going to a very different part.

As they entered, they made their way down to the morgue, stepping out of the elevator Jack froze. "If I go in there now, then it's real my son is gone;" "Jack you don't have to do this now, I know how you feel," Jack seemed to fly into a rage, "NO! you don't know how I feel your daughter is alive isn't she this great power, while my son is on a slab in the morgue, cold and I should have been there, but I wasn't was I no I was working on a case I have missed two weekends with him because we were working on who tried to kill your daughter. And now I will never get the chance to do anything with my son again." Conner knew that this wasn't jack that he was hurting, he needed time he was sure that he wasn't sorry for the work they had done.

Walking through the morgue doors Jack looked at the dark grey cold slabs, where the bodies of his son and ex-wife lay, he walked to the first one and raised the sheet covering the body, it was Megan still as beautiful as the day they met, her hair the colour of the sky at night her skin even though pale still radiant the differences between them now didn't seem so bad, they had grown apart due to the work and other problems. So why now while looking down at her lifeless body, he could not remember one of the reasons that they had discussed being that great, even though at the time they seemed that they could not continue with the relationship.

Conner was standing by the door giving him space, he could see the pain, he remembered the first-time meeting Jacks son, it was a beautiful Sunday morning and the south Wales police was having their annual football match, Jack had arrived with a shy reserved boy who jumped at his own shadow. But by the time they had finished he was a ball of energy every much his father's son, he had made friends with some of the other children who were there that day, including one Naomi Davies captain Davises daughter, they had gotten on so well they even become Facebook friends.

A noise brought him out of his thoughts; looking to Jack he had fallen against the freezers holding his son in his arms, the coroner standing looking at Conner not sure what to do. Conner walked over to Jack kneeling down he put his hand on his shoulder, jack shook his head, "No, this isn't happening he can't be dead, he's so cold I have to warm him up;" looking at Conner "please you have to help me"

Conner put his hand on his son's head, "Jack I couldn't imagine half of what you are going through right now, I know that you blame me and my tunnel vision into who tried to kill Sarah, I know you need to find who did this and I promise you that I will give this the same attention you gave to me when we were looking into Sarah's attack"

Jack held his son close he was inconsolable, nothing Conner said seemed to be getting through, he stood looking at the coroner and shook his head, it was then they heard the door open turning they look coming through the door was Catharine she was an officer and Megan's little sister, walking over to Jack she knelt in front of him and her nephew, placing her hands on Jacks hand and fighting back tears over the death of her sister and nephew she spoke softly, "Jack you need to let him go, they need to do their work they have to find out who did this and why;" "no you don't understand, I wasn't there when they needed me I

155

wasn't there to save him, I'm his father I am meant to protect him, I don't even know if he called for me in those final moments waiting for me to come and save him, I want to know" "Jack this is not your fault, this is not on you this is on whoever it was that did this, not you remember I have lost them as well." A sob broke through she had been trying to fight the urge to cry, trying to be strong she knew that her sister would want her to be, taking a deep breath she looked at Jack "the coroner needs to do his work,"

Gently she lifted James out of Jacks arms placing him back on the table, the sheet had moved once again revealing his ankle. This time Jack would not be stopped, moving the sheet they could see the brand that was on his ankle moving from his son to his ex-wife, they found the exact same mark on her ankle just above the ball there was a dragon burned into the skin all the hallmarks of the Jensing gang a gang that is known for the killings of around twenty different people they had been on the lookout for them for years, although over the past year there had been no chatter. Is this why? were they planning this?

Looking at Conner "Is this my fault I have been on that case for years I got close, just before Sarah's accident, is this their payback did they do this because they found out;" Conner put his hand on Jacks shoulder, "stop this you can't be sure who it was, there was no way of knowing this was going to happen." "But I could have moved them I could have changed everything; I didn't I chose to leave them in that house" "Jack calm down did you have any idea that the gang knew anything about your personal life, was there any sign while you were working the case that you had been compromised?" All Jack could do was shake his head; he knew that if there had been any chatter that his son had been in danger then he would have made sure that they were safe.

It still left one question unanswered how they got this close without any word, closing his eyes he still had one secret that no one knew, he had a daughter she would be about thirteen now, it was when he was in school, the girl's parents had taken her out when they found out she was pregnant. He was told when she was born but her parents being who they were wouldn't allow her to keep it so the child had been given up for adoption two days after birth, he had not been given the choice but back then, he wasn't thinking about long term he was thinking his life was over, he would have been lying if he said that he had not felt a sort of relief when he was given the news. It had been a closed adoption the only thing he knew was her name, now his sole purpose was to make sure that she was safe, if they had gotten to his family even years after his wife and he had decided to end it there was a chance that they may find out about this. "Conner, I have to talk to you in private."

Finally Conner knew everything it was the first time he had admitted everything to someone not even Megan knew he had another child, he had to admit when he had his son he started to think about what his daughter would be like, what she would look like, he had thought about trying to find, however always talked himself out of it not wanting to turn her world upside down; he had an appointment with Sandra O'Shay. She was the one who over saw the adoption if anyone would be able to help, he was sure it was her.

He walked in letting the secretary know he was there to see Sandra it wasn't long before he was led in to see her standing she smiled her eyes were looked like two emeralds shining in the dark she had a full pout, on a cherub face standing up she slinked around the desk looking like a panther she moved elegant and gracefully, stretching out a small hand that fit her frame she was about five foot two she had a slight frame. "Hello Jack, I guess you already know who I am, but as I said on the phone it was a closed adoption, there is nothing more I can tell you about the family that adopted your daughter, "Please there has to be something you can do, I was never told anything I never got the chance to say goodbye or even see her." Looking at him with a sympathetic eye she knew that he would have to petition the courts for the records to be unsealed. She explained everything to and him where to start but she did caution him that there was a chance that she would not wish to see him, but this was something he had to do, he knew there was a chance that the family hadn't told her that she had been adopted it was a chance he had to take.

As he left the social services, he noticed a car he had noticed a few days ago outside his house, being a police officer the first thing you think is are they following you? Then you tend to put it to the back of your mind and wait to see if you spot it again. This time he took note of the licence plate he would have dispatch look it up later.

Dropping into bed he thought about his next move he had an appointment with Judge Hughes in the morning, he understood that this was a long process but the thought that his child could be in danger. He wondered why he was doing this; was it because he had lost a child and wanted to fill the void that was left inside, or was it to protect her? Next thing he was standing on a cliff face looking down, he could see a small child in the distance it was her his daughter, he stood there helplessly watching men approach her "Run!" he was screaming trying to find a way down to save her but watching in horror as one pulled out a gun, she died in front of him. Screaming he jumped up in bed the sheets soaked with sweat, it was a dream heaving a heavy sigh he climbed out of bed looking at the clock 5:30 he decided that he was going to have a shower he didn't want to go back to sleep the thought of having that dream again was more than he could bare.

After the petition to the courts to have his daughter's adoption opened, they had weighed everything then granted the request. He finally knew where she was and who had adopted her, it was then reading the names that he was shocked she had been closer than he had known, for the names on the records were his aunt and uncle they had brought the child up, they would have had to know who her birth parents were. Yet in all the time he had been there welcoming the child as his cousin when in fact she was his daughter. He couldn't believe it why had they not told him that Ashley was his child? He had to find out he wasn't angry at them he was angrier that the child he had grown up with thinking that she was theirs when in fact she was his child, he needed to know why they had not once talked to him about it he had babysat for them many times and had grown to love her. Pulling into the driveway of his aunt and uncle, Ashley was in the garden playing on the trampoline not wanting to disturb her he walked quietly into the house for once thankful for the headphones that she always wore, as he walked in his auntie saw him, he knew by her face she knew what he was there for.

"Jack sit down" was all she said uncle ray walked in from the living room sitting at the table, "Jack we have been told you had the court records unsealed you know the truth now" "why didn't you tell me the child you had brought home was my child?" "If we had what would have you done? You would have never accepted who she was you would have fought against it, not wanting a reminder that the child you called cousin was your daughter." The clatter they heard behind them was Ashley dropping her phone standing there she looked at them, she knew that she had been adopted her mother and father had told her when she was old enough to understand she had been told that it wasn't that they didn't love her it was the fact that they had been young however they never told her whom her parents were looking from Jack to her parents she could not believe it he was her father, it was more than her brain could take turning she ran from the room Jack went after her as did Ray his auntie's knees quivered quickly she sat down before she fell, tears fell she knew that Ashley would find out one day as would Jack but not like this.

158

Ray and Jack followed her into the woods, the foliage was thick he could see her just ahead of him, the dream came to him at that moment thinking of her dying speered him on he had to catch up to her, she finally started to lose pace grasping hold of her shoulder he pulled her to him, screaming she started hitting him angry and hurt there were a thousand thoughts running through her mind all the time growing up she had known her father, he had been there the one she turned to when she needed advice and couldn't talk to her mum and dad the one who listened all this time he was her father. Did he know was it all an act why he hadn't told her the truth why had he never? All thoughts were hard tears streaming down her face she felt weak her knees gave way Jack caught her as she fell no longer having the strength to fight, she just lay there in his arms, the arms of her father she cried all the way home; by the time they had got back to her home she was cried out exhausted, she was asleep. Taking her up to her room he laid her on the bed he looked down on her his daughter the one he had been looking for had been in his life all along.

It had been three days since he had found out where his daughter was but with his aunt's wishes he stayed away he had told Conner everything even though he agreed with his aunt that there was a time for them to talk but she had just found out who he was; Jack started to plan his sons funeral, for now, his daughter was going to have to wait he thought for a moment if she knew that he was her father then she would have worked out that James was her brother. So, she had gained her father and lost a brother in the same instance, he had to put it to the back of his mind the one thing he could do was to make sure that his son had the best send-off he could give him.

It was a dreary Tuesday morning; Jack had not slept much the night before knowing this was the day he would bury his child. He had chosen James's favourite song to be played being eleven he had an unusual taste in music the song that was played was Lonestar's I'm already there, it was Megan's favourite as well. Standing outside the church they waited for the funeral car to pull up both his child and ex-wife would be buried at the same service.

Walking over he looked at the coffin such a small thing that held the body of his son, it was made by Jacks father who was a master carpenter and had insisted that he had wanted to do it, on the top was engraved his name with different characters around it the handles had been in the shape of Thor's hammer as he was James's favourite, Jack had seen it before it was moved to the funeral home, his father had lined it with Manchester United's colours for they were his favourite even though he had tried to get him to like Everton, the pillow was sewn by James's uncle Michael, with the words in diis manibus Meaning in god's hands, Jacks throat choked slightly when he saw the words to everyone else it may have seemed odd, but not to him he knew that every time he saw his uncle before he left they were the words he used to say with a smile as he ruffled the boys hair.

It was time the funeral director opened the door, Jack and Michael were the ones who carried Jame's coffin Megan's was carried by Conner her two brother's her father and her father's brothers. The path was lined by their closest friends' tears being fought back as they entered the church, finally they were at the alter where they gently laid the coffins down. The priest spoke looking to the coffins as he spoke about them, Jack stood he was to give his sons eulogy. He had decided to say a poem that he had read and felt that it was perfect not just for his son but for Megan also.

Wishing on your star
When you wish upon a star
You wonder what they are,
Are the planets, are they suns,
Are they real or just illusions,
When you wish upon your star you know how true it is in your heart,
You wish aloud so you can hear the truest thoughts or your greatest fears,
Sometimes you cry out into the night wishing your star would come to life,
To take the pain you feel inside and make it all OK,
But wishing is for children they say,
but we do it every day,
Whether it for us or the ones we love we wish on our star way up above,
We look out at the world by day,
But shed the tears at night and pray,
Let them know how you feel,
If it's emotional you know it's real,
So, look up at the sky to night and find your star you know it right,
It's the first star you see every night when you look up at the sky,
It's always there in your eye line,
We all have a star that we pick,
It's the one you chose as a kid,

The one that shines brighter than most,

The one you wished on when you saw Pinocchio,

It's there to remind you of those days when you were a child and carefree all day,

you chose on that night and remembered well, even when it was light,

it was then that you first wish was made,

So, look up at the sky to night and remember what it feels like,

To wish upon your star once more.

By the time he had finished, there wasn't a dry eye in the house, looking to his son's coffin "I wish that it was true because there is nothing, I wouldn't give to have you back in my life." He could not continue Conner rushed to his side as his knees gave way helping him back to his seat.

They watched as Alisha walked to the coffins placing her hand on James's coffin, she looked at it they had played together at family gatherings, to think that the boy who used to follow her around and pester her was her kid brother, "I wish I could have known you as my brother, instead of my cousin there is so much I could have said to you. So much we could have shared, I promise you brother that I will not hate father and I will do you proud." She placed a white rose on the coffin then in tears made her way back to her seat.

Finally, the day was over Jack fell into bed and cried himself to sleep; he could not believe that this had happened to one so young, he had done nothing wrong, yet someone had gone into his home and murdered him. Jack knew that he was not to be allowed to investigate, he had been told to hand over everything he had on the Jensing gang to Taylor and Mark. He had decided that for the best he would make sure that Alisha was safe then he would with Conner's help find who did this.

Chapter 9

The Awakening

It had been just over a month since Jacks son had been murdered and he had found his daughter, Sarah was getting worried she hadn't seen him she understood that he had just found his daughter and wanted to spend time with her; she was in training for the awakening, She kept losing concentration and master Yamatoya and Tetsuko were losing patients; she was sat in the meditation chamber trying to find focus but every time she closed her eyes all she saw was the funeral and Jack, Master Yamatoya walked into the room looking at him she stood, "I can't concentrate everything I have tried is not working," Master Yamatoya walked her to the stone room pointing to each of the plaques, "there are many of my brothers here, each of their deaths weighs heavily on me; there isn't a day that goes by that I do not think of them. Walking over he placed a hand on the one that read Tsutka Amashia this is the one I found the hardest, he was still young not much older than you when he died. I found him on the enlighten path he wanted to be a monk so bad that he decided to try and train alone; he knew the risks of trying that path but decided that he was ready for it. All I remember is not being able to find him, searching the monastery that was the last place I could think of, I prayed to Buddha that I would not find him, but he was there just past the Hackshia they say he had fallen and that his neck had broken, what I could not understand and still have trouble with to this day is why he had not come to me, it was then I changed the way I taught I became stricter but always open for those who needed extra guidance, all the time praying that the mistakes of the past never repeated. Do you know why I'm telling you this?" Sarah looked at him with a blank expression "I am telling you this because I can see you going down the same path, Sarah you are very talented but if you think that you are anywhere near where you need to be, so you are able to withstand the awakening then you are very wrong. Tell me what is it that is causing you to lose focus?"

Looking at him Sarah sighed "Its jack I haven't seen him since the funeral, my father won't tell me anything; every time I try to close my eyes to concentrate all I see is the day he buried his son. Master, I don't know what to do." Master Yamatoya patted the stone bench next to him, walking over she sat down hanging her head slightly she felt as though she wanted to cry, gently he placed a hand on her shoulder. "My child there is nothing you can do, Jack will come back when he is ready, we must give him time there is nothing worse than losing a child. We have to be patient with him and be here when he is ready."

Sarah knew that he was right sighing she stood up this time she decided to use the SheiKra, walking through the door she looked there it was the pedestal that she had first learned to use. Walking over she was about to climb up when a voice stopped her cold. She had heard that voice before when she was in the meditation chamber could it really be him, she hadn't seen him since that day. Turning around slowly she looked in the direction the voice was coming from, sure enough it was him master Yakamoto walking to the tapestry he stood there in silence for the longest time. When he did finally turn to look at her, she noticed that she could almost see through him, taking a breath if there was ever a time, she needed guidance this was it. "Master Yakamoto," she said in almost a hushed whisper, "what can I do I feel lost." Smiling he turned back to the tapestry, "Do you know who this is?" He asked, looking at the tapestry there seemed to be something familiar about it, master Yakamoto smiled pointing "Maybe this will help you see his likeness every time you walk into the great hall," looking at him she realized who he was he was the monk who had created this place.

"Ah, there it is realisation. Yes, this is master Yakasoto the man who created the frost temple, when he first comes to this country he fell in love with its people. the strange way they spoke he mastered the language in less than a year, he always used the language in his everyday life, you will find that all the monks here speak a vary of languages but the most is English, Welsh and Japanese along with many others, but the thing that's not commonly known is he had the same problems he felt lost not knowing what to do but he never asked for help, until he met someone most unexpected,"

"Who did he meet?" Sarah asked expecting him to say it was himself he was talking about and was shocked to discover that it was none other than master Yamatoya, "but that would make him over 400 years old," master Yakamoto smiled "Do you not know who master Yamatoya is?" she looked at him and shook her head "but can't you feel it when you are in his presence?" "Well when I am with him I feel more centred and as though nothing could go wrong" "Exactly this is because he Is the guardian of the human realm, the others don't know of course due to all guardian identities being secret they have to be because this world doesn't talk about magic; I suppose that when you're young myth and magic is all too real but when you grow then the thought seems preposterous, so everything is kept secret for their protection and to allow people to live their life believing that it's all nonsense." "But why would he not tell me who he was?" "Because of who you are, don't you realise all the temples know who every guardian is when you were found and did the training master Yamatoya it went against everything; he was questioned on it and his reasoning behind why he did, it was found that he was right due to the fact you have been out of that world your entire life, yes it's good that your mother left all you needed to learn, you have to understand that master Yamatoya has no one from his family left he has lived for centuries watching everything he loves go he outlives his students and every time one of them dies he comes to this tapestry and asks for guidance from the one person that he could always talk openly with because he knew who he was who he truly was. Then the day came the one they both knew would eventually come, master Yakasoto was dying that was when Yamatoya decided that he would not leave his side he would not allow him to die alone, when master Yakasoto named Yamatoya as his successor not many understood why but like all monks took it well, the night he died Yamatoya was sat by his side, watching his chest rise and fall until at two in the morning he finally took his last breath, that was the only time I ever saw him cry. He took up the rains and through his hard work and dedication what you see now is what he worked for; do you know how he managed it?" "I'm not sure that this has anything to do with my concentration." Looking at her he breathed deep "Just think about it there is a reason I'm telling you this, but you are not listening to it"

Sarah was supposed to understand something she just wasn't getting it; finally he turned to her, "using the SheiKra works to help focus but it doesn't help close off everything that you have going on in your mind," "then what do I do?" smiling "The answer to that question is right over there" he said she turned and saw a small alcove walking over she could see nothing except darkness, "I don't understand" smiling he walked over to her, "step inside," nervously she did as she was told it seemed the darkness enveloped her, she found herself feeling slightly scared master Yakamoto followed behind her, looking at him she noticed a slight glow she had not realized before, she noticed that he was slightly see through but now he looked Atherial to her and she was slightly happy the slight glow from him lit the room up slightly, "master Yakamoto, what is this place?" "this is the room of reflection, this is where the final stage begins for you, the only advice I can give you is allow your mind to guide you, don't allow fear to enter your head or your heart and with those final words he disappeared, standing there she felt slightly nervous but listening to his final words she swallowed her fear, taking a deep breath she steadied herself, she was wondering what the use her mind reference was meant to help; standing there she closed her eyes, taking a deep breath she allowed herself to see through her mind.

Memories flooded in she allowed them to stay for a moment then dismissed them, finally she saw Caradog and Gem they were stood there talking she concentrated on their voices, it was then one voice she never expected to here came in it was the voice of her mother, "yes my love it is me you are having so much trouble because you are not thinking of the awakening as a gift, you are looking at it as a curse, you are also allowing yourself to be distracted by the thoughts of jack, you have to allow him to find himself my love, only then will he find his way back to you, so let all thoughts of him leave your mind, put him in your memory box for now; you know the one I'm talking about you have had it since you were a child, its where you keep your memories of me."

With that her mother's voice faded away, a tear slid down her face, was it really her mother's voice she was hearing or was it just her mind knowing she needed her help and just made her think that it was her. She didn't know but she was sure that even if it was in her own mind, it was something she needed to know.

She did exactly that and placed jack in the memory box with her mother, she knew that if she didn't then she would never be able to get through this; constantly worrying if he was okay or not, so she finally knew what she had to do even if she didn't want to do it alone; it was something she had no choice on she knew that she would fail if she didn't concentrate, this was the final step the last few months she would have to be just ordinary Sarah, where she would always be Sarah but once she goes through the awakening, then she would have so many more commitments and that was the one thing that worried her, was she strong enough? she needed a way that she could stop her mind wandering, she had used all the tools that the monastery had to offer but she was still struggling to clear her mind she decided to talk to master Yakamoto if anyone could help her it would be him, but should she tell him she knew who he truly was or should just act like she did not know, she decided the best course was to treat him the way she always has.

As she went in search for him she noticed the others training, stopping she watched them for a moment thinking back to when she first started here and how she felt, was it such a short time ago it felt like she had been here years, she thought to the first test she had done and the training it had involved she had thought it was so hard but now she wished she was the same girl that was there, she had gone through so much that she felt like a totally different girl. With that she heard a sound behind her turning she noticed that both her and master Yamatoya seemed to have the same idea, "Sarah is everything okay?" "Master I am having trouble clearing my mind I have used everything the monastery has to offer but I'm still struggling what else can I do?" master Yamatoya smiled "come with me…" was all he said he then started walking she followed. Him but this time instead of going to one of the places that she knew he led her to a passage just behind the sculpture in the large hall, walking through all she noticed were steps leading down.

It seemed like they were descending for hours when finally they came to a stop, master Yamatoya led her to the back of the very large room she could hardly see as it was dimly lit, finally he pointed "Sarah go through the curtains you are finally ready for the last of your training," looking at him she didn't understand she thought she had weeks left, but unbeknownst to her she had completed all bar one of her lessons and that was the lesson of her own he could have nothing to do with it, once she enters the room the lesson will start, only once she had completed will it allow her to leave, but this is something he could not tell her, for if she was to know then there was a possibility that she would not do it.

Smiling at her "I will be right out here once you have finished" looking at him her eyes narrowed usually he would accompany her and give her some sort of direction why was it that this time she had to enter alone, "Master is there something you are not telling Me.?" He knew there was but to tell her the truth was hard as even he knew that when he had the final part of training to do, he was unsure whether to enter, so he just shook his head looking at him she knew that there was something that he was not telling her, she also knew the man, and it would be for a good reason that he had not told her.

Slowly she stepped past him and entered the room all of a sudden the path she had just walked in through closed and there was nothing but solid stone, running to the wall she pounded on it "no no no.. Master Yamatoya, can you hear me please anyone" with that she heard a voice behind her swinging around she looked and there in front of her was none other than master Yakamoto "I thought you said the alcove was the final step? He smiled "If I had told you about this final step then there was a possibility that you would have been too frightened to enter." "Why is it that no one seems to have confidence in me with every step all anyone has done is think I would run away, but I haven't I have accepted everything that was expected of me!" she started pacing back and forth why; she just didn't understand the more she thought the angrier she got. Finally, Yakamoto broke through her pacing "Sarah you have to understand to us you are a child, so yes we may treat you a bit fragile on times, but it's not meant maliciously it is done from a place of love and respect." "well to me it's just annoying plus I'm still annoyed that the room of reflection only help me with jack nothing else, my insides still feel like jelly, I still have no clue what is going to happen to me on the day of the awakening, I'm not even sure where it is going to take place, it's like I've been told but my mind has wiped it from my memory, plus all anyone around here seems to know how to do is speak in riddles. Is it so hard to get a straight answer out of any of you?"

Yakamoto smiled he understood but she needed to learn was that by deciphering the riddle would lead her to the correct answer, "okay so you are saying that you would prefer for us to give you all the answers? Let me ask you this if we were to do that then what would you learn, to give someone the answer without anything or to give someone all the knowledge they wanted without them finding the way is the wrong way, only by helping them to understand the knowledge do they learn."

She looked at him and smiled she knew he was right and that was just as annoying, "Wait a minute why are you here?" "I'm a spirit I can go where I please, when I realised that you were ready for the final lesson, I knew that Yamatoya could not be here with you to help you through it," "Yes, I understand that but why you?" "Sarah, I have watched you since you came here, I have seen the pain the tears but I have also seen the heart you put into everything you do, so when you were ready I knew that I would be here to help you for no other could be, that's the good thing about being a ghost I can go anywhere." He said the final part with a bit of a cheeky grin, "so what is it that I have to do here anyway, "the room will decide when you are ready to start the final lesson, once it has you will know when it starts, even though I cannot physically help you I will do my best to guide you." "So, what I just stand here and wait for the room to decide it's a room it's not like it has a mind or anything." With that it felt like someone clipped her around the ear "hey ouch that hurt!" she yelled master Yakamoto sniggered "yip looks like you were right no mind at all" she glared at him, "Yeah like I'm supposed to believe that the room did that huh I don't think so, I know that ghosts can hit the living." Yakamoto raised his hands "Hey that wasn't me I swear" she kept her eye on him and there it was again like someone smacked the back of her leg, "ouch okay so you have a mind quit it" suddenly, the room when bright looking around she noticed six chairs Yakamoto was stood by one of them, "Choose your six." "Choose my six what I don't understand. Hello creepy voice could you explain what six I'm supposed to choose?" but there was no reply standing there she looked at the chairs walking over she examined them, they had Japanese symbols on them, she had no idea what they said looking at Yakamoto "do you understand these symbols?" he nodded pointing at the first chair that is anchor the second is bind the third is hope the forth is friend the fifth is strength and the final one is courage" "Okay so anchor bind hope friend strength and courage, okay but does that mean I have to choose what order I want these in or the people I associate with the words, ahgg" she shook her head "okay if I were to say to you who would you think of first anchor?" "That's easy my dad" okay "Bind" "bind I don't know bind do you mean who I would like to be bound to or someone that binds me" "Sarah don't think the first name that comes to mind" "Okay bind tommy" "hope?" "Master Yamatoya" "Friend?" "Jack" "Finally strength" "That one is easy Caradog."

All of a sudden the chairs were gone and in their place were the six people she had just said the only difference was Caradog she knew how big he truly was but he was a lot smaller, they stood there and looked at her but not one of them spoke, "Dad, Dad!" but he said nothing just looked at her all of a sudden the voice was back, "you have chosen your six warriors now let's see if they agree," they looked down at the symbols that were now on the floor in front of them her father stepped onto his and a warm glow went around him, then tommy stepped forward but instead of a glow he burst into flames, screaming she ran forward but the heat was too much then he was gone, then master Yamatoya stepped forward and once again he glowed the same with jack and Caradog.

168

Then the voice was back, "you have to choose one more" tears were streaming down her face, "But what if I choose wrong, how do I know what the right choice is! Please tell me?" but the voice said nothing, Yakamoto looked at her "Sarah look within, you know in your heart who bind is, don't think of the meaning don't think of anything. Just close your eyes let your heart guide you, you got all bar one right clear your mind don't let what happened here taint your thoughts, breathe deep open your heart and your mind let them guide your focus on bind and allow the face to form in your mind no distractions, nothing." Sarah did as he had told her this time she would not think of anything she would allow the face to show her who bind was, she stood there for a while just breathing, and all of a sudden Gem came into her mind opening her eyes, "Gem" she said it without thinking, with that he was there stepping forward he stood on the mark and glowed she breathed deep. "I got it right" slowly they faded away once again it was just her and Yakamoto.

"Choose one" it was the creepy voice again this time there were four swords, walking over she was about to grab just one "Sarah stop!" she looked at Yakamoto "you have to choose the one that calls to you" "the one that what?" "The one is a true sword the others are not, allow your powers to choose the true sword" "my powers how?" "you have gone through all the training you have done the tests you know how to tap into your natural powers the swords are made of steel allow your earthen magic to find the true one," she looked at them and at Yakamoto slowly she sat on the floor putting her hands together she looked at the swords she allowed her hands to heat up until there was an orange glow coming off them, stretching her hands forward one by one she pointed at the swords the first one shattered like glass it was then she noticed a slight hum coming off the middle one standing she walked over stretching out she grabbed the hilt and pulled it to her the others disappeared;

"Choose one" it was the voice again but unlike her father and the others the sword did not disappear, this time there were three mirrors she walked over and looked into the first one there was nothing no refection nothing, stepping to the next one she could see her mother sat under a tree smiling, she blinked tears away and stepped to the final mirror this time she saw an alter but it seemed to be in a cave somewhere she could see bones on the alter and also blood seemed to be coming from somewhere, she just couldn't work out where it was coming from, standing back this time without prompting from Yakamoto she closed her eyes and pictured all three mirror's in her mind the first one seemed to warp out of shape the one with her mother in looked like it was going further away the final one looked like it was coming closer to her, opening her eyes she grabbed the last one, the others disappeared in an instant the one she was holding grew larger until it looked like a door way, she looked at it walking forwards she stepped through, she was stood in the cave near the alter looking around she noticed there were men she had never seen before stood there. Then one by one they rushed at her, and she systematically worked her way through all of them once the final one was gone, she was back in the room.

There was a loud rumble and then the sound of something cracking turning around she noticed her way was clear once more, but this time instead of losing concentration she walked through the curtains back to where master Yamatoya was waiting, he looked at his watch and then back to her and smiled "well done Sarah you have surpassed everything I could throw at you, you have passed all the trials and with you stood here you have completed the last of your training, how do you feel." Smiling she looked at him "tired but is Tommy okay." He looked at her for a moment and realised that something must have happened in there to make her feel like there was something wrong with him. "He is fine so is everyone else I think a celebration is in order we have two weeks before the awakening," "Wait what I thought I could not receive it until my twenty first birthday that's not for another wait what date is it" she looked at her watch and was surprised to see that she would be turning twenty-one in two weeks' time.

She had come a long way from the girl that liked to go out with her friends, to have a drink to now it felt like another lifetime, she walked with Yamatoya to the main hall where everyone was, once again a cheer went out when they found out that she had completed the rest of her training, the only thing now was the awakening she had to prepare for it.

The two weeks went by so fast it was the day before the awakening, she was in the garden sitting under a tree watching the birds fly about making their nests getting ready for the birth of chicks, oh how nice it would be for her to not have a care in the world, her peace was interrupted by master Yakamoto he appeared like before out of nowhere she smiled at him, "So are you nervous for tomorrow? "I thought I would be but for some reason I am actually calm, do you think that's normal?" he hovered by her "Well I can't actually say you see that although there has been three before you, you are the only one to get to this stage, but I think that you would know if it wasn't normal." With that he was gone, she was sure that he did that on purpose just to throw her off guard, with that she heard master

170

Yamatoya calling her name. taking a deep breath, she stood up "I'm over here," she called out to him he walked around the corner with a man that she had never seen before which seemed odd to her, as she thought she knew everyone that was here and very few visitors ever came.

"Sarah this is frank Phillips he is going to be your guide," she raised her hands "Guide what do I need a guide for, I know every inch of this place," master Yamatoya smiled shaking his head, "not for this place he's going to guide you through dream world, yes you passed every test you completed all your training but I've been told you scream in your sleep, well he is here to find why you scream in your sleep." "Master it's just nightmares everybody has those" "True… true but you are the guardian and when a guardian has dreams best to get to the bottom of it before the awakening okay, you go with him," with that he tugged at her arm frank laughed "don't worry child I am what is known as a dream walker that means I can come with you into your dreams and decipher what they mean okay," Sarah groaned and nodded "Fine but they are just dreams," "well hopefully you are right and nothing more needs to be done, but just for the old guys sanity please." "Old guy what old guy" Master Yamatoya squawked both Sarah and frank laughed and walked off leaving master Yamatoya shouting after them.

They were in her room frank handed her a drink and told her to drink it he also drank the same thing; all Sarah could think was it tasted like dirty socks. Before she knew it, she was in her nightmare and frank was beside her, "Sarah where are we?" he asked she just shook her head, "I don't know it's the same place every time the same dream." "Okay walk me through what happens," it goes by very quickly that's the thing," with that there was a brilliant flash of blue and a beautiful blue dragon appeared before them, it bowed its head to Sarah but when it came to frank there seemed to have anger in its eyes, "What are you doing in this place!" it demanded to know from frank, who was struck dumb with fear for the moment, "Speak or die" "I am frank Phillips I was called by master Yamatoya to help Sarah with nightmares but why are you speaking to me you are just a figment of her imagination aren't you?" with that the dragon laughed "I am Amuriel I am the last of my kind lying dormant for millenniums, before there was dinosaurs there was nothing we lived with in the nothing waiting we did not know what for until the day came that man was amongst us, we thought that we could teach man and help them but we found that man's hearts are easily corrupted, they would call but kill all my kind who answered that call, I was left

171

alone until the star of hope appeared, we have heard of it but thought it was nothing but an old legend until one day I saw the sign I followed it and have been with it ever since," "What was the sign?" frank asked with a slight shake in his voice. "She is the sign one of pure heart pure light that no man can diminish, I have been with her from birth, the day she receives her powers I will be hers to command I have pledged my life for her."

Sarah looked at Amuriel one whom she had been so afraid of her entire life the one she ran from in her dreams because she thought she wanted to kill her with a different light. "Amuriel I am so sorry I have been running from you please forgive me."

Amuriel lowered her head until her light touched Sarah, "Sarah you are not strong enough to hold me at the moment that is why I can only come for short periods of time, but soon we will be of one mind I will be yours I have found my other half," frank raised his hand "Wait hold on if you will be one then who will Sarah be will she be her or you?" Sarah looked at her thinking the same thing "I don't mean that we will be the same person our minds will link she will know my thoughts without speaking as I will know hers, she will be able to call on me when she needs help and I will give her my strength, I have been alone for so long to be seen by my master is what has kept me going, at the moment she can only see me in her, dreams but once she has received her powers she will see me as clearly when awake as she does while she sleeps."

Sarah opened her eyes and sat up Frank looked at her and smiled "Well of all the things I was expecting that was certainly not even anywhere on my radar," Sarah smiled and stood up as they opened the door master Yamatoya was stood there waiting, jumping "Bloody hell I am going to have to put a bell on you guys" she said with laughter in her voice, master Yamatoya looked from her to frank "well is she okay?" "Okay well let's say when she receives her powers I will not be pissing her off" master Yamatoya looked at him confused," "well yes that would be foolish" "Umm master Yamatoya her nightmare is not a nightmare what she has been running from in her dreams is nothing that would ever hurt her, it turns out that she is connected with a very old dragon called Amuriel who has chosen her to be its master it seems that they were around before life was around."

Master Yamatoya looked at him "The mythical blue dragon" he wobbled for a moment then walked over and sat down, "we knew you were special, but this is something completely different, my dear you are a mystic as well as a guardian for only a mystic could call upon Amuriel." With that he stood and bowed low before her, "master Yamatoya what are you doing please stand up," but he stayed low slowly he stood looking at her, "you no longer call me master for you are the true master" Sarah looked at him "Don't be so stupid I will always call you master for in my eyes that is what you will always be,"

A tear escaped him as those words left her lips, he knew that she had no idea what he was talking about, he had decided that no one was to know not even her father, he told both frank and Sarah that they were not to be told that this was something they were to find out after she had received her powers, with that he told Sarah to have food then to go to bed for she had a very long day ahead of her tomorrow.

Opening her eyes it was today, her twenty-first birthday but unlike most girls, her age she wasn't having a massive party today was the day she had been looking forward to and terrified of at the same time, she thought if only she stayed in bed a little while longer no one would mind, with that thought she heard an almighty crash that had her racing out of her room looking around she saw no one rushing to the window she saw Master Yamatoya lying on the floor instantly she thought he was dead, then realised that he couldn't die.

Running from the room she made her way down to master Yamatoya who was sitting up, "Master are you okay" she said breathlessly as she got to him, he smiled "I am fine" "if you are so fine then what are you doing on the floor and moreover what the hell was that crash?" Yamatoya laughed "Why don't you go and ask the other students what it was there in the main hall,"

Standing she walked to the main hall all she had to do was take one look inside to see where the noise had come from, all the tables had been upended the students were all standing around looking but she knew exactly who was to blame, walking through the door "Yakamoto where are you, come on I know that this was you get here now!" with that he appeared next to her the others look screamed and run which made his day he stood there laughing as Yamatoya walked through the door, "Master Yakamoto I should have guest." The students who were peeping around the door looked at each other and slowly started to walk back into the room, "Mm, master Yamatoya you knew there was a ghost here?" they seemed to say in harmony "well I'm not the only ghost here you know guys, but we have been watching over you for years making sure that everything was okay." Sarah laughed "Are you trying to tell me none of them knew you were here," "Well no out of respect we left them alone to do their

173

training but it's not every day that a guardian is to receive her powers is it, so as it was a special occasion we thought we would come and see how everything was going, what we didn't expect was this to happen we forgot when you have a lot of power in a concentrated space then it has to be let out some way, this is why we have limited it to just six of us the others are watching from a distance." "But why is it only you we can see." Just as the words left her mouth the others showed themselves and amongst them was the man who built the monastery, all there dropped to their knees and bowed out of respect smiling the master told them to get up.

Sarah was stood by the door once the commotion had died down and master Yashida walked over to her "Are you okay" he asked in a deep husky voice, she smiled "It's not going to be long now is it soon I will be stood at the top of the beacons waiting, master Yashida what if I'm not strong enough?" "You have done the training you have survived the tests that have been given you, you are not just physically but psychologically strong so don't fret you have the strength to undertake this," with that he bowed and left, one by one the other masters spoke to her the final one was Yakamoto "Look out there what do you see?" "Well, I see trees, training ground well I see home" he smiled "would you like to know what I see" she nodded "I see a world full of wonder a world that can be balanced and healed, I also see you in the sun the rain and the night for you are the one this world needs right now," with that he bowed and disappeared,

Night was approaching and her father Tommy, Jack and the others were waiting for her at the door master Yamatoya smiled and led the way but they were not making their way by car Gin was there to teleport them to the sight they needed to be at, "Are you ready?" he asked Sarah her mouth was dry and her hands slightly shook so all she managed was a slight nod, then in a flash they were there.

Sarah looked around the cave they were in she noticed that the alter lay beneath an opening, she looked up and noticed that all she could see was the sky. Master Yamatoya walked by her side placing his hand on her shoulder, "are you ready for this?" Sarah looked at him and with a slightly shaking voice "Yes, yes I am ready for this," he smiled at her and patted his hand gently on her shoulder.

Tokagine and his men had made their way to the top of Brecon mountain where the cave was, it wasn't the only cave that these rituals would take place there were altars all over the world, but this one held a special place for many, it was where years ago a group of soldiers who had gotten lost in the fog were saved by a monk in a long robe, telling them to go back it wasn't safe. However, what they didn't know was he was the guardian of the shrine and alter, it was his place to stop unwelcome visitors to enter.

Tokagine and his men knew of this apparition and waited just outside once he disappeared then they knew that the ritual was due to start, it was then everyone knew when he was there he would guide you away, if anyone inspected the area then all they would see would be quick sand, an illusion yes but no one would ever venture forward to find that out, however it was the path Tokagine and his men would have to take if he was to be there in time to steal her powers, he had researched the lore for years as did his ancestors before him, he had been brought up on it, it was he who had first discovered Sarah, the accident everything after was designed so that he could make sure that she truly was the chosen one, it also helped that he had a spy on the inside one that no one would ever suspect, he had gotten close to Sarah made her feel welcome helped her through her trials while through it all letting Tokagine know every time she passed a trial, it was the same person who told him she had completed her training and the day they would be at the altar.

Master Yamatoya held out his hand "Sarah its time;" she smiled shakily as she took his hand, letting him guide her onto the alter standing there she looked up she knew the words she knew the order to say them in but for the moment she was frozen fear gripped her like a vice, was she ready could she really do this.

Taking a steadying breath, she closed her eyes she would have to rely on her training, stepping to the centre of the altar she noticed that there were bones beneath her feet, they looked ancient she did her best not to break any, standing there she looked up she had to say the words in order.

Raising her right hand she looked up "I call upon the powers of earth, I call upon the powers of water, I call forth the powers of air I command the powers of fire, I am the one true guardian one that has stood the tests and trials I have succeeded, I have endured the magic lands I have fought through the earthen lands I have entered the dream realm I have conquered all fear I have taken on pain, I stand before you now as the one true immortal guardian I swear to uphold the laws of all and to break none, so as the moon joins the sun in the sky I your humble servant welcome the gifts you are to bestow upon me.

With that the sky darkened a loud roll of thunder echoed through the cave and a streak of lightning hit her hand her body started to glow as she welcomed the powers being bestowed upon her,

"Now!" Tim shouted with that Tokagine and his men flooded the cave master Yamatoya and the others rush to protect her, the fighting was ferocious blood bathed Sarah's feet but she knew to move would kill her, Sarah's auntie slowly crept around to the back of the cave grabbing Sarah she calls to Tokagine now, Tokagine runs forward raising the Ashanti dagger, as he thrust it towards Sarah Tommy jumped forward the knife plunged deep into his chest, "No!" Tokagine cried as he realised that his plan had been thwarted, Sarah's auntie let go as Sarah fell to her knees blinded for a moment as her eyes cleared, everything was blurry but she could see Tommy on the floor.

Falling off the alter she crawled to his side resting her head upon his shoulder tears streaming from her eyes weakly she cries "Tommy my love you cannot leave me, please open your eyes" with that his eyes fluttered open his breathing laboured, "Sarah I will always be with you my spirit will be your guiding light when you are lost, call to me and I will always answer." With that he was gone, letting out a cry that shook the cave toppling all those who were around, trembling she stood knowing the vows she had just taken it was a mortal man who had taken his life she had to obey the balance, but that didn't mean she could not avenge his death looking around, she heard Amuriel's voice "Sarah stop, you have to respect the balance if you were to kill you would be breaking your vow" "Amuriel they killed tommy I am not going to let them get away with that," "I didn't say for you to but they cannot be killed by your hand let me be your sword" with that she started to glow a blue haze surrounded her slowly it got brighter until you could barely see Sarah all you could see was the dragon she had within, Tokagine's men started to flee but with one blinding light were disintegrated, turning she set her sights on Tokagine, but the light of Amuriel looked into his soul and all she could see was blackness, he was a man of pure evil with evil coursing through his veins, "Why did you do this?" "You should have been mine if I had just taken her powers, you would be!" "No, I would not for I am not part of the powers that she received, I chose her she did not choose me, so if you thought you could have contained my powers without my consent then you are wrong." "No all the research told me that you would come to the one who had the power of the guardian it was foretold!" "that has always been the misconception of man, they believed that my kind went to the strongest, what you failed to see was it was our choice, we chose what human would be bestowed with our power the choice was never in mankind's hand, my kin were killed by those who thought to control the power we possessed, but that ability was taken from you when the dagger of Arthwen was destroyed, when that happened the power to kill my kind went with it." "Are you telling me that it's your choice, whom you go to; and you chose a woman why when men are the more powerful?"

With that Amuriel laughed and her body snaked around him, "little man you don't understand we do not choose power we choose heart, which is why you would never have called me to you." She spoke softly but coldly, man had always believed they were the ones that controlled her race, when in fact it was neither, her race didn't control humanity as humanity never controlled them, it was a symbiotic relationship they shared but her kind were systematically wiped out when those who had called them realised that they would never control them.

She had finally had enough with a slight blow he was engulfed in fire, ash was all that was left, Sarah's auntie tried to sneak out, "and where are you going?" Amuriel said with a dangerous voice, her auntie froze looking at her, "you whom chose money over family, you who's heart is as black as Tokagine's one who murdered her sister to get to her daughter," "He made me do it I loved my sister I wouldn't have killed her if he hadn't ordered it, I swear" "You swear are you forgetting that I know every thought you ever had I know what lies behind those eyes and in your heart?" her auntie fell to her knees, "Please great one spare me I swear that I will only do good in this world from now on please Sarah forgive me!"

Amuriel had heard enough she knew that Sarah could never forgive what she had done, for not only had she murdered her mother, but she had also tried to kill her. Raising her mighty arm in one swift motion she was gone, slowly Amuriel's light diminished, and Sarah fell to her knees heartbroken tears flowed freely looking at all the carnage that was around her all because someone had got the legend wrong, they believed that to take her powers would give them more power.

Master Yamatoya walked over to Sarah and placed his robe around her helping her to her feet the others gathered their dead, slowly they emerged from the cave Gin was waiting outside for them, and by his side the monk who kept vigil over the altar, he looked at those who came out and bowed his head, even though the attack was not his fault he felt that he had let them down. Gin looked and noticed the dagger that had no right being in the human realm sticking out of Tommy's chest, in a swift action he removed it to the shock of all those around him Sarah's eyes glowed brilliant blue for a moment, until he spoke "Sarah this

177

is the Ashanti dagger it has no right being in this realm," "Does that mean that I can help him?" "I'm sorry but he was killed by human hands the balance has to be protected," walking over he took a hair from Tommy's head holding it in his hand he closed his eyes, "This man has lived a true life, but it was never meant to be a full life, if he had not died by the hands of another on this day he would have died some other way fates hands were involved, his string of fate has always been short but tethered." Sarah looked at him, "what do you mean tethered?" Gin smiled "that is all I see." Then with a wave of his arm they were back at the monastery. Night was upon them Sarah was both mentally and physically exhausted. Walking over to where tommy was, she knelt next to his body a sob broke through, there he was one man that she had grown close to, and yet his life was cut short, looking around she noticed master Yamatoya was nowhere to be seen. With an outstretched hand she stroked the side of his face, if only there were more that she could have done. Jack walked over to her and placed a hand on her shoulder, "Sarah come on we need to take him to the coroner," "no… We know how he died and who killed him, why does he have to go can't we just lay him to rest?" her father walked over, "No love we have to follow the law he was murdered, we have to do this." Jumping to her feet "Yes he was murdered, we know who did it and what they did it with, but we cannot produce them can we!" "Love he was a police officer they will want him back, there is nothing we can do about that."

With that master Yamatoya appeared from the meditation garden walking over to where they stood, "I have given this much thought and I am going to contact his family myself they knew he was over here to help his brothers, the only thing we can do is tell them the truth; well as much of the truth as possible."

They came up with a plan and stuck to it the official report was that he had got caught up in the Yakuza war and had been killed, that was all that they knew to say they couldn't very well tell the truth about what had happened that night. The report was filed and accepted even though they could not produce the killer or the weapon that had struck the fatal blow.

Sarah Conner and master Yamatoya were to escort his body home for burial, to find out that his wishes were to be buried at the monastery. His family made their way over from Japan his brothers were inconsolable after all he had come all this way to save them, and when he needed them there was nothing they could do.

The day of the funeral came, Sarah looked at her father and master Yamatoya, "How are we supposed to say goodbye?" Conner walked over and hugged her "my little girl if there was only a way that I could take this pain away I would," she allowed herself to give into the grief, she had been bottling in for so long, Conner just stood there his heart-breaking with every tear, finally the tears stopped and she looked up at him, "Dad, I will never let you die." Was all she said before walking out the door?

As they stood at the graveside Jack stood next to her along with both of Tommy's brothers, they had heard everything about her from him and knew by the way he spoke that he had deep feelings for her, they just wanted to be near the girl who was in their eyes a sister, they made a silent vow to him that they would always keep her safe from harm.

The End